Stolen

and

Forgiven

A Branded Packs Novel

ALEXANDRA IVY
&
CARRIE ANN RYAN

Stolen and Forgiven

Branded Packs Book 1

Stolen

The first rule of being Alpha of the Canine Pack is to protect their secrets from the humans at all cost. One look at the dying human at his doorstep and Holden Carter knows he will have to break it. The broken woman with no hope at survival is his mate. When he forces the change on her to save her life, he not only sets forth motions that could risk both their lives, but the lives of every shifter in the world.

Ariel Sands grew up in a post-Verona infection world and under the care of the very humans she thought had cured the disease. When they betray her in the worst ways imaginable, she finds herself not only mated to the Alpha of a the very species she's been taught to fear, but the focal point of a traitor and path to destruction for everyone's way of life. It will take more than trust and a mating bond for Ariel and Holden to not only survive their enemies, but the burn of their own temptations.

Forgiven

Soren Slater is a Beta wolf who understands that duty to his Pack comes before his own needs. At a young age he takes a position as a liaison between his Pack and the other species of shifters. He never expected his enticing flirtations with Cora Wilder, a Tiger

Princess, would encourage her cat to consider him a potential mate. He's forced to walk away, choosing a partner among the wolves to try and strengthen his Pack.

Cora has no intention of forgiving or forgetting Soren's rejection. Not even when the Packs are forced to live together and she discovers Soren's former mate has died. But then, she's kidnapped by the SAU and she has no choice but to work with Soren to escape. Together they must put the past behind them if they're to survive the human's evil plot.

CONTENTS

Stolen

The Beginning

Twenty-five years have passed since the Verona Virus nearly wiped out human civilization. It was only when the shifters reluctantly came out of hiding to offer their blood as an antidote that the virus was brought to a halt.

Instead of creating harmony between the two species, however, the humans took control. The shifters found themselves branded, collared, and forced to live like animals. The Canine, Ursine, and Feline compounds are small and territorial, their populations on the edge of extinction. Each Pack is suffering from infighting, and even worse, the humans keep finding ways to enforce new laws that threaten their very existence.

The Alphas and other hierarchy are the only ones that stand in the way of their people's demise.

Or are they?

CHAPTER 1

If everyone didn't get the fuck away from him, they'd be responsible for the trail of clawed up assholes in his wake. Holden Carter, Alpha of the River Pack, ran a hand through his hair. His muscles strained, and his wolf prowled far too closely to the surface for his liking. It didn't matter that they sat on old couches and the scarred wooden floor in his home. He'd take them out one by one if they wouldn't let him breathe.

"You look ready to kick someone's ass, Alpha, you'd better rein it in."

Holden turned to his second, Soren and narrowed his eyes. The smug bastard might be a Beta, but there wasn't a submissive bone in his body. The only thing that kept Soren from leading like Holden was his wolf.

The wolves determined dominance, not the strength of the man beneath.

Instead of smashing his best friend's face in, Holden lifted a lip in a semblance of a smile. Of course, from the look on Soren's face, it must have come out as more of a grimace than an actual smile.

Oh well, the man deserved it. As did the rest of them. Hell, he needed to run. Or a drink.

Anything at this point.

Holden turned back to the wolves in front of him and let out a low growl. Each man and woman quieted, the collars around their necks a stark contrast to the color of their skin. He fucking hated the collars his brothers and sisters wore more than the metal one wrapped tightly around his neck.

It reminded him that the Pack wasn't free.

Weren't equal.

Weren't human.

They were caged and branded, but not forgotten.

He'd make sure his Pack was never forgotten.

That was his duty as Alpha. One of many.

"You've aired your grievances," Holden growled out, his wolf clawing at him. "The collars can't come off. It's a death sentence at this point. You know this." The collars themselves wouldn't kill them if they took the metal cages off their necks. No, it was the humans who held that power. They had eyes everywhere, a hold over their lives and future.

"But we can overpower the humans," Theo, a younger wolf, bit out. He had been born within the compound walls and had never stepped foot outside as a free man. Between the need to find some semblance of who he could be and the natural aggression of a new adult wolf, Theo always toed the line of wolf and man. "We're wolves. We're powerful. Not like the fucking cats and bears in the other compounds."

Rumbles from the other wolves who agreed with him.

Holden suppressed a growl of agreement. The cats and bears were in their own compounds and had their own troubles. Many of the wolves in the Pack had never seen another type of shifter. The humans had broken from their brethren, and the results weren't a shared connection of pain. Instead, the old taunts of cat vs wolf vs bear had turned to something far more feral.

Again, Holden didn't want to think of that. Instead, he wanted—no *needed*—to run.

"That's enough," he growled, his wolf in his voice. "We're not all dominants. There are submissives, non-fighters, and children to consider." Holden let out a breath. Always so much to consider and never enough leverage to protect his people from atrocities of the worst kind.

Humans.

The wolves, cats, and bears had been locked within their own compounds for twenty-five years. Two and a half long decades where a new generation had been forcibly denied a glimpse the outside world; destined never to breathe the air of freedom, never to run on four paws for as far as their legs could take them.

Instead, they'd been collared, imprisoned, and branded like cattle.

Holden rubbed his left forearm where the brand of his species, his people, burned as it had when he'd turned fifteen and been forced to wear the mantel as Alpha and savior of his kind. The tribal wolf howled at an unseen moon—ironic since the humans who'd designed the brand had done their best to cut the wolves from their nature and their need to be one with the earth. The act of defiance in tattooing the left side of his Pack tattoo had cost him dearly, but he'd never regret the ink on his skin.

Not when it meant his people had a chance at life.

Holden squeezed his forearm, his claws breaking through the tips of his fingers slightly before receding.

He had better control than any wolf here, but sometimes, the wolf needed to *run*.

The men and women who sat in his home were his council. Not a true council since wolves didn't work that way, but they were the pillars of their Pack, their compound. Each of them wove within the den, learning what they could and keeping the peace. For if a wolf stepped out of line, it wouldn't be the Alpha in all cases to punish them. Instead, the humans would take that on their shoulders and make them an example. The people in front of him helped him keep his Pack in line and let him know of problems that he could be unaware of as Alpha.

Soren, as Beta, did most of the legwork when it came to that, but he couldn't do it alone. Not when their numbers grew monthly, but the space they'd been provided hadn't. The walls became more confining daily, and soon they would have to find a way to glimpse freedom. However, today was not that day.

"We cannot fight against the humans with what we have," Holden continued. "We are gaining in number, gaining in strength, but it is not enough. Not yet."

"When will it be enough, *Alpha,*" Ana, another young wolf, snarled.

Holden clenched his jaw and met her gaze. Her wolf whimpered and lowered her eyes after only a moment of meeting his. Ana wasn't a weak wolf by far, but she wasn't anywhere near Holden's dominance. Between her and Theo, Holden had reached his limit in dealing with cocky attitudes and far away dreams of a freedom without thinking of the cost.

"We're done," Holden bit out. "We are dealing with the problems we can control, and the rest are tabled." He let out a breath, his arms threatening to shake. If he didn't get out of there soon, he'd start shifting right then. "Go to your families."

The others shuffled out, their own wolves reaching out to him. He could feel their power brush his own, but that didn't calm him like it should have. Instead, it only egged him on.

"You need me to run with you?" Soren asked, his voice low. His best friend understood him like no other, but Holden needed to be alone right then. It didn't help that he knew Soren needed to run off his own demons, but it was not Holden's place to help him. Some scars could never be healed.

Holden shook his head. "No. Go back and make sure Theo and Ana don't start shit."

"They're young," Soren said simply as the two of them walked out of Holden's home into the night.

A breeze brushed over Holden's face and he stopped to inhale the sweet scents of nature. As much as humans wanted to close them in and never let them breathe free air again, that hadn't worked. When the compounds were built twenty-five years ago during the first months after shifters had been discovered, the wolves, cats, and bears had been forced to live in warehouses of sorts, breathing recirculated air with no trees around them or soil beneath their feet.

Holden stifled a growl at the memory of their brutal captivity. The chain-link and razor wire electric fences surrounding their newer compound clawed at his soul, but it was nothing like before. When his packmates had started dying, he'd begged—fucking *begged* on his hands and knees—to let his people have fresh, unfiltered air and the space to run on four paws that they needed to survive.

In the end, he'd bargained with his life and won. At least as much as he could. He refused to rub between his shoulder blades; the puckered scars there a stark reminder of what he'd endured for the facade of freedom his Pack now held. Between the blood he'd lost and the brutality he had been forced to endure and take part in monthly, he'd found the cost of that small freedom.

But his Pack's lives were worth all that and more. "Alpha?"

He shook his head, his hands fisting at his sides. "Go." One word, a growl on the wind, and Soren lowered his gaze. Holden didn't miss the sadness there. Soren alone knew the pain Holden endured to keep his people safe, but there was nothing the other man could do—nothing Holden would require his friend to do.

Soren gave him a tight nod then loped off after the other wolves that had gone their separate ways. Holden knew Soren would hold the fort while he ran along the forested edges of their compounds. He couldn't hunt as the humans had done all in their power to keep game and other animals out of the wolves' territory, but he could at least run hard between the trees.

He made his way to the forested area on the westernmost edge of the compound. From there he could barely make out the shadowed peaks of the Rocky Mountains. After the humans had found out about shifters and done their best to kill them off, the rest of those with two natures had been forced into compounds around each major city in America—and across the world if what Holden had heard back then was correct. Denver loomed in the distance north of them, but he couldn't quite see the lights of the big city. That was on purpose, of course. God forbid humans were forced to see the atrocities those in power had created—manmade camps where freedom was nonexistent and torture was a way of life.

The Canine compound sat between the Ursine and Feline compounds, with the Ursines to the west nearer to the foothills, and the Felines to the east, their compound brushing the plains. By law, Holden and his people were not able to visit the others. In fact, they were never allowed to step foot off their compound unless the humans took them out. And even then, it was only for questioning and study.

He swallowed back the bile that rose in his throat at that thought. He needed to run, to forget those who had bled at his hands and out of his control. With a sigh, he stripped off his shirt and undid his pants. While he could shift fully clothed, he'd only end up disengaging anything on his body that wasn't etched into his skin or a special metal. The collars, of course, were made of a metal that adjusted to the size of the shifter's neck after they changed into their animal form. Such ingenuity from a people who had all but killed his own.

He let out a breath then pulled on his wolf. The change was quick, a breath of sweet agony, and soon he found himself on all fours. In his animal form, he stood a little larger than a natural wolf. The moon wasn't full so he'd be able to hide easily within the shadows if he felt like it. It helped that his midnight-black fur blended so well with the dark. The only real color was a white stripe on his nose.

His mother had loved that little stripe.

He repressed a growl and buried the pain of her loss. When the Verona virus had hit, most of his people were safe from the disease, but not the carriers. He'd lost his parents, his siblings...everyone.

A growl escaped his throat, and he shook his body like he'd stepped out of water, and *ran*. His paws slammed onto the ground, the force of the impact vibrating in his jaw, but he didn't care. He had dirt between the pads of his feet, and a slight breeze through his fur. If he could ignore the stench of metal and burning electricity, he could almost forget that he lived within a cage.

He'd been running for only a few minutes when he scented another wolf.

Well, hell. He wasn't in the mood for this, but Theo needed to get it out of his system. As Alpha, it was Holden's job to help the younger, dominant wolves find their place within the Pack. That meant fielding dominance challenges and takedowns when necessary. Theo wouldn't win tonight, but the wolf would be able to let his aggression out. Too much suppressed aggression within a system, and that system would break. Holden had seen firsthand what happened when a younger wolf not only didn't learn to control their urges but didn't learn to let them out, as well.

Holden lifted a lip in a snarl as Theo padded toward him. The younger wolf had grey, tan, and white patches, much like many of the wild Timberwolves outside the compound. Theo's human side had finished growing, though Holden knew he would gain more muscle over time. However, Theo's wolf wasn't quite finished growing. Holden had a feeling Theo would soon be as large as Soren. That would be good for the Pack since they would need all the strength they could get in the coming months and years. Right then, though, Holden had more pressing matters on his mind.

He let out a warning growl, but Theo didn't stop moving. The animal within Theo maintained control, and Holden would mold and shape that into a dominant wolf worth having in the Pack. Theo snarled but didn't lower his gaze.

Challenge issued.

Theo pounced, a quick movement that surprised even Holden. It seemed the young wolf had some speed. Good, but not good enough. Holden moved out of the way at the last moment and nipped at Theo's flank. The younger wolf snapped his large teeth, but Holden didn't get bit. Instead, he threw his own body at Theo, smashing the young man into the dirt. Theo struggled, but couldn't fight Holden's greater size. Knowing it had to be done, Holden bit into the back of Theo's neck, marking him has his lower. Pride swelled inside, even if it warred with frustration. Theo would make a good enforcer or tracker one day, once he'd found his calling. He just had to refine his balance with his wolf. They all had to do it, though Holden had accomplished it far younger than most.

When Theo relaxed in his hold, Holden released him and stood back. He nudged at the other wolf and they both shifted back, Theo panting in exertion.

"Feel better now?" Holden bit out. He'd needed his run and a dominance challenge hadn't helped his wolf.

Theo ran a hand through his too-long hair and grimaced. "Sorry, Alpha. I...I tried to hold back."

He waved him off. "Your wolf needed a fight. I get it. It's what makes us wolves and not human. But, next time? Try Soren or someone else first."

Theo let out a breath. "Yeah, I know. I just...I don't know."

Holden had a feeling he knew. Theo would one day be one hell of a strong wolf. Perhaps not as strong as Soren to be Beta, but he'd be up there. Theo's wolf needed to seek out the strongest of them all, even if he was certain to lose. Holden understood it, but he didn't have to like it.

"Go back to the center of the den and get tended to by one of the submissives." Holden grinned as Theo flushed. "I meant your cuts and bruises, boy. You know those submissives hold the power while we just think we do."

Theo raised a brow and stood up on shaky legs. "True. Sorry for fighting you."

"Never be sorry for fighting when your wolf needs it. You did the smart thing. You waited until we were alone and not in the middle of the den center where someone would take it as a clear challenge, rather than just aggression." He frowned. "If you're still feeling it, talk with Soren about more duties. If you have all this energy, we might as well use it to our advantage."

Theo snorted and ran a hand over his brand—an absentminded gesture that clawed at Holden. He remembered the day Theo had been branded. He remembered the day each of them had been.

The two of them stood naked in the middle of the forest, but it didn't matter. At some point, he'd have to go back and find his clothes since his run had been cut short, and he didn't know where Theo had left his before he'd shifted.

"Thanks for not making me truly bleed," Theo said wryly.

Holden rolled his eyes, his wolf huffing. "Go to the submissives."

Theo grinned then ran off, leaving Holden alone in the forest once again. The fight had helped him release some energy, but he still sat on the edge of control. Fighting or fucking would help with that if the run didn't, but he figured he wouldn't be doing either tonight. Fighting Theo hadn't been nearly enough. As for fucking, he had to be careful when it came to females in the Pack. None of them called to his wolf so he wouldn't be able to truly mate with them. Most of the others in the Pack could find a mate their wolves would tolerate, even if it weren't a true mating; however, as Alpha, he needed the balance, a complete bond in every way that mattered.

And unless she magically dropped from the sky, it wouldn't be happening. Unlike the stories of legend, shifters didn't live forever. They only had a short time on this planet, like humans, to find the one for them and make it work. He was already in his forties and unable to meet new wolves.

He had no chance for true happiness.

His wolf pushed at him, and he let out a frustrated growl. Fuck. Between the lack of options when it came to humans and now mating, he needed to punch something. For months now, he had been running on the edge of control, and he wasn't sure what he could do about it. He needed something to center him, and running with his wolf wasn't cutting it anymore.

He was about to shift back to his wolf—something that would hurt to do this close to his previous shift—when the wind changed. The scent of copper hit his nose and he went on alert.

Blood.

Human blood.

Knowing full well he could be running into a trap, he padded on human feet toward the origin of the scent. If he didn't, he could be risking his Pack even more. Human guards patrolled the gates, but they didn't come out this far often. There weren't any homes out here, and his people only used the forested area for runs and hunts.

It could be something as simple as a human guard having cut themselves accidentally, but he had a gut feeling it was something far worse. His wolf at the surface, he crept toward the source of the metallic scent. He couldn't scent any humans other than the injured one. In fact, the stench of near-death became so potent, he was afraid he was too late.

This was a body dump.

A shadowed lump lay in a macabre pile on the shifter's side of the fence. He let out a low growl and prowled closer.

Shit.

Someone had sure done a number on her. They'd cut her up so old and new scars covered her body. When they'd dropped her over the high fence, they'd broken her bones—and perhaps had done that before she'd come to them. She lay naked with her long, tangled hair covering her face. Her chest rose softly in pained gasps, and he knew she lived—but not for long.

Whoever had done this had sliced her up in ways that made his stomach want to revolt. He'd seen unimaginable horrors in his years and had even been on the receiving and giving ends of such memories, but this...this was too much.

He crept closer and sucked in a breath.

They'd fucking vivisected her. How the hell was she even alive?

Death edged closer; it was only a matter of time before she'd let out her last breath. There was nothing he could do. The humans who had done this—he scented their stench around her—had placed her on the shifter's land for a reason. If he had to venture a guess it was to place blame. It wasn't the first time the SAU—Shifter Accommodation Unit—had played this game. And it wouldn't be the last.

He let out a breath, knowing this woman suffered. He could either let her die in agony, or make it a swift death for her. His wolf whimpered, and he frowned. That was an odd response. His wolf didn't whimper. Ever.

Mate.

It wasn't a whisper. Not a word. Not even a true voice. But a feeling along the bond to his wolf where he'd only felt aggression and pain for so long.

It had to be a mistake. There was no way this dying human was his mate. It *couldn't* be. With a shaking hand, he brushed her hair from her face and fell to his knees.

Mate.

Her eyelashes fluttered but she didn't wake. A single tear mixed with the dirt and blood on her face slid down her cheek and he brushed it away. Fuck. This couldn't be happening. He'd found his mate only to watch her die.

He knew what he could do—knew what he could have done in an age past. But it was truly forbidden now. He licked his lips, and his wolf pounded at him to do the *one* thing he couldn't as Alpha. Not anymore.

Only he wasn't sure he could hold himself back.

Knowing he was about to break the one rule as Alpha that held his people together, he pulled away from the woman and shifted back to wolf. It hurt like fucking hell, but nothing compared to what she must have felt just then.

Once he did this, he'd risk everything he and his people had fought for. As Alpha, he shouldn't do this, but as a man, he couldn't not.

He said a prayer asking forgiveness and bit into her shoulder. She let out a gasp, but didn't thrash—she was far too close to death for that. The sweet, tangy taste of her blood settled on his tongue and he pulled away before biting her belly and thighs. The more fleshy places he bit, the stronger the chance the change would take.

If she lived, she would shift as he did.

If she lived, he would have to hide her from the prying eyes of the humans who collared them. For the humans had no idea how to make shifters. As far as the humans knew, shifters were born, not made. With this one bite, he risked the secret they'd kept since revealing their existence twenty-five years ago.

Yet his wolf pushed him and he knew he'd made the right decision.

At least that's what he prayed. Because if he hadn't, he'd sentenced himself and his people to certain death.

Once again.

CHAPTER 2

The overwhelming agony that had become a pulsing, steady presence in her life slowly receded to a dull roar. That couldn't be good, and probably meant only one thing.

Ariel Sands was dead.

Though after so many weeks, months—was it years?—straddling the line between death and the unyielding fire of life, she wasn't sure she could be too upset about her life coming to an end. Maybe this was for the best. She wouldn't hurt anymore. Her throat wouldn't burn from the screaming. Her nose wouldn't itch from the scent of her own blood as the butchers played with their new toy.

Bile coated her tongue and she swallowed.

Wait. Could she swallow if she were dead? That didn't make much sense, but she'd never been dead before so she didn't quite know.

"What the fuck did you do, Holden?"

The deep shout startled her and she pried open her eyes. Well, hell, it seemed she wasn't dead. But where the fuck was she? She almost tried to move, but froze. What if her captors heard her? It never failed to be worse when the so-called doctors found her awake after a long sleep.

A few things had changed since the last time she'd woken up after passing out. First, it felt as though she was lying on a bed with a comfortable mattress and blankets rather than a hard metal table. She held back the instinct to scream out or even let out a relieved breath. This could be a test. The doctors could want to see what she would do once she thought she was comfortable...or safe.

She'd never be safe again.

She'd known that from the first needle prick against her will.

"I did what had to be done, Soren."

That voice. Ariel stiffened at that voice. It wasn't familiar, at least it shouldn't have been, but for some reason, she felt as if she'd heard it before. Or maybe someone like it. The deep timbre slid over her, increasing her heartbeat yet calming her at the same time. What the hell was going on?

"What you had to do?" the other man, Soren, she thought it was, yelled once again. "You broke our laws. You *turned* her, Alpha. You risked the lives of our people, our way of life because, what? She's a pretty face? How the fuck could you have seen that with all the blood on her?"

Turned? Alpha? Laws?

Ariel shook, this couldn't be happening.

She had a bad feeling she wasn't inside the SAU lab anymore.

A really bad, freaking feeling.

"If you weren't fucking yelling, you'd hear her heartbeat has changed, Soren. Now go. I will take care of this."

A low growl came from one of them, and Ariel clutched the bed sheets. Shit. She needed to get out of here. If these where who she thought they were, she needed to find a weapon. Fuck. Did he say turned?

No, that couldn't have been right.

Shifters were born, not made.

Everyone knew that.

Didn't they?

Oh, fuck.

How was this man, this Holden, going to take care of this? She opened her eyes and quickly closed them again. The bright light overhead made her head pound, and her stomach wanted to revolt. Her heart began to race at the sound of footsteps coming closer, and she waited for whoever it was to see her. She'd fight them off if she could, but if these were shifters, then she was screwed.

Those animals killed people.

Everyone knew it...or at least that's what she'd been told.

"You're awake."

She tried to sit up at the sound of his voice and winced. She might not hurt as much now as she had before, but she still wasn't up to a hundred percent.

"Don't move. You're hurting yourself." The man barked the order, as if he were used to people following his every command. For all she knew, he was.

Knowing she needed a good look at her captor, she once again pried her eyes open. This time, it felt as though someone had knocked her in the chest.

Dear Lord, was her kidnapper supposed to be that sexy?

His dark hair spiked a little on the top of his head, but the rest had been cut short to show off the hard angles of his face. His tanned skin looked as if he worked hard outdoors and used his hands. Every inch of him was toned, muscled, and rock hard, but he didn't look like one of those scary, body builders who couldn't walk through a door without turning sideways. His eyes were a piercing blue, like two pools of water that went deeper and deeper. He fisted his hands at his sides, and while she wanted to think he was trying to keep himself from doing...something...she didn't want to find out what would happen when he let go. The dark brand of a tribal wolf on his forearm looked like it still hurt, while the tattoo on one side didn't look as bad. The metal collar around his neck stood out and confirmed what she'd already suspected.

He was a shifter.

"Who are you?" she croaked. Hell, her throat hurt.

Holden frowned and stalked over to the side table, the muscles on his thighs bunching as he moved. Why was she so fixated on his thighs? She needed to find a way out of here and get back home...wherever home was.

He poured her a glass of water from a pitcher and handed it to her. "Drink."

"Bossy much?" she rasped. Probably not the best idea to antagonize the literal beast, but she couldn't help herself. She was scared, and when that happened, she acted like she was a tough bitch.

He merely raised a brow and reached out with his free hand to cup the back of her head. She tried to pull away but he held her in place. Damn, the man was strong.

"Drink."

She did not trust this man or his attitude. Instead of complying, she pressed her lips together.

Holden sighed and took a sip of the water himself. "It's not poison."

"If you're a shifter, then you're not going to die from poison." She immediately closed her mouth again. Fuck. She hadn't meant to say that. What if he wasn't a shifter and just a normal kidnapper? The fact that she'd just thought the words 'normal kidnapper' made her want to reevaluate her life choices.

Holden's eyes widened a fraction, betraying his surprise at her words. "Drink the water and soothe your throat. We have a lot of shit to talk about, and you pussy-footing around isn't helping."

"Don't say pussy-footing. It's degrading to women." Dear, God. She needed to shut up before he killed her for being annoying.

Holden snorted then shook his head. "You're right. Considering the women I know can kill most men with just one claw, I should stop saying that. Habit. Now drink the motherfucking water."

Her throat ached so she opened her mouth and let him press the glass to her lips. He tilted it slightly so she could drink without choking. The water instantly cooled the burning ache, and she greedily gulped more before he pulled it away. Her chest lifted quickly, her breathing back under control.

"More?" he asked, and she shook her head. She hadn't had a decent meal or drink in who knew how long, and while she craved it, she didn't want to hurt herself more by doing too much, too fast.

He nodded and put the glass on the table. "We have a lot to talk about."

They did, but she wasn't sure she wanted to hear it. "You didn't answer my first question. Who are you?"

He folded his arms over his chest, making him look even scarier. "I'm Holden Carter, Alpha of the River Pack."

So he *was* a shifter. "I've never heard of the River Pack. I thought all of you lived in SAU compounds."

Holden lifted a lip in a snarl. "The Shifter Accommodation Unit labeled our compounds. This one is Canine Compound G. But we have our own names, our own traditions. We are the River Pack."

Canine. That meant he was a wolf. The freaking Alpha wolf, leader of all the others in the compound, or Pack—whatever he wanted to call them. All she knew were the stories of shifters she'd been told since she'd been born. At twenty-five, her birth had come at the end of the Verona virus outbreak, and she'd never met a shifter. At least she didn't think so. The animals had been put in their compounds during her first few months of life. Looking at the man in front of her, though, she internally winced at the word animal. He looked so...*human*. Maybe using that degrading word put her in the same camp as the so-called SAU humans who had cut her open to watch her bleed.

Bile once again rose in her throat and she closed her eyes, the nausea receding slowly.

"Your scent is off," Holden said, bringing her out of the memories of screams and blood. "What's wrong?"

"I'm fine," she lied.

"You're lying, but we will deal with that later as long as you are physically okay." He narrowed his eyes but she didn't look away. She had a feeling if she did, he'd feel as if he'd won. Why she thought that, she had no idea. Maybe the doctors had messed with her brain when they'd been slicing up everything else.

"Why did I find you on the perimeter of the compound, broken and bleeding?" he asked, bringing her to the present.

"What do you mean?" she asked, trying to sit up. Only then did she look down at herself and gasp. "Where are my clothes?" She might be wearing a sheet, but that was it. *Why am I covered in dried blood? Where are my cuts? Why do I have so many old scars?*

Holden cursed and knelt down by the bed so he was at eye level with her. "Tell me you aren't a plant. Tell me you had nothing to do with what happened to you, and you're an innocent bystander in all this."

Her hands shook, and she pulled the sheet closer. "Why am I here?"

"Answering questions with questions will get us nowhere."

She glared. "Well, you're doing it, too."

He gave a curt nod and let out a sigh. "You need to answer me, woman. I don't even know your name, and you are in my territory. I need to know if you will harm my people. Then I can work on what you need, but I can't do that if I don't know where we stand."

"My name is Ariel," she said, knowing that much she could give away. Of course, she didn't have many secrets to hide anyway. She still didn't know why the humans had taken her to study in the first place. For some reason, she had a feeling this Holden would tell her more than the SAU ever did, but she'd have to be careful. She wanted to go home, get clean, and forget the sound of her screams. Only she didn't think that would be an option anymore—not when she found herself in the middle of a wolf Pack with no memory of how she'd gotten there.

Holden's eyes darkened a moment, and he let out a breath. "Ariel. Like the mermaid."

"It was big around the time I was born," she bit out.

"You're a baby then," he murmured.

"I'm old enough." For what, she didn't know. And now they were getting off track. "As for where you found me, I don't know how I got there." She swallowed hard, knowing she might be making the biggest mistake of her life. "The SAU took me from my home and into their compound. It was like a hospital of sorts. I don't know how long I was there, but they..."—she took a deep breath—"...they studied me. Cut me up. Watched me bleed. Called me Test Subject A. I don't know what they wanted or why I was there, but I didn't have anything to do with it. The last thing I remember was screaming because they were cutting into my stomach and didn't use any anesthesia. Knowing the way the bastards work, they probably just dumped my body here to blame you."

Holden let out a small growl that sent shivers over her skin. "I think you are probably right on that account. The fucking humans like to blame the shifters for everything, though we are the ones locked up in cages, while they commit the atrocities that feed into the nightmares of the public they pretend to protect."

She licked her lips, wanting to defend her people, but couldn't. She'd seen the bloodshed and pain that had resulted in the unification of humans after the Verona Virus had been wiped out. The government had created a fourth branch—the SAU—that worked outside the checks and balances the other three had fought to maintain. The rights of the people weren't what they had been before she'd been born.

Yet, she'd been told only the worst about the collared shifter in front of her and those he represented.

"I'm human, Holden. I shouldn't be here."

He growled again. "You *were* human, Ariel. That's what we need to talk about."

Her head ached, and her ears buzzed. What he'd said couldn't be right. She'd heard him say something similar earlier, but it was wrong. It had to be.

"Shifters are born, not made," she rasped. "I'm human. I need to go home."

"You can't go back to where you came from, Ariel. For now, *this* is your home." He didn't look too pleased about it, but then again, neither was she.

"You're wrong. I'm going home."

He took a deep breath, truly looking into her eyes for the first time.

"Ariel, to save your life, I had to turn you."

She shook her head and tried to get up. Her body hurt, but far less than it should have considering her injures. "Leave me alone. You're crazy. I'm human and nothing can change that."

"A bite of an Alpha or a mate can change that."

She blinked. Nope. Not going to believe that.

Holden ran a hand over his face. "Fuck. I'm doing this all wrong. You were dying, Ariel. Dying and in pain, and I did the only thing I could do."

She shook her head, trying to remember what that other man—or was it wolf—Soren, had said. "You can't make people wolves."

"We're not supposed to, no. But I had no choice."

"I'm not a shifter! I'm human!" Her hands shook and her mind whirled, unable to get a hold on what she thought, what she wanted to think.

He gave her a sad smile. "You didn't die from the bite, Ariel, so yeah, you're a shifter. There's still a small chance you won't make it through your first shift, but you're not human anymore."

She tugged on the sheet and tried to get off the bed. "Seriously, if this is your way of telling me I'm one of you, you suck at it. You can't just tell someone you've bitten them, and that I could still die if I try to shift. It doesn't work that way. You're supposed to ease into it. Or you know, not bite someone!"

He gripped her arm and she froze. "I've never turned another person, Ariel. So yes, I'm probably going about this wrong, but you're making it hard to keep my thoughts in a straight line."

She swallowed hard at the look of his hand on her skin. Her body felt...off...and she didn't know why. "I want to go home," she whispered. She wanted to wake up and know this was all a dream, a nightmare. What he said couldn't be true. She wasn't a shifter. She was human. She had to be.

Holden, crouched near the bed, reached out and cupped her face. The action seemed to surprise them both from the look in his eyes. "Let me begin this again. Ariel, you were almost dead in our forest. Not only would the humans have blamed us wolves for what had happened to you, I couldn't let you die like that."

She licked her lips, her mind going in a thousand different directions. "Why? Why couldn't you just let me die?" Not that she wanted to die, contrary to her first thoughts when she'd woken up. She wanted to know *why* this man, this wolf, felt he had to break his law according to the other wolf, Soren.

"You're my mate," he said simply. Only it wasn't that simple.

"You're crazy. You are fucking batshit crazy." She tried to pull away, but he held her in place. The feel of his hands on her arms, holding her so that she couldn't move, caused her to panic as the memories of what the doctors had done to her smashed into her consciousness. "Let me go." She'd meant for her voice to sound firm, only it came out a broken mess of a whisper.

"Fuck," he muttered then let her go. Only she didn't move once she had the opportunity. "I'm sorry. God only knows what those bastards did to you, and me grabbing you like that didn't help. " He raked a hand through his hair. "Okay. Let's take this one step at a time. We'll get you cleaned up and changed so you'll feel a little less grimy." He wrinkled his nose. "The smell of blood is a little much."

She could smell it herself, and she tried not to think about how much more intense it smelled than before. She was *not* a shifter.

"I'll explain everything once you're clean and have food in you." He nudged her chin with his knuckle and she met his gaze. "You're my mate, Ariel. You don't have to believe that right now, but you'll feel the connection." He frowned. "At least I hope you will. We'll deal with what that means at another time, but first, let's get you cleaned up."

She blinked. "You *changed* me. Is that what you're saying? Because if that's true, you didn't give me a choice." She ran a hand over her chest. "I...I don't know how I feel about that."

He winced but didn't defend himself. "Shower, Ariel. Now."

"Don't order me around."

"I'm the Alpha, siren. You'll have to get used to listening to my orders."

"Siren?" she asked, her head spinning.

"It was either that or mermaid." He shrugged then picked her up, holding her close to his chest.

She let out a yelp and wrapped her arms around his neck so she wouldn't fall. "I can walk," she snapped.

"Can you?" he asked in that annoyingly arrogant tone.

She actually wasn't sure she could walk at the moment, but that didn't give him the right to pick her up wearing only a sheet. She didn't even *know* this man. Mate or not.

Jesus, what was going on in her mind?

Holden strode to the bathroom, but she kept her attention on the space around her. The place looked like a small cabin with dated furniture and electronics. She'd never been to a shifter compound before and hadn't known what to think of it. Right then, though, she didn't want to think of it. Instead, she needed to find a weapon and get the hell out of there. He might say she was his mate, but she didn't miss the fact he hadn't said she was safe.

He set her down on the bathroom counter, the sheet safely tucked around her. "What are you doing?" she asked, her throat still a little raw.

"I'm getting you cleaned up. I'd let you soak, but we need to get the filth off of you and we don't have enough hot water for a long bath anyway."

She shook her head, trying to clear it. "Why don't you have enough hot water?"

Holden looked at her like she was crazy. Considering she was trying to have a normal conversation with a shifter who claimed she was his mate while she wore only a sheet and was on the hunt for a weapon, maybe she *was* crazy.

Her hand slid over to the hair shears lying on the end of the bathroom counter. They weren't large, but they were at least something. For a moment, she thought his gaze had caught the movement, but she wasn't sure.

"The SAU regulates our hot water supply." He snorted. "They regulate everything. I might be Alpha, but I don't have small children who need a warm bath while I don't. So I don't take up much of the supply. Now come on, let's get you out of that sheet and in the shower."

Before she knew what she was doing, she had the scissors at his throat and her foot on his hip. She hadn't known she could move that fast. In fact, she'd *never* moved that fast—not even in all the fights she'd had in the orphanage as a kid.

He let out a sigh, which surprised her considering the position they were in. "You don't have to fear me."

"Excuse me? You're a freaking shifter, and I'm not supposed to fear you? No. I don't think so. I don't know you, and now you want me naked in a shower? I had to be naked, dirty, and strapped down for those bastards. I'm not doing the same for you."

He thrust his hand out and took the scissors out of her hand, throwing them in the other room before she could blink. "We will discuss what the butchers did to you soon. I'm curious as to why they would study you, though I have a feeling it is just one more thing in their long line of demented procedures. As for getting you in the shower? I'm a wolf. We do not care about nudity as much as humans do. We need to be naked to shift or we'll lose our clothes. We're not perverts or whatever you think we are. But we do respect the modesty of others if they so require it. As for you at this moment, you can't stand on your own. I know you think you can, but you're weakened from what they did to you as well as the bites I had to make to save your life. I am not going to cop a feel or pound you against a wall to have a taste of you. I have more control than that. However, I'm also not going to ask a female to walk in here and help you. You're my mate, and my wolf won't allow another in the room with you in your fragile state—even a woman who is sexually attracted to men."

She never thought she'd ever hear so many words come out of this man's mouth all at once. She also had no idea how to take anything he'd just said.

"Set me on the floor or something so I can wash off," she said, her voice firmer than she thought possible. "I'm strong, Holden. Stronger than you think I am. I won't let you take over my life." It was a life, she knew. Oh, she was strong, but she didn't know about the world of shifters and everything that life entailed. She had a feeling she was as far out of her depth as she could possibly be.

He tilted his head, looking so much like a wolf she had to blink. "You might be strong, Ariel, but you are not as strong as me."

"Bullshit. If you say I'm a wolf like you, then I'll learn to be strong."

He looked surprised for a moment then nodded. "And I will teach you to take care of yourself."

"I can already take care of myself."

"Then I will teach you how to take care of your *new* self. Because, Ariel, your life has changed; every decision you make from here on out will affect more than just you. I will protect you, however. Know this."

"I can protect myself." If she kept saying it, then maybe it would be true. She couldn't rely on him, not and still remain who she was.

He let out a low growl that made her shiver in all the right places. Or wrong places, rather.

"We can do both."

She wasn't sure what he meant, but she had a feeling she'd soon find out. Nothing made sense, and she knew this was only the beginning. Her world had shifted, as soon, according to him, so would she.

What did this mean, and what the hell was she going to do about it?

She was Ariel Sands, orphan, Test Subject, and able. Only she wasn't sure if she was anymore. If she weren't human, if what Holden had said about mates was true, then who was she?

CHAPTER 3

"This is crazy. I shouldn't be here."

Holden let Ariel continue her tirade as she sat on a stool in his kitchen. The fact that his *mate* sat in his home while he prepared food for her was not lost on him. However, he knew he didn't have time to dwell on that fact. He not only needed to ensure Ariel knew that this would now be her future, but he had to protect his Pack.

A Pack that, at this moment, knew Ariel sat in his kitchen.

He might be Alpha, but there were things he couldn't keep secret from them. Having a mate and knowing she had been human was one of those. People had seen him walk inside his home with a naked and bleeding Ariel in his arms. The rumors would have started there with Soren outside trying to alleviate some fears.

Soon, Holden would have to venture outside and deal with the situation—preferably with Ariel on his arm. It wouldn't matter that she wasn't marked, collared, or branded at the moment—but he needed to show a united front for his people. If they saw him falter, it would hurt their Pack.

He closed his eyes and let out a sigh. He didn't want to have to tell Ariel what would come next—the branding and the collaring. It was a torture she shouldn't have to face, but he would have no choice.

"You're not even listening to me."

Holden opened his eyes, put down the spoon he'd been using for the pancake batter, and walked over to Ariel's side. It would have been nice to play domestic and act as if things were normal. But they were far from normal, and sitting around pretending that things would be would only hurt the situation in the end. He turned her stool so she sat between his legs, small, terrified, and still somewhat human. Honestly, he had no idea what he was going to do, but he knew what he *needed* to do.

"Ariel, your life has changed. You can't go back to what you had before."

Her eyes clouded. "I knew I wouldn't be able to once the SAU took me. But I can't stay here, Holden. I'm not a wolf."

He cupped her face. "You will be soon, Ariel. In fact, I can already scent the change on you." He hadn't been able to scent the sweetness of her before under the grime of blood and dirt. But now that melded with the underlying scent of wolf on her skin.

He liked it.

She pulled away, her eyes wide. "You can't just tell me these things and not explain. You can't just tell me I'm your mate and expect me to jump on board. It's barbaric, Holden. I'm not like you."

He brushed his thumb along her cheekbone, the soft skin addicting. He never thought he'd have a mate. After all, he was already in his forties, living in a world where finding someone his wolf would have was a rarity. The fact that he'd found Ariel, a woman his wolf wanted and, therefore, the human half of him would learn to care for and love, was surprising, to say the least.

"Ask me what you want to know, and I will tell you what I can."

Ariel searched his face and let out a breath. "Why do you think we're mates?"

"Because my wolf told me you would be perfect for us. He chose you."

She looked at him, obviously skeptical. "So this wolf inside you just goes around picking people and forcing them to mate? That's a little weird."

He snorted and shook his head. "It's not always like that. Not for shifters in our den, nor in the other dens from what I know. Others do not find their mates like that. Most of us marry and mate the same way humans do. We find someone who is compatible, fall in love, and our animals eventually fall in line. It's not magical—it's not fate, and there is no real mating bond like in some of the stories humans like to write about us."

Ariel grimaced. "I might have read a few of those."

"Humans have a fixation with us because they aren't allowed to know the real shifters. So they make up stories. I've read a few and laughed my ass off. But in reality, our wolves are a part of us, but not the full part."

"Then why did your wolf decide that I was yours? It doesn't make any sense."

This was where it became tricky. Until she shifted and found her own wolf, it wouldn't connect fully to her, but he'd try. "Some wolves find their mates before their humans have time to fall in love. It's not love at first sight, but instinct."

He the out a breath he'd been holding as she frowned.

"I am Alpha, Ariel. I cannot mate with a woman my wolf doesn't choose. In the past, it wasn't a problem because there were so many of us spread out, our wolves would eventually find someone. Locked up in cages as we are, it limits us."

Her eyes widened. "So you've never found a mate before now?"

He shook his head. "I haven't. I found a couple women in my life I could have maybe married, but could never mate. And I would never put my Pack stability at risk being with a woman who couldn't survive the role as an Alpha's mate."

"Survive? What the hell do you mean?"

He closed his eyes. Fuck. He hadn't meant to put it like that. "You might not realize it, but you're fucking strong, Ariel. You had to be to survive what you did. When it's time, you will find your wolf is strong, as well. My wolf just happened to see it before anyone else did."

"I'm not sure I believe that," she whispered.

"That you're strong? Or that you're my mate?" He held his breath, waiting for her answer. He didn't know this woman beyond what she'd told him, but damn, it would hurt if she pushed him away outright. She was hope of something more for him, even if he wasn't quite sure what that was.

"Both maybe?" She sighed. "How do you know if someone is mated? Is it like a marriage or something? What does it mean? And it scares me that I'm even talking about this, you know. Last time I checked, I was a human trying to find my way in the normal world. This is all a little unbelievable."

His lips twitched at that. There was no way the world any of them lived in was normal anymore, but he'd let her think that for now. She'd find out the truth soon enough.

He pulled back and held out his forearm. Her gaze traveled to the brand and ink there. When her fingers traced over the ridges of the tribal wolf he sucked in a breath. She moved her hand back, her eyes wide.

"Sorry! Did I hurt you?"

He swallowed hard and shook his head. "No one really touches it," he said softly. "It's okay. You asked about mating, and this is part of it. When we are mated, we get the right side of the brand inked with the tattoo that we choose to signify our pair. The life side of the brand is a tattoo of our particular Pack. The brand itself...well it is different than just a tattoo. Each wolf, bear, and cat wears a brand to signify their species."

She blinked then looked down at her bare arm. "Why would you do that?" she whispered. "It looks like it hurt like hell. Can't you just smell each other or something?"

He clenched his jaw and tried to relax when she looked up at him. "It was not our choice."

Her mouth parted, and she reached up to her neck where the absence of a collar stood out like a beacon. That would have to change soon to keep her safe—to keep them all safe.

"What do you know of our history?" he asked.

She frowned. "I know what TV and books tell me. When the Verona Virus hit twenty-five years ago, it wiped out a lot of humanity. That's when you guys couldn't hide anymore and came out in force to try to attack us." She pressed her lips together and winced. "Sorry," she whispered. "Anyway, the SAU found the cure and then saved the rest of the human civilization by putting the 'animals' in cages." She used air quotes around the word animals to apparently indicate she didn't quite believe the prevailing propaganda. It didn't make it any easier to stomach hearing those words from her mouth.

"The SAU is a decrepit and violent organization that uses fear mongering to keep humans unaware of what's going on around them. If they keep the fear heightened just enough, then humans will turn the other cheek when it comes to locking up, in camps, women and children who have done nothing but be born with the ability to shift." He let out a small growl, holding out his arm. "The SAU did this to me. They force us to brand *children* so no one can hide what they are. They are the ones who make us wear collars and try to force us to forget that we are shifters and once held power. Now we don't even have to power to free ourselves. We are outnumbered and weak because *we* were the ones who saved you. Not the doctors. But us. The shifters."

Ariel put her hand on his chest, her palm right above his heartbeat. His wolf calmed immediately, brushing at her touch, nudging beneath his skin.

"I grew up in an SAU orphanage, Holden. My parents died from complications from the virus when I was born. I know the SAU isn't the perfect pillar of society they claim to be. If I hadn't known it when I was a child, hungry and alone, I would have damn well known it when they cut me open to see if they could make a shifter."

Her eyes widened, and she clamped her mouth shut.

He gripped her arms, his wolf coming to the surface. "They're trying to make *shifters*?" He couldn't believe it. Or maybe he could. He wouldn't put anything past the SAU, but fuck, this was bad.

"I overheard one of the doctors talking about it when they were putting me under for some tests. I don't know why they want to do that or why they kidnapped me from my home to do it. The latter probably because I have no family and no close friends due to where I grew up."

His wolf raged at the thought of her hurt, bleeding, and alone, but the man knew he needed to think about the consequences of what she'd just told him.

"Fuck, Ariel. This is bad. But you need to know *how* bad first. Shifters came out of hiding because we couldn't get sick from the Verona Virus. Humans started to notice that whole groups of people and families seemed to have immunity. We came out on our own terms, contrary to the SAU propaganda. We gave what we could and searched for a cure. We might not be fully human, but we aren't fully animals either. There was no way we would allow people to die while we stood back and did nothing."

"You saved us?" she asked, her voice low.

He gave a tight nod. "And in thanks, the humans brought in their military and killed many of us. They were scared of what we were and what we could do if we wanted more. They might have lost people, but they still outnumbered us. The SAU formed soon after, and they threw us in camps and made up arcane rules and regulations to keep us in check. We have no rights, no future beyond the walls and fences that surround us. They put wolves together with other wolves, regardless of different Packs. They did the same to the cats and bears, not thinking one minute about the numerous species within those sets of shifters. We had to quickly form our own hierarchy within the dens or we'd have been lost." Flashes of memory from that time assailed him, and he swallowed hard, clenching his fists.

"What do you mean?" Her hand hadn't moved from his chest, and he wasn't about to let her move it. He *liked* her touch and damn well wanted more of it.

"Human society needs leadership and rules to survive. Shifters are the same way. We need an Alpha, Beta, and other parts of the Pack to function. Even in the old days, it was like that. We took what we had before and made it into what we needed here."

"Are all Packs like this then? In the other compounds?"

He hesitated for a moment, not sure what to tell her. This was his mate, though, and he needed her to know all she could to survive what was to come. "Yes. The humans cut us off from the other dens around the cities as well as the feline and ursine ones around Denver. However, we have our ways."

She blinked at that. "So you're in communication with the others."

Shit. He was breaking the rules left and right for her today. "Yes."

"And you can't get into more of it because it's your secret," she said softly. "I get it. You probably shouldn't have told me this much, right?"

He snorted. "Right. I also shouldn't have changed you, Ariel. There are reasons for our rules."

She licked her lips. "The SAU and the rest of us think shifters can only be born." She frowned. "That's probably why they're using me and others...to find a way to make their own."

"And if they find out that an Alpha or a mate can change a human into a wolf..."

"Oh God, they'll force you to make others."

He nodded. "They already force us to do so much, we can't be forced to do that." He cupped her face, trying to convey the gravity of the situation. "We have to hide you, Ariel. The humans don't know every single shifter in their compounds. They tried at one time, but when we first started, the SAU wasn't as organized. They killed hundreds of us and kidnapped others for experiments." Bile rose in his throat and he let out a breath. "They didn't keep good enough track, so they don't know how many they keep within these walls. But they *do* know every single person inside has a brand and a collar."

"That's barbaric."

"That's reality," he snapped. He could sense Soren outside the door and knew their time alone had come to an end. He'd have to take her outside to face his Pack and be branded. Fuck, this wasn't going to end well. "If I hadn't bitten you to change you, you'd have died. Maybe you would have been okay with that, but I wasn't. Not only did I want to save your life because of what would happen when the humans found you dead on our doorstep, but you are my mate. I know I took your choices away, but we can't go back now. Only forward."

Her jaw tightened and her nostrils flared. "I'm grateful to be alive, but everything's changed so quickly, and I'm not up to speed. You're going to have to give me a minute or two to think."

"I'm afraid you don't have a minute." He cursed. "This is what's going to happen. We're going to dye your hair so you at least look a little different than you did before." He pulled at the dark strands. "I think you can go a little lighter and you can cut some off if you want."

"You want to dye my hair," she said dryly. "Because that will save me. Just like Clark Kent and his glasses."

He snorted. "Not quite that severe. You're my mate so it's not like you're in a low profile position, but we can try to hide you until the others forget

about you. The hair job might work for a little while."
He let out a breath. "We will have to get you a collar. If
you don't have one on and an SAU guard sees you, it's
an automatic death sentence."

"You have to wear them all the time? Even in
bed?"

He nodded. "Always, Ariel. We aren't people here.
We're lab experiments and zoo animals. You'll have to
blend in to live."

"And you said you aren't strong enough to get
out."

He winced at that. "Not together. We have
submissives who don't fight—they can't because their
wolves nurture. We have children and elderly who
would be caught in the crossfire. It's not as simple as a
war." If war was ever simple. He cupped her face once
more. "Ariel, you'll need the brand and the tattoo. I'm
sorry."

"I don't have a choice, do I?" She didn't cry,
instead she looked resigned. He wasn't sure what to
make of that.

He shook his head. "No, for that, I am sorry. But I
can't apologize for saving your life. I know it's too
much right now, but I'm yours, just as you are mine.
We will have to face that reality at some point. First,
we must protect you and our Pack." He didn't miss the
look in her eyes when he'd said 'our.' "After that, we
will work on the next steps. I'm in a position of power
with my people. I cannot let them fall because I fear
my choices and let you fear yours."

"It's a lot to take in at once, Holden," she said
then pulled back from him. She scooted off the stool
and stood by his side. She was so tiny compared to
him, but he knew the strength within her. She
couldn't be anything but strong to survive the torture
she'd endured. If taking back a semblance of control

helped her survive the memories, then he'd try to make it happen.

A knock at the door interrupted them. "That would be Soren, my Beta."

She wrapped her arms around herself and looked toward the front door. "Your second in command?"

"Yes. He's also my best friend and pissed as hell about what I risked."

"Meaning he doesn't like me."

Yes. "He doesn't know you."

"You don't know me," she said dryly.

"I'm trying to," he countered.

She rolled her shoulders back. "So there is the Alpha and Beta. Anything else I should know?"

"Tons," he said with a laugh. "But we'll get there. There is usually an Omega within a Pack, a healer of physical and emotional needs. However, our Pack is lacking one. Hard to complete the set when we can't meet new wolves over time."

Soren knocked again, this time louder, and Holden held out a hand. "We need to face the Pack. They're out there and will want to know what we're doing." He tugged her close and looked down at her. "You need to stand by my side and don't fight me. I know you want to scream and rage for what I did to you, but that will need to stay between us. We can't look as if we aren't united. If we do, the Pack will fracture."

"That sounds so political."

"It is. We have our own rules and problems within the den. Add in the SAU and what could happen outside these walls? It's a shitstorm. That's why I need you to at least pretend you are happy by my side. You don't have to lie and say you love me and want that future with all of your heart, but don't tell the others you'd rather have died than be one of us."

She sucked in a breath. "I *never* said that."

"You didn't have to."

"You're an idiot. Don't put words into my mouth. I might not be happy I had no choice, and I might be confused as hell, but I am not going to let others get hurt because I'm confused. Now, let's go see this horde of scary, dangerous wolves so I can get my flesh burned and hide from the humans who tried to kill me. Because *that* sounds like a fun way to spend the day."

He snorted then pulled her close, wrapping his arms around her. She hesitated a moment, before sinking into his hold. She used humor and sarcasm to get her through the pain, but he knew the agony lay right beneath the surface. The fact she felt so good in his arms meant he'd have to deal with his own feelings as soon as he took care of his Pack.

As always, Pack first, Alpha second.

Holden pulled her toward the door and opened it, his wolf once again at the surface. Soren stood on the other side, his face grim, his hands fisted at his side.

"Ready?"

"Yes," Holden lied. He looked down at Ariel who had squared her shoulders, her gaze on the people behind Soren. "Come, Ariel." Time to face the consequences of his decision to save her life... and to find a slice of what happiness he could.

He stepped past Soren, Ariel by his side, and met the gazes of the wolves that he called his own. Some openly gawked at the woman at his side, others smiled or glared. Their emotions ran the gamut, and he knew he'd have to defend his choice of not only a mate, but what he'd done to save her life.

He'd broken Pack law, and now he would have to face Pack judgment.

"This is Ariel. My mate." Grumbles and shouts rang from the others, but he held up his hand. They soon quieted. "The humans left her nearly dead. It was the only way to save the woman my wolf has chosen as his own. I will not regret what I have done, but I will ask for your patience."

"The humans will kill us!" Ana called out.

"Not if we hide her," Theo said, surprising the hell out of Holden.

"Is she really yours?" Mandy, a submissive asked, her eyes downcast.

"Yes, she is really mine."

"Then we will protect her," Mandy whispered then leaned into Theo. The two of them were friends only, but the dominants and submissives always cared for one another. The fact that this submissive was the one to say what she did spoke volumes about her own strength.

Soren came to his side, the flash of metal in his hand making Holden wince. "Are you ready?" his Beta asked Ariel, ignoring Holden all together. It seemed his best friend wasn't happy with him at all.

Holden turned Ariel in his arms so she was forced to look up at him. "We need to collar you and brand you quickly. The Pack ink can come later because the humans don't look for it, same as the mating ink. But we need to do the rest now."

She let out a breath then met his gaze. "I guess I should get used to my new normal."

"I guess so." Soren held out the collar and Holden took it in his hands. "I'm sorry," he whispered, so low that only she and Soren would have been able to hear.

"Don't be. Not for this." Her gaze remained on his as he snapped the metal in place. The collar was more than a way for the humans to know who could shift. It was the embodiment of all that his people hated. It showed the world they were animals locked in cages. That they had no freedom and lived on the whim of a government that considered them nothing more than a blood bank in case the Verona Virus hit again. His hand traced over the cool metal on her overheated skin, and he held back a sigh.

He'd locked the one woman who would be his into a fate she had no way of escaping. Selfish did not begin to underscore his actions. Yet he couldn't regret it. Not even then. Soon she would find her place within the Pack and learn who she was a shifter. His friends and people would welcome her or shun her, but they would learn to respect her as their Alpha's mate.

Soren cleared his throat and Holden looked into the eyes of his best friend. "The next part must be done now, Holden. She will need time to heal, and since she has not shifted yet, it will take her longer than others."

Ariel let out a breath, the held out her arm. "I feel like I'm in another world or dreaming." She licked her lips, bracing herself. "More like a nightmare, right?"

Soren held out the branding iron, hot from the fire and Holden gripped it. "I'm sorry," Holden whispered.

"You have to do it?" she asked, her lips thinning.

He met her gaze. "Yes. I have to brand each and every one of my people."

"Oh, Holden," she whispered. "Those bastards deserve to rot in hell."

From the snickers and hollers from the people around him, they'd heard it, too. He swallowed hard then met Soren's gaze.

"Ariel is it?" Holden's friend asked. "I'm going to hold you down so Holden doesn't hurt you more than he needs to. You can scream and shout and do everything you need to. Okay?"

Holden held his breath as his best friend wrapped his arms around Ariel, holding her back to his chest. His wolf raged, not wanting to do this. Fuck he wanted to run away and take her and whomever else he could with him. That wasn't an option, though, and he needed to do this to protect her.

"Breathe for me, siren," he said softly. "Breathe."

"I forgive you," she whispered back.

He let out a sigh then touched the hot iron to her flesh. Ariel's eyes widened, and she screamed. It pierced his heart, and his wolf slammed into him, wanting to kill whoever had dared hurt her. Only the fault lay in his hands, not another's. It would always be in his hands. He was the Alpha. The one to protect. The one to brand.

He pulled back then blew on her burnt flesh. He would never forget the sound of her pain or the smell of her seared skin. He threw the iron to the grown and pulled Ariel to his chest and away from Soren. She whimpered in his arms, clutching her own arm to his chest. He ran his hand down her hair and murmured to her, trying to soothe her hurts.

It was just one more thing in a long line of regrets he had to bear. He knew it might be for the greater good, but he'd never let the memory of her pain leave him. He'd been the one to do this, the one to make her cry.

And this was only the beginning. Their true agony would be waiting for them. Of this, Holden was sure. Because no matter how hard he would try to hide her and keep his people safe, they were still prisoners.

They would never be safe.

CHAPTER 4

Less than a day in her new body, and Ariel had no idea who she was or why she'd given in so quickly. It made no sense. She shouldn't have held out her arm, shouldn't have allowed him to brand her as cattle. It was like an out-of-body experience. Holden had said it was to save her life and the life of his Pack.

She deliberately ignored his use of the word 'our' when it came to Pack and Holden. One minute she'd been a normal human, trying to earn a living and find her place in a post-Verona world. The next she'd been strapped to a metal table, screaming in agony. Take another breath and she'd been dying in a man's arms. If she thought really hard about the memories and tried to clear the fog away, she could almost hear his voice, assuring her she'd be okay. Maybe it was just her trying to make up a memory of what he'd done. Now though, she wasn't that woman dying in a forest. She'd woken up to find her whole world had not only changed, but she'd have to change with it.

The lies she'd been told her entire life about what the compound held and *why* they were there in the first place made her uneasy. It wasn't that she was gullible—far from it—but she'd seen the evidence of what shifters truly were when she'd stood out on that porch, her arm out, ready to be branded. The men, women, and children who had stood there, staring at her with so many differing expressions on their faces, weren't the monsters who filled so many humans' nightmares. They weren't the boogeymen in the closets used by human parents to keep human children in check—or even the boogeymen the SAU propaganda used on those human parents to keep them in check.

They were alive. They were collared. They were branded.

They'd been forgotten by so many people who once knew them as humans twenty-five years ago. But she knew she would never forget them, never forget the pain on their faces as they watched her being branded...never forget the anguish on Holden's face when he'd been forced by the very humans he'd saved to do an unthinkable act.

All in the name of his people and their safety.

It killed her.

She fingered the unfamiliar collar at her neck and frowned. They lived with these every day, a solid, heavy reminder of their place in the world. Maybe one day she could forget the scarred flesh on her arm and cover it up, but she'd always feel the weight around her neck. How the hell had she ended up here?

If she had been a different person, she might not ever be able to forgive him for turning her in the first place. But she wasn't that person. Instead, she was the woman who'd been through hell all on her own and had to learn to see things from numerous perspectives in order to stay alive.

So, no, she didn't blame Holden for turning her into a wolf. She couldn't. Not when the alternative would have meant her death. But she wasn't sure what she was going to do with this new information, this new life of hers. It wasn't only that she had to learn to shift and do everything that came with being a wolf. It was that she actually had to learn to *be* a wolf. Comprehend that this wasn't a dream, that this was her new life. It didn't make any sense, but sitting around trying to pretend it wasn't real wouldn't help anyone.

She'd already noticed she could hear and see better than she had before all this had happened. And earlier, she'd been able to smell Holden's cooking in a way that startled her. It was as if she could scent the delicate trace of cinnamon, whereas before, she never would have noticed the spice's presence at all.

This wasn't her going crazy. Something had changed within her, and she'd have to deal with that. There would be no burying her head in the sand when it came to being a shifter.

If only she could do the same when it came to the *other* part of Holden's presence. Mates and bonds and tattoos that signified a connection made no sense to her. She'd never been in a real relationship, let alone one with a man she didn't know, which from the sound of it, was a permanent one she would never be able to get out of.

His wolf had chosen her.

But what about her wolf's choice?

What about her choice?

Yes, he was fucking sexy as hell. With those long lines of muscle that spoke of strength, he was the epitome of her type. He'd forgone shaving that morning so he had just the slightest edge of beard that made her want to feel the scrape on her inner thighs, feel his tongue sliding between her wet folds as he tasted every inch of her.

She blinked and pressed her legs together.

What the hell?

Where had that image come from? She'd been worrying about her place and what it meant and now she could only think about him sliding between her legs and eating her out? There was something definitely wrong with her. Maybe it was a symptom of her new wolfiness. Maybe shifters were perpetually horny, and they couldn't help themselves.

Ariel closed her eyes and pressed her face into her hands, only to suck in a breath and immediately drop her arms.

Fuck that hurt.

Soren and the others had said she wouldn't heal as fast as the other wolves until she made her first change, but she knew the brand had already begun to heal. In fact, she'd healed already from the bites and torture from the SAU, so there was no denying she'd been changed, as much as she wanted to. Soren had mentioned that her major healing was a one-time thing since she'd just been changed, but she was foggy about the details. The brand hurt like hell underneath the bandage, but it itched just enough that it had to be healing ever so slightly.

Perhaps it was her wolf that had made her feel almost...safe...in allowing Holden to brand her. Damn, she needed to stop thinking of Holden as the one branding her. It wouldn't help her decide what to do next.

The truth was, Holden may have held the metal iron, but it hadn't been him branding her, hadn't been his wolf.

It had been the humans who had forced him to do it. Who had forced him to do it to countless others.

She hadn't seen all of the Pack yet, but she'd seen enough of them to know Holden must have carried out that trial to the point he might never be whole again. The pain that came from being forced to hurt another person wasn't something a man like Holden would get over.

"And how the hell would I know what kind of man Holden is at all," Ariel muttered.

"You need only ask."

She turned on her stool, her heart racing. "Holden. I didn't know you'd come back inside." After the branding, she'd gone inside to heal alone once Soren finished bandaging her up. Holden had offered to come or send someone to be with her, but she hadn't wanted to face someone when she'd been so weak. That trait wasn't a wolf thing; it was an Ariel thing. Even with the new senses, she at least had that much of her remaining the same.

He'd remained outside to talk with his Pack. It made sense that he'd needed to do that without her there. Oh, he might have said she could be there, but she knew it differently. He'd risked the lives of so many just for her—a woman he didn't know. People had the right to vent without her being there. Soon she'd have to deal with the consequences of his actions, but not now. The others needed space to hear the details of what Holden had done, and Ariel needed the freedom not to be lashed at when they first heard.

"I just came back in," Holden said softly. He frowned and strode into the kitchen fully holding out his hand. "Let me see your arm. You shouldn't get an infection, not with the change working its way through you, but I want to see the brand."

Soren had covered up the burn with gauze and tape before heading back out to the porch with his Alpha. He hadn't spoken a single word, but had glared enough to show her his disapproval. Not only did she need to deal with a Pack in danger because of her, but Holden's best friend apparently hated her, too.

Perfect.

"If you want to see, sure," she said, holding out her arm for him. "Soren said it would take a while to heal though, so it's probably pretty ugly right now." She'd marred her skin because of the situation and would never be able to take that back. She honestly didn't know how she felt about that, or frankly, how she *should* feel about that.

He frowned and gently took her arm in his hands. His calloused fingertips scraped against her skin, but didn't hurt. In fact, it made her...need. Hell. What was with this man? One look at him and she wanted to rub up against him like a cat in heat. Or maybe it was a wolf in heat?

Oh crap. Now her brain was making wolf sex jokes. She needed a drink. Or a nap.

He traced his finger along her skin, gently lifting the bandage without pulling too hard. She sucked in a breath before looking down. She hadn't known what she'd expected to see, but the angry red flesh wasn't it. Holden's and the rest the Pack she'd seen had dark brands that looked like raised tattoos surrounded by their Pack tattoo. She hadn't seen a mating tattoo on the right side, but she figured it would look similar to the Pack tattoo.

"It's healing nicely. Faster than what I would have thought. That's good. It means your wolf is strong." He cleared his throat, his eyes still on her skin. "I can't believe I did this to you."

"Its not you," she whispered. "It's what they made you do."

"And if I were a stronger Alpha, I wouldn't have to do it at all."

She wasn't sure that was the case. She saw the size of him and some of the others. They had to be strong. But they were highly outnumbered and outgunned. It would be harder than one man fighting against another to win. When she told him as such, his head raised and he gave her an odd look. She didn't know what it meant, but she felt as if he were seeing her in a light he hadn't before.

"Why is yours darkened in?" she asked, trying to get the feel of Holden's touch out of her mind. She also wanted him to focus on something other than his perceived weakness. There wasn't a weak thing about the man in front of her.

He cleared his throat and tore his gaze from hers. "We add ink to the flesh once it's fully healed. We can't tattoo over all of the scarred skin, but enough of it that we can make the brand as much of ours as we can."

She nodded and looked down at the brand. If it had been a pure tattoo, one of her choosing, she would have thought it was beautiful. The long lines of tribal blended into a wolf howling at the moon. Instead, all she saw was ownership she had never wanted to claim.

Holden brushed a piece of her hair behind her ear and she froze. "Are you okay?"

She swallowed hard, too aware of the man in front of her. She truly wanted to reach out and rake her nails down his chest and tilt her head up so he could brush his lips across hers. Was this the wolf? Or the woman? Because if she couldn't tell, she wasn't sure she could do anything about it. She didn't like being out of control, and as it was, she didn't have much control, if any, of her life anymore.

She needed *something* that was hers.

"I don't know," she answered honestly.

He nodded and cupped her chin. "What's going on in that mind of yours?" His thumb stroked her skin, and she had to keep from turning in his hand. Seriously, what was wrong with her? She didn't even *know* him.

But she wasn't going to get out of her situation by living in her mind. Not voicing her thoughts—at least some of them—wouldn't change the brand on her skin or collar around her neck.

"I don't know what part of my reactions are me or my..."—she cleared her throat—"or the wolf. I haven't shifted, so I have no idea if I'm really a shifter like you say, but I have all these extra senses, and I want do things I know I shouldn't, and now my head hurts." She closed her eyes and tried to wish herself back in time so she could say what she needed to say eloquently rather than the ramble she'd just done.

Holden let out a breath then lifted her chin. She opened her eyes cautiously, praying she wouldn't see laughter in his eyes. She wasn't sure she could deal with that right now.

"I know it's a lot for you, Ariel. Hell, it's a lot for any of us when we're dealing with another half of us we've always had. I can tell you it's been since we were first put in this compound that one of us has changed a human. So I think I almost forgot that it's going to be ten times as worse for you. For that, I am sorry."

She licked her lips, her pulse racing at his touch. They had so many more important things to talk about, yet all she could think about was how he would taste. There was truly something wrong with her.

His nostrils faired and his eyes darkened. "Well fuck, siren."

"What?" she croaked.

"I can scent your need, darling, but I'm not going to do anything about it right now. Only because we need to talk first, and you need to find your way. Me pawing you won't help that, but fuck, you make it hard." He grinned. "You make *me* hard."

Her cheeks heated as mortification rolled over her. She was embarrassed before, but this surely took the cake. "Oh."

He rested his forehead against hers. His breath brushed over her skin, and she fought keep steady so she wouldn't tremble.

"Don't be embarrassed, Ariel. With our heightened senses, it's hard to keep secrets. Most of us aren't animals and try to ignore it. I shouldn't have said anything to you about it at all, but you keep me off kilter."

"So you can scent when I...when others...?"

He let out a rough chuckle, his face still close to hers. "Yes, but it's usually mixed with all the other scents out there so I ignore it. But with you? You're mine, you see, so I'm attuned to it, to you. It makes my wolf want to ease your need."

She pulled away, frowning. "So it's just your wolf? Does this mean the fact I can't focus on what I need to focus on is because of my wolf? I don't know how I feel about that."

He shook his head. "That's only part of it. For those of us who were born with our wolves, we've learned the delicate balance of control." He ran a hand over his face. "It's not that my wolf is making me want you; it's that he chose you for my mate in the sense that he knew you'd be perfect for us. What that means? Well, that will come once you and I learn each other. As for wanting you? That is all man. Yes, my wolf might push at my emotions and make me growl more when it comes to wanting you, but he's not in control that way."

Well, that wasn't at all what she'd expected him to say. "So...I want you, but my wolf is just...enhancing it?"

His lips twitched, and he nodded. "That's one way to put it." He played with the ends of her hair, his face set with concentration. "We're going about this in every wrong way possible, but we'll figure it out. It'll take a while for you to find your wolf and shift for the first time. If I remember right, it'll be on our hunt that you can shift. That won't be until the full moon."

She raised her brows. "So you can only shift at the full moon?"

He shook his head. "No, but the pull is stronger then. You'll feel it, an itch under your skin and a tug between the two sides of you that you're just now feeling. We can't go back to the way things were, but we can figure out how to make things work the way they are now. Okay?"

He said the same things she'd been thinking, so it wasn't a stretch to agree with him. "Okay."

Holden let out a relieved breath. "Good." He looked so uncomfortable for a moment, she took pity on him and tried to lead the conversation.

"So what do we do now exactly?"

"We need to finish hiding you fully within the Pack. The SAU doesn't watch our individual movements as much as they used to. They don't keep count of us, so honestly, you can blend in as a woman they hadn't noticed before. Since you have the brand, they'll ignore you for the most part. You need to keep your collar on at all times and don't bother the guards when they are around. As long as we keep your true origins secret, that'll be the easy part."

She swallowed hard. "And everyone will keep the secret?"

He met her gaze, the torture within his eyes slicing through her. "It would mean our death or something so much worse if the humans found out how we can change others. They'll keep the secret, though I know a few aren't too happy I changed you."

She reached out and put her hand on his chest. His heart beat firmly against her palm, and she sucked in a breath. "They have a right to their anger. I don't blame them for that."

"Nor do I, in all honesty. But I need to figure out how to make it right."

So did she. He'd saved her life, and now, somehow, she would have to prove that she'd been worth it. She might not know where she was going with respect to Holden and his claim, but she couldn't be weak and useless when it came to the Pack. She'd find a way to prove her worth.

Somehow.

"You will. Once you're healed, you'll come with me and I will introduce you to the Pack fully. We'll find a place for you, Ariel. There are always things to do."

"I won't be a burden," she whispered.

"You could never be," he said softly, coming closer to her again. So close she could feel the heat of him, the *need* of him. "You've already taken this better than anyone could have thought. You'll pull your weight and find your place." She watched the long lines of his throat as he swallowed. "You'll find your place with the Pack...and with me."

Her heart raced, and she tilted her head up so she could see his eyes. He licked his lips and her gaze followed the movement.

"I want to kiss you, siren. Will you let me?"

She cleared her suddenly, dry throat. "I thought you were Alpha, yet you're asking like that."

He cupped the back of her head and lowered his face so barely an inch sat between them. "I don't ask anyone else. For you? You, I will always ask, always let have a choice. You're my mate, Ariel. You're *mine*."

She said the only thing she could say right then; the only thing that made sense in a long line of confusion and pain. "Then kiss me."

He growled softly, sending shivers down her spine. When he lowered his lips to hers, she broke. The softness, the tender care in which he moved made her shake, made her *crave*. With one hand still on his chest, she gripped his shirt, pulling him ever so closer. He kept one hand on the back of her head and used the other to cup her face, gently running his lips back and forth over hers. Since she sat on a stool and he stood between her legs, they were the perfect height for this.

She moaned against him, wanting more, and he didn't let her want more for long. His tongue traced her lips, and she opened for him, letting her tongue brush along his. He growled, deepening the kiss. When he pushed closer, she moved her hand from his chest and wrapped both arms around his waist, pressing her breasts to his body. He kissed her, nibbled at her lips, and sucked on her tongue. Her body shook, her need for him an ache she'd never felt as deeply before with any other man.

Too soon, he pulled away, his breath coming in pants to match hers. He rested his forehead on hers once again, as she fought to catch up.

"Wow," she whispered then shut her mouth.

He let out another rough chuckle, and kissed her forehead. "I like the sound of that wow."

"Pretend I said something eloquent and meaningful just then, okay?"

"As long as you pretend I didn't just paw you after all you've been through."

She pulled away and smiled. "I don't think I can do that. I liked the pawing, even if I'm still confused as hell."

He smiled full out, his face brightening. Hell, he was so handsome, so freaking sexy. It was no wonder she'd latched on to him like a drowning woman, and he was a life preserver.

"Confusion we can deal with. It's not going to be any clearer with just one day of explanations. But what we just did? I'm not going to lie. I liked that. A lot."

She blushed and bit her lip. "Okay, then. Maybe we should do it again. Just to be sure." Who was this woman, and where had she come from? Ariel kind of liked her.

Holden just snorted then leaned forward and brushed his lips along hers. She moaned into him once more. She could get used to this.

"It's true. I thought it was a lie, but it's true."

Holden froze and Ariel stiffened at the woman's voice. He let out a growl then turned on his heel, blocking Ariel from view.

"What are you doing in here, Claire?"

Claire. Who was she? Ariel shifted so she could see around Holden and tried not to frown. The woman stood at the edge of Holden's kitchen, her arms folded over her ample chest. She had to be a full six inches taller than Ariel and looked like a warrior princess with her long flaming red hair.

"I heard what you said out there about *her*, but I thought it had to be a lie. You must have just used the mating excuse to keep her alive since you had a moment of idiocy in changing her. You wouldn't have taken a mate you didn't know after *years* of saying you wouldn't mate anyone. You wouldn't mate me. It doesn't make sense, Hold."

Hold.

This woman knew him, knew him intimately if Ariel guessed correctly. It had occurred to her that Holden would have a past, but she hadn't thought he would push someone aside for her. She didn't know enough about mating, but she knew enough about cheating and broken hearts.

Cold, she pulled away from Holden and wrapped her arms around herself, ignoring the ache in her forearm from the brand.

"Claire. This is my home. You cannot come and go as you please."

"You're kicking me out," the other woman whispered.

"This is not your home, Claire. It never was. We aren't mates, and haven't been together in a year. I don't know what you're trying to accomplish by coming in here and making a scene, but this is not like you." Holden took a step to the side and clasped Ariel's hand. "Despite what you thought, Ariel *is* my mate."

Ariel wanted to crawl in a hole and hide. So one of Holden's exes wasn't happy with the mating. That wasn't surprising, but this was *so* not the way to go about it.

"Holden."

"Go home, Claire. We will talk about this later." He looked down at Ariel. "All of us will talk."

Ariel met Claire's gaze and didn't like what she saw. This woman had loved Holden, probably still loved him despite Holden saying they hadn't been together in a year. Ariel didn't blame the other woman for the animosity, but this was not how she wanted to start her new decision in becoming part of the Pack.

Claire shook her head then turned on her heel and stomped away, slamming the door behind her.

"Fuck. I'm sorry about that. I was so focused on the taste of you, I didn't sense her coming in. I need to be more careful about that. You cloud my brain."

She shook her head and hopped off the stool. "I don't think I should be flattered that I cloud your decisions."

Holden scowled. "That's not what I said."

"But that's sort of what it came out as. As for Claire, you say you haven't been together for a year, but she looks pretty hurt, Holden."

He let out a curse. "I haven't been with *anyone* in a year. My wolf didn't want any of the women here so I had to be careful who I was with. I'm Alpha, siren. I can't just mate with anyone and let them lead the Pack with me. I needed who my wolf wanted, too. We both want you, not Claire. I'm sorry that she's hurt, but she shouldn't have come in here like she did. There had been a distance between her and I, and now she's tried to come closer."

"It's a lot, Holden," Ariel whispered. "Each piece seems difficult, the Pack, the SAU, my wolf, and now Claire. But put it together? It seems insurmountable."

He moved forward and cupped her face. She didn't move away, needing his touch more than she wanted to admit. "It might seem that way, but it's not. One step at a time and we will figure it out. Together. I promise you, siren."

He could make those promises, but that didn't mean it would all work out. So much was out of their hands. Even if they could overcome that, she still had a fate she would need to learn to accept.

Because she might have craved his touch, his taste, but that didn't mean she would be able to survive the burn of a world that she didn't know.

CHAPTER 5

The next day, Holden's wolf ran him hard. Between Claire, Soren, and some of his packmates, he and his wolf were already on edge. Add in the fact that he'd put Ariel in his bed last night—he'd spent the night on the couch—and he was ready to jump out of his skin. His wolf wasn't happy with the decision, but neither Holden nor Ariel was ready to sleep all night next to the other.

She needed space, and he needed the ability to breathe since he wouldn't have been able to hold himself back once she curled into him. He could just imagine the feel of her lush ass pressed against his cock when he spooned her.

Holden growled and adjusted his dick in his pants. Sporting a hard-on while trying to think of how to integrate Ariel into the Pack that day wasn't making any of this easier. In fact, it was damn near impossible.

"Holden?"

He turned as Ariel made her way to him. She tugged on her long-sleeve shirt covering her brand. Every time he looked at it, he wanted to howl, but he held back for her sake. He needed to act like everything was as normal as possible. Going off about something he couldn't change wouldn't help anybody.

One of the submissives in the Pack had dropped off a few things for Ariel to wear and use. He was so damn grateful for those in his life. While he did his best to protect what was his and make the tough decisions, it was the submissives who nurtured the Pack and provided comfort through the little things, and sometimes, even the big things they did.

"Everything okay?"

His mate gave him a small smile before pulling her hair back from her face. The long locks curled over her shoulders and down her back—sexy as hell.

"Yeah. I wanted to thank you and whoever brought me the clothes. And well, everything they brought." She shrugged and let out a sigh. "I can't even say I only had the clothes on my back when I came here since I was naked at the time."

He winced at the memory of the blood covering her body and held out his arms. "Come here."

She raised a brow. "Why?"

He rolled his eyes. "Because I'm a wolf and you are, too. We hug. We touch. It's a shifter thing. Let me comfort you."

She looked hesitant but walked into his arms anyway. He wrapped his arms around her body and sighed before inhaling her sweet scent. "Am I comforting you, too?"

He let out a low growl and she froze. Damn it. He *knew* she wasn't used to the ways of the wolf, but he couldn't help his reactions sometimes. "Yes, siren, you comfort me."

"Good," she mumbled then relaxed in his hold once more.

They stood there, holding each other in silence for a few minutes until someone cleared their throat. Holden had heard his friend and Beta enter the house, but he didn't want to let go of Ariel.

Ariel moved away from him and turned. "Soren, hi."

She was so damn awkward around the man and Holden didn't blame her. Soren hadn't been welcoming, but then again, he couldn't blame his friend, either. It was all a big clusterfuck, but he hoped they'd all find a way to fix it.

Soren nodded at Ariel before turning to Holden. "We have a problem."

Holden cursed. Of course there was a problem When wasn't there a problem? "What is it?"

"The sentries spotted the guards at the entrance," Soren explained. "The SAU sent a few guards and soldiers into the compound. They should be in the den center in the few minutes. They want all of us there." His Beta leveled a look at Holden. "They've come in for inspections, but this smells different."

"Fuck." Holden ran a hand over his face and turned to Ariel. "We drew in the Pack tattoo this morning, so don't rub on it just in case they look too deeply at it. We'll have to get you properly inked tonight or tomorrow. The wound looks a little red still, but you're healing enough that the brand won't look out of place. Just act as calm as possible and stand by my side..."—he cursed again—"...unless it looks like they're trying to get me to act out or shift then go to Soren." He looked at his best friend who gave him a nod. "We'll be fine."

Ariel's eyes widened, but she nodded. "You're lying, but thank you for trying. I won't say a word, and I'll do my best to blend in. But, Holden, what if any of them are the guards or doctors who held me? You won't be able to hide me."

He nodded. "I know. But if we hide you right away and they find you, it will be worse for all of us. Hopefully, if we group together, they won't bother looking at any of us specifically. They don't usually look at our faces. They look at the brands and move on. We aren't people to them, Ariel. That prejudice has saved our lives before and, hopefully, will again."

Soren cleared his throat. "They won't be looking for you as a wolf or amongst the people Ariel. They're looking for a dead girl. They want to place the blame for the body they dropped. When they don't find it, they're going to keep looking, but they won't find you. We'll just have to be careful."

Some of the tension that had plagued Holden since he'd first bitten Ariel eased. He was sure Soren would protect his mate. Of course, Holden had enough tension that he didn't quite feel as relieved as he thought he should have.

"Just don't let me screw up. Okay?"

He leaned down and kissed her softly, surprising them both. "I won't. Now let's go. We can't be late, and I don't want us to be the last ones there. Remember. Blend."

He gripped her hand and followed Soren out of the house. They made their way to the center of the compound, their senses on alert. Holden felt his wolf growl, but he remained silent. As they walked, others came out of their small homes and joined their party, flanking Ariel, shielding her from outsiders. If he hadn't been watching it, he would have missed it. They'd done it so subtlety, that it looked perfectly normal. But he knew his wolves; this was deliberate. He didn't know if they were protecting her for themselves or for Ariel's sake, but either way, he loved his Pack right then.

She would be their Alpha along with him. It wasn't an easy task, but if they got through this, then they would be one step closer to Ariel taking her place at his side.

They gathered with the others in the center of the compound, the tension rising with every passing minute. The place wasn't that big so it wasn't as if anyone had to walk far to get anywhere. However, the guards and SAU liked to demonstrate their power by taunting the Pack with a casual urgency in their movements that kept him on edge.

There was a reason Holden had gone for a run the night he found Ariel. Being Alpha was almost too much for any one person. Ariel being by his side almost soothed him even with the added complications and secrecy. He couldn't explain it, but maybe one day, he'd ask another true mated couple to see if it was the result of the mating or was it Ariel herself who helped him breathe again? She should have been a wreck after what happened, yet she kept it together, holding her head high as she rolled her shoulders back.

He'd never been so fucking proud.

He scented the humans before he could see them. The others around him shifted from foot to foot, the anxiety mounting. Ariel put her hand on his back in order for him to keep his hands free. Smart girl. The guards knew he was Alpha, even if at first they'd tried to deny any from of hierarchy when it came to *animals*. After all, they made Holden brand his Pack because of the position he held. They kept a watchful eye on him whenever they entered the compound and would notice a woman by his side. He just hoped they didn't recognize her. The SAU, though organized, held too many cards too close to the chest. He'd noticed over time that not all arms of their organization talked to one another. It wouldn't be out of the ordinary if not everyone knew what she looked like. If they did...well he was fucked.

They all were.

"We've heard there's a dead human on your grounds," a member of the SAU announced with no preamble. "We will be searching the dwellings and the forested area for her remains. Once we find the body, there *will* be repercussions. You know the law. You kill one human; we kill ten shifters. It's only right, after all. You're lucky we don't exterminate the lot of you animals."

Holden ground his teeth together. As far as he was aware, none of his people had *ever* killed a human. They'd fought for their lives after the Verona Virus and before they were collared, but that had been during what was essentially a war and long before the laws that now held them captive were passed.

He didn't answer their taunts, didn't tell them he had nothing to hide. After all, that was a lie. He could hear Ariel's breath coming in pants even though he knew she tried to calm herself. As it was, his hands were fisted at his sides, and he could sense the aggression of the others around him. Being told they were nothing, that they had no rights and deserved death and not being able to do anything about it was the worst from of impotence. He couldn't protect his mate, couldn't protect his people...he could do nothing but take the verbal lashing while the humans searched their homes, as if they meant nothing to them.

Soren leaned closer, brushing his shoulder against his. Holden calmed down fractionally. His best friend, his Beta, was there. At least that was something. If it weren't for the children held in their mother's and father's arms, and the submissives who couldn't fight because their wolves craved nurture instead, they might have had a chance. But the bullets in the guards' guns tore through flesh and bone, taking out life in swift and too casual measures.

Protecting his people wouldn't come from teeth and claws.

It would come from words and secret alliances that, if they were to come out in the open, would kill them all.

However, he couldn't think about that. He could only think about the men in front of him, taunting him with their power, and the woman behind him, the one who could destroy his fragile hold on control.

One of the guards moved forward, his gaze on Holden. The man held his gun to his chest, his finger near the trigger but not on it.

"Is there something you want to say, *Alpha*?" The man sneered the title, but Holden didn't care about that as much as he should. This peon wasn't Pack, but an extension of hatred that didn't have a true cause. Fear led them and their actions. Holden wouldn't allow that to be the same of his people.

He tilted his head, looking more wolf than man. A clear taunt, but with so many witnesses, it would be hard pressed for the guard to do anything about it. Sure, he could try to beat the shit out of Holden— again—but that would only lead to more tension.

"Did you hear me? I asked you a question." The young guard looked as if he hadn't been born during the Verona Virus. So fucking young and so little brains.

"I have nothing to say," Holden said as calmly as he could. Ariel's fingernails dug into his back but she didn't make a sound. Good girl. This had to be scary as hell for her, but there was nothing he could do. She'd never see the cruelty of those who thought they owned the shifters. She'd seen the depravity of her own torture, and that was enough. He hated that he had to show her this as well—that he'd brought her fully into the fold with the bites that had saved her life.

The guard moved into Holden's space, trying to look bigger than he was. In reality, Holden stood a good four or five inches taller than the little-pricked bastard.

"Do I sense an attitude, *Alpha*?"

Holden smiled broadly, making sure he showed as many teeth as he could. The guard's eyes widened, and he took a few steps back. "I have no attitude. I am merely doing what I was told. I'm a good, powerless shifter." He let his eyes change to wolf, a subtle power play that might not have been smart, but was needed.

The guard paled and scurried back to his friends.

It didn't matter they were collared and caged; they were still wolves. One on one, he could slice the little bastards up before they could even reach for a weapon.

And the guards knew that.

That was why they always came in force. They knew with one move, the tables could turn—at least until the other guards showed up with the big guns. These guys didn't much care for risking their lives to wait on the others to save them. They were frightened underneath all that bluster.

And that's exactly how Holden wanted them.

He stood there, glaring at the guards who thought they held the shifters' lives in their hands. Only that wasn't the case. Not now. These individual guards could be taken easily, while some of his soldiers protected the young and those who couldn't fight.

Holden had his own sentries, his own soldiers and fighters who would lay their lives on the line for the good of the Pack.

And it was with that in mind that no one moved.

It wasn't the time to fight.

The humans would find nothing and then be on their way. And one day soon, they'd find the perfect way to take back the control they'd long since lost because they'd refused to kill those that were weaker than them. That mistake, in some shifter's eyes, had caused their branding, and Holden wouldn't allow that to happen again.

More guards joined the others and Holden frowned. These must have been the ones who had been searching their homes and outlying areas for the body they would never find.

The guards grumbled, and Holden shifted ever so slightly so he could keep them in his sight. One of the older guards, who had never once hit a member of Holden's Pack, came forward.

Holden didn't like this man—he didn't like any of them—but he knew this one wasn't as cruel as the others. This was a job to him and didn't take pleasure it in. One day, Holden would use that.

"It seems there isn't a body in any of the homes or wooded areas," the guard said slowly. He narrowed his eyes at Holden but didn't move forward. "We'll be back later to check again, but for now, you are free to go about as you were."

He nodded at Holden and moved back to the others. Soon the guards were gone, and the tension within the Pack eased marginally. Holden nodded at a few of his wolves who loped off after the guards. He wouldn't put it past the humans to lie and say there were leaving when they clearly weren't.

When the shifters were first captured, they had no freedoms and no privacy or breathing room. Now they could at least run within their territory and shift when they needed to. Yes, the guards could come in at any time and for any reason, but they didn't often. It gave a sense of peace to the young ones who had never seen the outside world. If Holden could make that peace a reality, then one day he'd earn the name of Alpha.

"Holden," Ariel croaked out.

He turned on his heal at the sound of fear in her voice and cursed. Her skin had paled to an almost greenish-gray color and her teeth chattered.

He picked her up and brought her to his chest. "What is it, Ariel? They're gone. You're safe for now."

Soren frowned at Ariel in Holden's arms and shook his head. "They didn't notice her. What's wrong?"

"I don't know," Holden ground out.

"I...I remembered some of them." Ariel closed her eyes and pressed her face to his chest. "They were there. In the room. I *remember*."

Holden froze, his body straining as pure rage poured through his system. "You're saying some of those that hurt you were here today?"

She nodded then shook her head. "Maybe? They wore the same uniforms." She wrapped her arms around herself in his arms and shivered. "I'm sorry. I...I don't mean to react like this."

Mandy, Theo's submissive friend, walked forward, her hand out. She met Ariel's eyes then Holden's. He gave her a nod and she put her hand on Ariel's arm. "Honey, it's okay. We'll protect you, darling. Now go with your mate and take a nap or cry it out. We're here for you, Ariel. You're one of us now. We won't let them take you."

Ariel sighed and relaxed slightly in his arms. Damn, he loved the submissives in his Pack. They knew how to soothe when all Holden wanted to do was rip the limbs off of whoever had hurt his mate.

He nodded at Mandy who gave him a small smile. "Come on, siren. Let's get you home."

He met the gazes of others in his Pack, knowing they'd seen his mate at her weakest. Normally, that would have been fatal to an Alpha's mate. But this was no normal wolf. This was a woman who had been tortured and brutalized, yet stood on her own two feet, facing those who had hurt her to not only protect herself, but the Pack she didn't know. It was only after the guards had left that she'd broken down.

She was far stronger than anyone had given her credit for, and the others saw that.

He got her home and into his bed, knowing Soren and the others would deal with the outside world for now. He'd go back to his full role as Alpha soon, but he couldn't do that when his mate was in pain.

He took off her shoes and socks before doing the same himself and climbing into bed with her. When she curled into him, he let out a small sigh and moved so his back was pressed against the headboard and Ariel lay on his lap.

She clutched his shirt and relaxed her body. "Thank you."

"For what?"

He ran a hand through her hair and used his other hand to stroke her back and bottom. He couldn't help himself; his mate was in his arms and not running away. Even if the worst had landed him here, at least he had her for now.

"For holding me when I couldn't walk or hold myself up." She nuzzled into him, and he had to swallow hard. Soon she'd be able to feel the evidence of his desire for her pressing against her ass if she didn't stop petting him.

He couldn't help it. She was his mate, and he was a man who wanted her more than anything. He just couldn't rush her.

"I will always be here to hold you, Ariel. I know we're just learning each other, and you're finding your way in this new world, but know this, I will *always* be here. Just because we're going about this mating thing the wrong way around doesn't mean we're actually doing it wrong."

She snorted and looked up at him. "The way you said that, it actually *does* sound like we're doing it wrong."

He winked and lowered his head to kiss her on the nose. He'd made her smile just a little. Progress. "You know what I mean. We're not doing things in the traditional way, but as you don't know the traditional way, we can just do it *our* way."

Great. Now he was rambling like a teenager rather than a man in his forties. He couldn't help it. Ariel made his brain go dizzy. It could have been his wolf reacting to her, but he knew it wasn't only that. The man wanted her to. He craved her strength, her beauty, her sacrifice.

Ariel was the one for him—body and soul.

Now he just needed to make sure she knew that and thought the same of him.

She slowly traced her finger along his chest, and he stiffened again, his cock filling. "I...I want you, Holden. Is that wrong?"

He cleared his throat and lifted her chin with his finger. "Never. That is *never* wrong. But I don't want you to want me if you're scared of me. I don't want this to be something you feel forced into because of the circumstances."

Why he tried to talk her out of this, he didn't know.

She shifted so she straddled his lap, his jean-clad erection pressed against her heat. Dear God, she was going to kill him.

Ariel cupped his face, her fingers playing with his beard. "I want you, Holden," she repeated. "I wanted you in the kitchen before, and I want you now. I know the world doesn't make sense, and we're far from understanding who we are together and who I am within these walls, but I know one thing. I want you."

He licked his lips before sliding his hands up her thighs and settling on her waist. She was just so tiny. One wrong move and he'd break her. He wasn't a small man in any respect and this wasn't any woman.

This was his *mate*.

"If we do this, there's no going back," he warned, his voice low.

She tilted her head. "There never was a way to go back," she whispered. "I don't know what will happen next, nor do I know how I'm going to deal with all these changes. But I do know I want to feel you inside me. Make me feel good, Holden. Even for a moment."

He ran his hand up her back and gripped her neck, her hair wrapped around his fingers. "It'll be for longer than a damned moment, siren. That I can promise you."

"Then kiss me."

"And that's all?" he asked before rotating his hips.

Her mouth parted and a gasp slipped out. "I want it all. Make me *feel*. Make me remember the good and forget the bad."

"Anything, Ariel. Anything."

She lowered her head and brushed her lips against his. "I don't know who I am or what I will be, but I know I want you, right here, right now. Is that enough?"

"For now, siren. That's enough for now." He pulled her closer and kissed her fully, his tongue diving in and out of her mouth, craving more, craving *everything*.

And soon, he'd have it all.

CHAPTER 6

A riel *burned.* Her body ached, and her mind whirled. She knew they were going way too fast, but she didn't care. She wanted Holden, and damn it, she would have him. She wasn't back in her small apartment trying to figure out life in a world where those with power held it all, and people like Ariel had nothing.

She existed with Holden in a place where they had the power. She flashed back to a time when she'd cried in agony, but she wasn't going to think about that now. It would *always* be there, and if she let it, it would take over her life, and she would never be able to breathe again.

She pushed those thoughts out of her mind and focused on the man who held her in his arms. He was kissing her like he wanted to fuck her hard right then and there. His hand rested on her ass, and she rocked into him, wanting his touch everywhere. He moved his lips down her jaw and licked her neck, forcing a groan out of her.

"You taste so fucking sweet, like peaches." He bit down gently on her shoulder and she shivered, her pussy aching.

"It's the lotion I found in the basket someone gave me," she said, painting. "Peaches and cream."

Holden growled softly, molding her ass in his hands. "I can't wait to taste your cream."

Ariel wanted to laugh at the line, but she couldn't. Not when Holden moved his hips just enough that the long ridge of his cock pressed against her clit. Dear Lord, she could come just from that alone.

Just when she thought she could come, Holden lifted her by the hips and set her off his lap so they were sitting in front of one another, him on his knees with her on her bottom.

"Hey!"

He grinned and kissed her soundly. "I need to taste these breasts of yours, siren." He cupped her with both hands, her breasts overfilling his palms. "I dreamed about these nipples."

She raised a brow. "Seriously? Already?"

"Hey, don't underestimate the power of your nipples." With that, he pulled her shirt over her head and undid her bra. She blinked as he threw her clothes off the side of the bed and cupped her breasts once again, his heated skin on her cool flesh.

"Jesus."

He licked his lips and rolled the tight buds between his fingers. "Perfect. Fucking perfect. So tight and sensitive," he growled. "All pink and perky. I bet if I suck on them they'll go red. What do you think?"

She rolled her eyes even as she moaned. "You have a fascination with my nipples."

"I also have a fascination with your ass, if you must know. For a small girl, you sure know how to fill out your jeans. It makes the wolf *and* the man in me want to bend you over and mount you."

"You know, that should be a turn-off, but for some reason, I just got a little wetter," she teased, and he let out a groan. She took that as a hint and reached over, pulling at the bottom of his shirt.

He let go of her and helped her strip off his shirt. Ariel about swallowed her tongue. Long lines of lean muscle and hard ridges. Holden was sex on a stick and Alpha in every sense of the word.

She reached forward to touch him and suddenly found herself on her back, Holden between her legs, his mouth on hers. He devoured her, kissing her like he couldn't hold himself back while his hands roamed her sides. She wrapped her legs around his waist and kissed him back, wanting more than she ever thought possible.

He reached between the two of them and undid her jeans. She let her hands move from his back, helped him strip off her jeans and then helped her do the same for him. Soon they were both naked, pressed tightly against one another and kissing like this was the last moment on earth. His thick cock rested on her mound, sliding over her clit with each movement. She could feel herself get wetter as he continued to kiss her, taking his sweet time with her mouth and not moving downward.

When she pulled away, needing air, he finally kissed down her neck. He licked and sucked, worshiping her body in a way no one had ever done before. He looked up from her collarbone then knelt between her legs, taking her arms in his. His gaze remained on hers as he kissed down her arm to her almost fully-healed brand. When his lips brushed over the raised flesh, she knew she could love this man.

Even in the heat of the moment, he cared for her and ached for the pain he thought he'd caused.

This wasn't time for pain, however. Instead of letting him mourn his duties as Alpha, she reached out and gripped his cock.

"Mine," she growled, and Holden sucked in a breath.

"If you want," he grunted then lowered his body, pulling from her grip. "But first, I need to taste you like I said I would." He cupped her breasts, pressing them together before laving her nipples. She bowed off the bed, her pussy contracting at the sensation of him tugging and biting at her nipples before soothing the burn with his tongue.

"Holden," she moaned, arching her back, pressing her breasts in his face.

He growled then lowered himself even further, licking down her stomach. He dipped his tongue in her belly button before going lower. He blew a cool breath on her core, and she shuddered.

"So pretty and pink," he said gruffly. His fingers traced her lower lips, spreading her. "Look how wet you are for me, my mate. So wet and *mine*." He lowered his head and latched onto her clit, flicking the tight nub with his tongue.

With that, she shattered, her eyes closing and her body bowing. She came hard, but he didn't stop licking her and biting down on her clit. When he teased her entrance with his thick finger she whimpered.

"You're so tight, siren. Are you going to fit my cock in this wet cunt?"

She licked her lips and opened her eyes. "I don't care if you're big and I'm tight. I want you inside me. *Now*."

Holden grinned, his lips wet from her pussy. "I need a condom," he grunted. "Most mated pairs don't need them, but we're taking this slow."

She rolled her eyes, even as her heart panged. "You're between my legs and just made me come with your mouth. That's not that slow."

"We're taking other things slow, siren." With that, he lifted off the bed and reached for a condom in the nightstand. He slowly rolled it on his length then positioned himself at her entrance. She lay beneath him, her eyes widening as he slowly pushed forward. "Tell me if it's too much."

She shook her head, unable to speak as he slowly filled her. She couldn't think, couldn't breath. He wasn't just big, he was *hers*. The part of her that she didn't know, the part that she knew would one day be her wolf yearned for this—knew it was their future.

The other part of her knew things would never be the same. The brand might have started her choices in this new life, but this was the step that told her she'd made her choice. She wanted Holden. She wanted this life how it was and how she would make it hers.

He lowered his body so he rested on his forearms on either side of her head. "Ariel," he whispered. "Mine."

She reached up and cupped his face before lifting her hips, allowing him to slide fully in. They both moaned in unison. "Move."

He grinned then kissed her. Hard. Before she could take a breath, he *moved*. With each thrust, she swore he grew bigger, filling her until she wasn't sure she could fit anymore in. She wrapped her legs around his waist, urging him deeper.

"Fuck, Ariel. I'm going to come." He kept moving, but put his hand between them, playing with her clit. "Come for me, mate. Come for me."

She met his gaze and came, her cunt tightening on Holden's cock. He let out a growl then came with her, filling the condom. She could feel him pulsate within her and knew one day she'd want him without the condom so he should have him bare.

He lowered his forehead to hers, breathing heavily. He didn't speak, and she didn't need him to. He'd pushed away the thoughts she'd feared and brought forth more she knew she'd have to deal with. This was her mate, her man, and her future if she let him be.

And yet, right then, all she wanted to do was think of the man in her arms and nothing else. All of that would come, and soon. But for now, she had Holden cradling her like she was precious to him.

Nothing else mattered.

There came a time for a woman to face her fears and try to be an adult. This was that time. Yet Ariel had no idea what she was doing. Today wasn't about her and Holden or even about how she would deal with whatever came with the SAU.

Instead, today came from another threat...or rather problem.

The Pack.

She'd been inside the den for almost a week, waiting for her body to fully heal and for Holden's tattoo artist, Gibson, to finish up the Pack ink on her forearm. She'd yet to leave the house as Holden had wanted her out of prying eyes from the guards, who had been prowling around under the guise of searching for a dead body.

Ariel's dead body.

So instead of trying to come to terms with her new life and integrating with the people who had protected her without even knowing her, she'd been forced to hide from them. She might have grown closer to Holden and given him her body, but she hadn't been able to do anything else.

As it was, she'd only met a few of the wolves in Holden's inner circle, but no one else. Even though the den was isolated to the point that they weren't allowed outside the walls, they had their own structure and daily routines. They farmed on the small plots of land they had near the edges of the den as well as held normal day-to-day jobs that they'd made themselves. Apparently the SAU didn't provide for much so Holden and the rest of them had found a way to make what they had and what they could make work for them.

Of course, it would have been nice if Ariel could have seen any of this firsthand. Instead, she'd been told by Holden and a reluctant Soren as she asked question after question about her new home. She had a feeling her hiding out from the others wouldn't put her on their good side. They'd already risked their livelihood because of her mere existence, and now, she hadn't even had a chance to say thank you or learn their names.

Today, however, she would get that chance.

Holden had felt it safe enough for her to venture out of his home and into the community. Well, he'd felt that after she'd begged and yelled a bit, but it got the point across.

They might be mates—a point she wasn't a hundred percent on board with until she had more time to process—but he wouldn't be allowed to walk all over her.

He'd have to learn that eventually.

Hopefully.

The Pack worked as a unit with each member contributing in some way. The dominants watched the borders for signs of threats and did other things Ariel wasn't sure about. She had a feeling those runners and soldiers did more than Holden said they did, but she didn't want to question him. Not yet. The walls might be solid and the humans might try to keep them inside, but Ariel knew these men and women wouldn't take captivity lying down. In fact, from the way some of them talked, she felt as if some of them had seen the outside world.

However, that wasn't her business. Yet.

Today, she'd be working with the submissives with canning and other food preparation. The submissives were the wolves who cared for the other wolves through calming and influential ways. They didn't want to fight if they didn't have to and would rather let their Alpha and dominants protect them, while they protected the dominants in other ways. Ariel was happy to hear that men and woman both made up the submissive group, meaning wolves didn't segregate based on gender. Ariel wasn't sure what kind of wolf she'd be, and Holden wasn't letting on if he knew, but she wanted to learn as much as she could. She'd given up hope that this was all a dream, and it was time to learn to live in her new life.

Holden ran a hand down her back, and she looked up at him. "You ready?"

"As ready as I'll ever be," she replied honestly. His nose always wrinkled when she tried to lie to him about how she was feeling, so she'd quit trying to make him feel better by lying about her nervousness. It wasn't as if she'd been good at it anyway.

"Let's go, then. I need to meet with the inner circle today, so I'm leaving you with Mandy and the others."

Mandy was one of the few wolves she'd met. After her panic attack at the sight of the guards, Mandy had not only helped her then, but she'd come by every day to see if there was anything she could do. It was nice to be able to just talk with another woman, even if Ariel felt out of sorts. None of this made any sense if she truly thought about it, so she'd done her best to try and go with the flow. If she did that, maybe she'd figure out how to be the new her.

A wolf.

One who hadn't shifted yet, but that was another problem in itself.

"I have no idea what I'm doing, Holden," she said right as they made it to their destination.

Holden frowned and turned to her. He tucked a piece of her hair behind her ear, his finger brushing along her skin. She let out a sigh, holding herself back from leaning into his touch. She didn't understand this connection between the two of them, but whatever had changed inside her wanted him.

And again, if she were honest, the old part of herself wanted him, too.

"You will figure it out. I can help you in only so many ways without harming your efforts. You will need to find your place within the Pack on your own, although I will be by your side along the way, if that makes any sense."

She nodded. It did, but that didn't make it any easier to stomach. Again, she had to push out all thoughts of what life had been like before her kidnapping because there was no going back. Only going forward and pushing her way through the chaos that was finding herself a wolf in a new land.

"Good." He lowered his head and brushed his lips along hers. "I will be here when you are finished finding out how this section of the den works. Soren

and a few of the others will be over for dinner later."
She widened her eyes and he winced. "They usually
come over for a meal after a meeting like the one we're
having now. Should I have asked?"

While her life had changed dramatically, she
needed to remember that Holden's had changed as
well. He was not only the leader of the Pack, but had
lived for years on his own without having to worry
about another person in his home. They were bound
to misstep.

"Let me know what I need to do," she said finally.
"It will be nice to learn more about everyone." If she
kept trying to say the right things, then maybe she
wouldn't mess up as much. One day she'd probably
fuck it all up, and they'd have to deal with it; however,
there were only so many changes in her life she could
take before she fumbled it all.

He nodded and kissed her once more before
leaving her on the doorstep. They'd both decided she
would enter the place on her own as his mate. She
might not bear his mark on her arm, but Holden said
she smelled like him now and no one would dare
harm her.

Only she didn't quite believe things worked that
way. This meeting would tell.

She made her way inside and stopped short at the
sight of twenty or so men and women working on
various stages of canning and boxing. Each person
held a station and looked as if they knew what they
were doing. Most had been in the middle of a
conversation or laughing when she'd walked in. As
they realized she was there, they stood or sat in
silence, their gazes on hers. Two or three bowed their
heads like she'd seen some do before, but others
looked at her like she was an outsider.

Because that's what she was. An outsider and interloper. She was the reason their lives were in jeopardy, if the humans found out what Holden had done. She was the reason things were changing since Holden had taken her as his mate. She wouldn't back down, but she would find a way to blend.

From the looks on these people's faces, she had a feeling things wouldn't be easy.

"Ariel, you're here." Mandy walked right up to her and tugged her close for a hug.

Ariel wrapped her arms around the tiny woman and tried to smile. At least one person was happy to see her. God, she needed to stop sounding so whiny and lost in her own pity party. Once she got over herself, she might be able to actually fit in and become friends with these people.

It wasn't as if she had anywhere else to go.

"Thanks," Ariel whispered. "It's good to see you," she said a bit more loudly.

Mandy smiled as she pulled back. "It's good to see you up and about. I know you had a few injuries that took a while to heal. Let me introduce you to everyone, and you can see what we do here. Once you're able to shift, you'll find where your dominance lies. Then you can figure out what job you do here."

Ariel nodded, feeling slightly more relaxed in Mandy's presence. Holden had explained Mandy's roll as a submissive, and if Ariel hadn't felt the affect for what it was, she wouldn't have believed it. The woman had a caring nature and knew how to put people at ease. What a talent to have. Being able to fight and protect the Pack would be nice as a dominant, but Ariel held great respect for those who knew how to take care of the inner health of those close to them.

Ariel met each person, holding out her hand to them in hopes that they wouldn't shun her. Every single one shook her hand while others hugged her close. She wasn't sure what it meant, but she did feel a little bit more at ease. No one looked like they wanted to be her best friend, but at least they weren't lashing out at her.

"And this is Claire," Mandy said finally, an odd note to her voice. "I think you've met before, though."

Ariel's gaze shot up to the amazon's face and held back a curse. "Hello, Claire."

Claire didn't respond. Instead, she folded her arms over her chest again and glared.

Mandy cleared her throat. "Each person in the Pack takes shifts in here as well as most of the other roles. This isn't Claire's normal job, but everyone helps out where they can. We can't leave the den, but we make the den as much of ours as we can."

"I see. That's nice." Ariel knew she sounded off, but she couldn't help it. The only time she'd met the other woman, she'd lashed out and claimed Holden as hers in every way but marking. From the look on Claire's face, there was no love lost on Ariel's account.

Ariel cleared her throat, knowing she needed to push the jealousy away. She still wasn't sure if she truly believed in wolves choosing mates and a forever kind of future with one man, but she *did* know whose arms she'd slept in the night before. That counted for more than something she couldn't quite comprehend.

"Holden said I'm going to do something similar over the next few weeks. That way I can see how the Pack runs. I'm glad I won't be the only one moving from place to place."

It was the truth, even if she'd forced a smile when she said it.

Claire narrowed her eyes. "I don't get it. How could his wolf choose you? You're not even a full shifter? A human hasn't been changed in decades, yet he deemed you worthy? It doesn't make sense. Holden risked all of our lives for you, and the lives of the countless shifters locked in cages because of *humans* like you, and you don't even look like you care. You're acting like this is just a new job or new day camp or something? Humans *torture* us, and we don't get a choice in the matter. We don't have rights. We have to lie down and watch those we love die at the hands of those who think they're better than us. And here you are, looking like you're one of us when you aren't. You don't shift. You grew up in a world where you had freedom; you were human. And now you're taking our Alpha along for a ride."

Ariel's eyes widened at Claire's tirade. So much *hatred* and yet not one word of it was because Ariel had taken Claire's ex. Oh, that might have been the underlying motivation for her words, but Claire spoke as a shifter, not a woman scorned.

"I know I am not a full shifter yet because I haven't changed," Ariel said slowly.

"And you might not ever be," Claire snapped. "You could die during the first hunt because your body can't take it. Did you even think about that? Did you think about the fact that you could harm our Alpha in the process? Because if you die, he'll be a broken shell of a man. That's how mates work. It's not sparkly and pretty like human marriages. It actually *means* something. You'll leave our Pack with a man who can't protect us, all because you want to latch onto someone to protect you."

Ariel blinked. She'd known the hunt would hurt her because it would be her first time shifting, but from the way Claire put it, it sounded as if there was a higher chance Ariel wouldn't survive. Holden had mentioned the possibility, but he'd either lied about the percentage or Claire was trying to scare her.

Ariel had a feeling it was a little bit of both.

However, none of this meant Ariel had to sit back and take it. "I didn't ask for this, Claire. The SAU took me from my home after raising me in their orphanage where I had *no one,* not even a Pack, to love me. The doctors tortured me, cut me up and injected me with so many different chemicals that I will never know exactly what they did to me. They tossed me over the fence like garbage and wanted to use my death to punish you. I didn't get a choice in what Holden did, but I can't regret it. I'm alive because of him, and I will always be grateful for that."

"Claire, stop it," Mandy said softly. The woman shook, and Ariel had a feeling it had to do with the other woman's wolf not wanting confrontation. "Please."

"Shut up, Mandy," Claire spat. "Go back to following the dominants like a little puppy."

Mandy winced and Ariel moved to stand in front of the little woman. "Hey, if you have a problem with me, you lash out at me. Not Mandy. I don't know the full dynamics of your Pack, but being a bitch to someone who is just trying to help just makes you look bad."

"Stay out of this. You aren't Pack."

Ariel held out her arm, the brand fully healed and her knew Pack tattoo freshly inked. "This begs to differ. I might have come from different circumstances than all of you, but that doesn't give you the right to speak to me like you have. And do the math, Claire. A few of the older wolves here might have been changed while human for all you know. Many of the people here were alive to live outside the walls, your Alpha included. I might not be able to shift yet, but that doesn't mean I'm *nothing*. I'm learning.

I'm trying. That's a hell of a lot more than you can say at this point."

She let out a breath and turned on her heel, done with this for the day. She'd already made a scene, even if she hadn't started it, and she could feel the stares of others on her back. She'd find a way to make this better, but forcing others to deal with her wouldn't help right then.

As soon as she took a step, she ran into a solid chest and almost fell back. Holden gripped her arms to keep her from falling.

She let out a breath, trying to not let his presence soothe her. If she let him soothe her, then he would think it was okay for him to come into her life and take over. Again. Of course, he was here to witness this. Of course, he was.

"Ariel."

"Let me go, Holden. I do not want to get into this right now. I will go back to the house, and we can try tomorrow."

"Do not let Claire win this," he said softly.

She moved her head back to look into his eyes before turning and looking at the others who might have stood up for her against the humans, but had done nothing against Claire. Yes, they were submissive in nature, but they wouldn't meet her eyes. She wasn't sure what that meant, and right now, she wasn't sure she wanted to.

"She already has," Ariel said simply then moved around Holden so she could head home. She didn't want to speak to him, not when she couldn't help but feel a slight edge of anger toward him.

He kept secrets, she knew that, but now she had no idea where she stood within the Pack, within his heart...and within herself.

The unknowing hurt more than the knowing when it came to the pain of a new life born in blood. She didn't want his touch, didn't want his comfort, not when she didn't know where they stood.

She needed to find the reason to stay, the reason to be. And letting him cloud her judgment wouldn't allow that to happen. She buried the hurt at the lack of his touch and left him standing there in a room of wolves who she might not ever gain the trust of.

Her life had changed and once she might have been able to move forward, but now she didn't know. And that hurt worst of all.

CHAPTER 7

Holden wanted to punch something. When Mandy's friend Tonya had run to him saying Claire had confronted Ariel, he'd dropped everything to see if he could help. He couldn't step in if it was a true dominance fight, but since Ariel hadn't shifted yet, he could try and ease tensions.

He had no idea why Claire kept acting like this, but there had to be a way to stop it. Of course, he blamed himself as he'd been the one to break it off with Claire, and apparently, hadn't done it well enough. He'd also been the one to bring Ariel into the fold.

Kicking himself in the ass, however, wouldn't do anyone any good. Only when he'd tried to help, Ariel had turned him away. She'd walked away from him in front of his Pack and hadn't looked back. He knew it didn't look good to others, but right then, he could only think of his relationship with Ariel, his mate.

He didn't know how to fix this. It wasn't as if he'd ever been mated before in the first place. She hadn't spoken to him except to say she needed time to think about what had happened. It was as if all the progress they'd made with each other in the past week had been washed away with one conversation with Claire.

Ariel hadn't allowed him to protect her and the wolf in him wasn't sure how to feel about that. He was Alpha, the protector. Without that, he didn't have much left. He'd used his body and his life to care for others and do what he could for them. Since Ariel had pushed him away, he wasn't sure where he could stand.

At least she'd let him sleep next to her the previous night, though they hadn't touched. His body ached for her, but his heart and mind knew he needed to think. He admired her perseverance and the way she did her best to overcome the life she'd been dealt, but she'd still pushed him away.

That was not how he'd ever expected to have a mate. And now he didn't know what to do.

Today, though, he knew he'd likely pushed her even further away, and that killed him. He hated this day of the month above all others. Today he'd shown Ariel the true cost of being Alpha—of being mated to him. She'd probably sever all ties she could once she saw the brutality that came with his role in life.

Oh she couldn't leave the den and would forever be a shifter once she went on the hunt, but now she'd find a way to leave him fully.

And he wouldn't blame her one bit once she saw what he'd be forced to do yet again.

He rubbed his hand over his own brand and tried to mentally prepare himself for what he must do. It should have gotten easier over the twenty-five years he'd been forced into this role, but it never had been. It might have been the hand of the humans that forced him into this position, but he had his own blame as well.

Enough of this shit. If he kept wallowing, he'd have to grow his hair out and form a band where all he did was moan and gripe.

He stalked toward the back of the house and took a deep breath. "Ariel? We need to go to the den center now."

She lifted her head from the book she was reading and nodded. Mandy had given her a book of Pack history for Ariel to study that morning. Holden would have to find a way to thank her for finding ways to care for his mate when he couldn't.

"Okay," Ariel said softly then stood up and kicked the floorboard. It popped up and she slid the book into the space before carefully putting the board back in place. She'd adapted so easily to keeping their secrets. He should have been grateful, instead, all he could think about was what he would have to do in a few minutes...what she'd have to see him do.

Holden stood in the doorway so Ariel couldn't walk past him. He needed to make sure she understood some of what was happening before she faced the fray.

"Today is the day of the branding," Holden said softly.

Ariel frowned and looked down at her own brand. "What does that mean?"

He closed his eyes for a moment before speaking. "It means today is the day I am forced to follow through with the SAU's sanctions. They require all shifters, ages two and above, to wear the brand of their species."

Ariel's eyes widened and her face paled. "Two?" she whispered.

He fisted his hands at his side. "Two. I was the one who branded you, and I will be the one to brand them, as well."

Ariel swayed on her feet, and he reached out and gripped her arms. "They force you to brand *babies*?"

He growled softly. "Yes. I know I've mentioned something to that effect before, but I didn't go into detail. The SAU forces me to brand every child in our Pack. I have been doing it since I was fifteen and became the Alpha."

Ariel looked up at him, and he expected to see revulsion, instead, the pity he saw there made him frown.

"Oh, Holden, I'm so sorry. I can't believe they make you do that. Those fucking bastards. They are killing you each time they force you do to that."

He leaned back. "You don't think I'm a monster?"

She shook her head and put her hand on his chest. "No, of course, not. I think those who put you in this position are. They are the same ones that gave me nightmares and made me scream. I will never blame you for what they make you do. But I have to ask, how do the babies fare? I mean, I know they heal quickly, but Holden, that's *horrible*."

He cupped her face and looked down at her, his jaw set. "What I am about to tell you must not leave this room. The Pack knows because they have faced it before, but like our secrets of the change, this is another."

"Of course, Holden. I would never hurt you or the Pack. You saved me. Took me in, even if it was against your best interest."

He relaxed marginally even though he wasn't a hundred percent sure she truly felt that way. The Pack hadn't embraced her like they might have in the past before the Verona virus had hit. But that was a discussion for another time—one they *would* be having.

"As Alpha, I can take the pain from them in this. I can't do it often, and keep my reserves for the branding."

Ariel's eyes widened and tears formed in her eyes. "Oh, Holden. You take the pain from *each* child."

"Of course," he said simply. "Every month, we tell the children they must scream and lash out as if they are in pain while I take the agony into myself. I can feel each burn, each stroke, but I can't show it. Some slips through and the humans believe it's because I hate what I am doing. It only eggs them on to keep at it. They want us to treat ourselves as monsters so they can continue to do the same."

"Holden," she whispered. "There are *hundreds* of Pack members inside these walls."

"I know."

A single tear fell down her cheek, and he brushed it away. "Don't cry for me, siren."

"I will if I want to. You're in pain because you are protecting your Pack like a good Alpha should do. And the children have to scream and pretend it hurts. I hate all of it."

"The children will feel it heal, I can't stop that, so they will have some pain later, but it's mostly itchy at that point. They wear their collars and keep their secrets. Even the babies know not to share with the humans who cage them." He frowned. "If we had an Omega, things might be different. The role as healer, for both the physical and emotional needs of the Pack, can take away that pain and diffuse it while all I can do is take it all in. But we don't have one, so I make do."

Ariel shook her head. "And if you can't meet other Packs to mate in, you might not find an Omega until the next generation."

"If at all," he said softly.

"I will need you by my side for this as my mate, Ariel. I know we aren't surefooted yet, but we need to stand tall for the parents who have to watch their children come into a fold we never should be in to begin with. We keep having children, because if we don't, the humans win, but it's a harsh reality out there. The guards will once again be there, but there is still a good chance you can remain hidden as you are."

She shook her head, her shoulders deflating. "We'll never be truly safe with me inside the den walls."

"We never were before, Ariel. I brought you in, and I'll be damned if I'll let them take you." He hadn't meant to be that honest, but she'd left him bare with her words about the branding. He'd underestimated her, and he needed remember not to do that again.

Ariel froze for a moment then frowned. "Wait. If you could do that, then why did I feel the brand marking my skin?" She held up a hand. "Not that I want you to feel that pain for me. You do enough already, and I don't want you in pain for me, but I don't understand why you didn't. Does that make sense?"

He let out a breath. "You're my mate, siren. We might not have the ink on our skin, but my wolf is yours. We're too connected for the Pack magic to work. I had trouble with my control over that power when I first started and children of friends of mine are even harder to keep a rein on the pain." His chest felt hollow, and he let out a shaky breath. "That's why people tend to stay away from me if they plan on having children. The closer I am to them, the harder it is to keep my connection in a way that allows me to keep their pain and not have it go back to them. If we have a bond in any way, it almost makes my powers null."

Ariel put her hand on his chest once again and lifted on her toes to kiss the bottom of his chin. "Never take my pain, Holden. If you want me to be a partner, then let me help. I won't leave your side today. I'll help you in any way I can. If that means holding you while you grieve the part of you the humans ripped away, then I will. I know this isn't what we thought it was, but I'm yours, Holden. All I ask is that you let me find my place."

His wolf pressed against him, wanting out, wanting to run and be with Ariel until the end of days rather than being merely the Alpha. Yet, he couldn't do that. Instead, he brought Ariel in his arms, inhaled her scent, and knew they'd find a way to make this work.

He pulled away and rested his forehead on hers. "We need to go. If we're late, the humans will take it out on us."

"The SAU," she whispered. "Call them the SAU. Not all humans would do this." Tears glazed over her eyes, even if he saw the fury in them. "But I still hate that I fell for the lies the SAU told us. I hate myself for not finding a way to free you. I'll never forgive myself."

He kissed her softly and led her away from the house. "Propaganda works wonders, siren. We'll find a way to our freedom." They had to. She slid her hand into his, and his wolf brushed up against his skin, wanting more. The wolf had already fallen for the woman—had at first scent—now the man knew her strength, her determination and wasn't far behind.

"So the guards just watch?" Ariel asked, her voice low.

Holden growled and took a deep breath. He needed to remain in full control today. If he didn't, he'd slip up and the children would feel the pain.

There was no way he could take that chance. He owed it to his Pack to protect them—even from himself.

"Yes, they watch. They also take out some of our wolves and make examples of them if we're not showing the proper respect." He clenched his jaw and allowed his wolf to once again rise to the surface. His wolf would aid in what they had to do as long as Holden held the reins.

"Examples?"

"They use Tasers and electric sticks to hurt us when we're not doing what they want."

"Barbarians."

"And yet we're the ones with the collars." He looked down at her, only to see her fingering the collar at her neck. If there had been another way to keep her safe without forcing her to endure captivity he'd have done it.

There might have been another choice...one that only a chosen few knew about, but Ariel wouldn't have survived outside the walls in that circumstance. He pushed that unnecessary thought from his mind.

They made their way to the center of the compound, Ariel's hand firmly clasped in his. A few wolves had already gathered there, waiting for Holden to begin. Not every wolf would show up for this. There was only so much everyone could stomach year after year. At first, every single Pack member had shown up as a sign of solidarity, but Holden had pushed them away after a few years. Forcing everyone to witness the brutality that came with captivity and being Alpha only hurt the morale of the Pack. So only a chosen few would stay behind and guard Holden when he was at his weakest. Friends and family members of the children who had just turned two would also be in attendance. No children other than the ones who would be branded today were there.

They didn't need to see this as they'd already lived it once. When they were adults, they would be able to come back and help Holden and those who would forever be changed. Of course, if Holden and the others had their way, by the time the children were old enough to choose, they wouldn't be behind the walls anymore, under the thumb of the SAU.

Time would tell if plans came to fruition.

Once again, he pushed those thoughts from his mind. He rolled his shoulders and let go of Ariel's hand. She brushed his hip, and he looked down at her.

"Let me hold you," she said softly.

He shook his head. "I need to concentrate," he whispered, knowing the guards were near.

She lifted up on her toes and brushed a kiss on his cheek. "Then I will be here when you need me."

He nodded, emotion clogging his throat. He shouldn't have brought her here, not when he wanted to keep her as his, but he hadn't had a choice. The Pack needed to see her, and Ariel needed to know *everything* about what it meant to be the Alpha's mate.

In his mind, once she shifted, she would be a partner, one who could stand with him and help him keep his Pack safe. She would be strong, fearless, and soft only for him. Though she hadn't shown her true wolf yet, he could taste the dominance of her soul, the strength of her heart.

She would be an Alpha's mate in truth. Of that he was sure.

There were six children today.

So many.

Of course, they hadn't had a branding in four months. The guards hadn't come to force it and Holden had held off, knowing the SAU wanted its hands in all things shifter. He'd branded more than six at one time before, but today would be long. He met Soren's gaze, and his Beta nodded. Holden would be out of energy at the end of this. It would take all in his power to keep on his feet and make it home, before he passed out in agony and sheer exhaustion. Soren would have to do his best to keep the peace and the Pack safe while Holden was out of commission.

His wolf huffed at the thought, but Holden held back a shrug. This was his lot in life, and he'd do it over and over again if it meant the relative safety of his people.

The children had wide eyes and pale faces. Three boys and three girls, all so tiny that Holden wasn't sure they even looked two years of age. Soon they would be able to shift into their wolf form, little adorable pups who would one day be the large wolves humans feared.

"Are you ready?" he asked softly, trying to keep his face emotionless. If he looked like he cared, the humans would know. Oh, the guards might not be in sight, but he could scent them. They were watching, waiting to see what Holden would do.

Each child nodded, their little hands in their parents'. They children would know their role. They would scream and hold their breath so their face would turn red. If they could, they would cry. A few children faked passing out so they wouldn't have to scream. At two years old, these pups had to endure the worst in humanity but only had to act in true pain. It was sad how good they were becoming at this.

Soren walked to his side, six collars on his arm and the branding iron in his other fist. As Beta, Soren would place the collars around the children's necks before each branding—much like he had done with Ariel.

Holden let out a breath, aware the guards had shown themselves, slowly surrounding the small group of people who had come to lend support. Every once in a while, Holden could forget they were in a cage and think worry about inter-Pack issues and dominance fights. Then things like this happened, and he got shoved to the front of their existence.

"We don't have all day, Alpha," the younger guard spat. Holden and Soren recognized him as one of those who had come looking for Ariel. "Brand the little monsters and we'll leave. I'm not in the mood to deal with your stench for longer than I have to."

"Jesus, let this kid breathe first," Theo mumbled on Holden's other side. The younger wolf's eyes widened and Holden cursed.

"What was that, bastard?" The guard flicked a switch on the electric wand and let out a weak human growl. "Did you just talk back to me?"

Holden snarled and put himself in front of Theo. The younger man might be a full grown adult, but he was still a pup in transition in some respects. He couldn't control his temper all the time, and that was a liability.

"Let's get on with the branding," Holden bit out.

The guard tilted his head up and glared. "Get out of my fucking way, or I'll tase all of you. Get me, *Alpha*?"

Theo stepped out from behind Holden, his head held high. "Come at me." Holden could hear the regret laced in Theo's tone, but did his best not to react to it. Theo would pay for his outburst.

Holden fisted his hands at his side, forced to do nothing as his Pack repeatedly bled for who they were. There was nothing he could do without harming the ones who couldn't take care of themselves. One day that would change, he had to believe their plans would work. But for now, he was powerless.

Theo stood tall as the guard slammed the edge of the stick into his side. The wolf let out a pained whimper, but only those with enhanced hearing would have been able to pick up on it.

Holden let the guard hit Theo two more times before he'd had enough. Frankly, he'd had enough years ago.

"Enough! If you want to get through the branding today, then you will let us get to it. If not, we can do it another time."

The guard spit on the ground near a still standing Theo. "Want the other end of my stick, too?"

Theo snorted. "Sounds like you want dick, asshole. Not sure why you're hiding it. Nothing wrong with that. But if that's the case, don't take your frustrations out on us."

Holden closed his eyes even as he felt Ariel's hand on his back. "Theo."

The younger wolf lowered his gaze then moved so he stood behind Ariel, flanking her just in case.

"That little bastard is going to get what's coming to him."

Holden raised his chin. "Remember, human, you can beat us with full force, but you are one tiny man with only a few other tiny men behind you. Keep taunting us, and I might lose my temper." He let his wolf rise to the surface. "Try me."

The guard gulped then gestured toward Holden's hand. "Get on with the branding."

Ariel snarled behind him and Holden froze for a fraction of a second. Fuck, her wolf had to be close to the surface, as well. Soon she'd have to shift. The hunt was that night so she didn't have long to wait. But fuck, this was bad timing.

"Sorry," she whispered, so low that only he could hear it.

He reached around with his free hand and squeezed her arm, letting her know it was okay. In most cases, becoming wolf was natural, a way to show emotion. Right then though, they had to be careful, and Theo had already tread far too close to the line.

Holden pulled her to the side so he faced the children. When he held up the branding iron, two of the children paled while the others widened their eyes. They might have been told this wasn't going to hurt them, but they were babies, they might not believe it.

One day, for every brand he'd been forced to make, he would take it out of the skin of those who had captured them. His people were branded, but not forgotten.

Ariel put her hands on his back. "I'm here for you."

He took in her strength, knowing he would need it. "Come."

The first one, a little boy with dark hair and trembling parents came forward. He held out his arm, his head held high. One day this little boy would be a dominant wolf, strong and powerful. For now, he needed to keep the innocence the humans would deny him.

Soren took the branding iron from him and stuck into the fire. The metal, a special amalgam that heated quickly, burned red hot. Holden reached for the handle, bracing himself for the pain that would come soon.

He met the little boy's eyes and gave a slight nod. The child let out a breath and screamed as soon as Holden pressed the hot iron to his skin. Only Holden knew from the look in the kid's eyes it was all an act on his part. The little boy didn't feel a thing—thank God.

Red hot flame scorched through Holden—burning through his soul. Agony swept through him, his brow starting to sweat. He was used to this, but something was off. He wasn't feeling as much as he should have. He looked at the kid again, but didn't see an ounce of real pain on his face, nor did he scent pain coming from him.

No, the pain he scented was from himself...and from the woman holding his back.

"Fuck," he cursed. The guards snickered beside him but he didn't pay them any mind.

"Keep going," Ariel whispered, pain laced through her tone.

They might not share a physical bond like so many humans thought they would, but they still had a sense of belonging, a connection like no other. Because she was his mate, the mate of an Alpha, she could take some of his pain, some of the child's pain away.

It wasn't supposed to be like this.

"No," he grunted as he pulled the iron away. "Go home," he grunted. He'd been thinking she'd see him as a monster for what he had to do, but now it was different. Now he was hurting *her*. Again.

She shook her head then reached up to cup his face. "Holden Carter. I am your mate," she whimpered then looked over her shoulder at the humans who were studying them with avid curiosity. "Let me help."

He cursed then kissed her forehead, knowing he couldn't do more with so many prying eyes. She was just so fucking strong. She'd been thrust into this situation and was talking like a dominant Alpha. He couldn't ask for anything more from her.

He'd hurt her with every brand, but she'd soothe his soul and he'd find a way to soothe hers. The humans had forced this on them, but he'd find a way to make his mate heal in all ways.

She'd already started with him, and he could never repay her. Despite the brevity of the situation, he wanted his mate, wanted the other half of his soul. And he'd found her.

CHAPTER 8

Ariel's body ached. Not only did she still feel the remnants of the branding with Holden, but her wolf, or whatever it was, kept pushing at her. According to Holden, after most brandings, he was out of commission and in need of rest. She had no idea how he'd thought he'd be able to go on a hunt tonight after that.

But he didn't need to think about that now. Apparently, her being mated to him and taken some of his pain and bled it into her. It might have hurt like hell, but it wasn't as bad as the actual branding she'd faced. She'd have done anything to protect those children and Holden. For the first time since she'd woken up in this strange place, she felt as if she had a purpose.

She was Holden's helpmate. The one he could lean on in times of strife.

And it felt damn good.

Now, though, would be another test of fate. Her first hunt. Soon she'd figure out how to shift into a wolf and know her new life was truly real and not a figment of a dream she'd never thought she'd have.

"We aren't out in the wild, so we can't hunt game or anything like that," Holden said from behind her. She didn't turn, instead inhaling his spicy scent as he wrapped his arms around her waist.

Things had changed that afternoon, and they both new it. She'd felt the connection between them and had taken as much pain from him as she could. She'd do it again in a heartbeat. They were a true mated pair even if she didn't have the tattoo on her arm yet. That would come though, she knew. She wanted it. Her wolf wanted it. *Holden* wanted it.

"So we're just going to run around in wolf form?" She never thought she'd say those words. Even though it scared her, she *wanted* to run, to shift. She wanted to let whatever was burning inside her to come out and be free.

Holden brushed her hair away from her shoulder and kissed the side of her neck. Shivers rocked her body. "It's more than that. You're letting your wolf out so she can breathe and *run*. You've felt the higher energy you have, even if you ache. You need to burn that before it turns to aggression or an anger you can't control. Running allows that. We do it as a group because we're not human. Running together brings forth our need to be a Pack and not be alone."

She turned in his arms and wrapped hers around his waist. When she nuzzled into his chest and growled softly. "The nudity thing might be a problem."

Holden didn't laugh at her. Instead, he squeezed her once and laid a kiss on the top of her head. "We're used to it since we've always had to shift. For now, you'll strip down behind me, and only I will see you naked." His eyes darkened and he let out another growl—this one louder, deeper. "I don't want anyone to see you but me."

"That kind of goes against the whole okay with nudity thing."

"I'm a male with a mate. I don't need to make sense."

She rolled her eyes, feeling a bit more at ease. It was surprising how easily Holden did that to her, and she had a feeling he wasn't aware of it. She hoped she did the same for him.

"So we'll be at the edge or something?"

He nodded and patted her ass. Cheeky man. "Yes. Soren will be the closest to us." He lowered his head and Ariel frowned.

"What?"

"He might catch a glimpse of you, but he's already seen you without clothes when we first found you."

She groaned at that. "Oh, good. Your best friend's seen me naked."

Holden snorted. "He couldn't help it. And believe me. He wouldn't do anything about it. Not only are you my mate, but..."

"What is it?"

"I don't know everything, but I do know that Soren went through hell already when it came to a woman. I don't think he's going to want to mate again."

"Again?" she asked, surprised that the broody man would have ever had a mate."

Holden shook his head. "It's not my story to tell. When he's ready, he'll talk to you about it. That is, if he's ever ready."

She sighed then kissed Holden's chest. "I can understand that." She let out a sigh. "I guess it's time to go?"

"Yes. The moon is rising and I can feel your wolf, mate of mine. Let's see what you look like after you shift."

She swallowed hard. As much as she'd been thinking she could do this, fear still threatened to take over. She hadn't actually *seen* anyone shift before. She'd only seen the videos the SAU had shown over the news when they wanted to scare the human population. Only she hadn't known that was the case at the time.

Not only could she die tonight if the change didn't take, but she'd see Holden as a wolf for the first time as well as so many others. It was a night of change, and hopefully, she'd be able to handle it all.

Holden cupped her face, his gaze serious. "It will all work out. Trust me."

She turned and kissed his palm. "I trust you, Holden. That won't ever be an issue."

Something flashed over his eyes and he nodded. "Let's go to the edge of the clearing, then. It's time."

He moved away and held out his hand. She placed hers in his, knowing this was another step toward a future she didn't quite understand, but she knew was the best for her.

By the time they made it to the edge of the clearing where she'd shift, most of the Pack who would hunt that night had already gathered.

"We don't shift as a group or hunt every week or even every month. But when we have a new member, a child who is now grown, we like to welcome them. You'll need the strength of the Pack tonight, and we are here for you."

She leaned into Holden's embrace, her mind going in a thousand different directions. Men, women, and older teens stood in groups, laughing and talking to one another. She hadn't seen much laughter within the den, and she liked seeing it now. They might have been forced into their roles in life, but they weren't letting it take everything from their spirit. There was something to learn from that, and Ariel would do her best to take in the lesson.

Mandy came up to them with a smile on her face, though Ariel could sense the worry in her gaze. After all, Ariel could die tonight. It had been so long since anyone had changed a human that they weren't sure if she'd survive. Not everyone did, and sometimes, the change just didn't take.

Her hands shook as Mandy held open her arms. Ariel pulled away from Holden to hug the woman who had become her friend.

"You're going to do great tonight," Mandy declared, and Ariel snorted.

"Thanks for trying to keep me positive."

Theo came up from behind Mandy and slid an arm around the submissive's shoulders. Mandy relaxed in Theo's hold, but Ariel wasn't sure if it was a sexual and romantic gesture or one between friends. She had so much to learn about the Pack's dynamics.

Her Pack's dynamics.

Soren moved slowly toward them, his gaze on the perimeter rather than the wolves. "We need to get started. I don't think the guards are going to venture in any time soon, but I don't want to risk it."

Holden nodded and gripped her hand. "I agree." He let out a breath and she licked her lips, knowing it was time.

Holden threw back his head and howled. The sweet timbre echoed through her bones, sending waves of need of a different sort through her body. The others howled back, their voices a perfect harmony that brought tears to her eyes.

"To the hunt!" Holden yelled and the others howled once more. Before she could figure out how to join in, the others started stripping off their clothes.

Ariel might not be a prude, but this was still a first for her.

Holden moved so his body shielded hers. "Mandy, Theo, turn your backs but shift near us."

"You've got it, Alpha," Theo said, his voice deeper than usual. The two of them quickly stripped off their clothes and went to all fours.

Holden tugged at the bottom of her shirt and she took a deep breath. "You're going to strip down like them and then get on your hands and knees." She blushed and he let out a rough chuckle. "We can do that soon, siren. First, though, I want to see your pretty wolf."

She quickly took off her clothes and did her best not to look at Holden as he did the same. He'd told her wolves could smell arousal, and she didn't want to swoon or something in front of the rest of the Pack.

When she got to her hands and knees, Holden kneeled beside her, his hand on her back. Again, she refused to look at him since one of her favorite parts of him was dangerously close to her face.

And enough about sex. This wasn't the time for that.

"Close your eyes and think about the part of you that feels different than before. That edge that you haven't been able to grasp in the past couple of weeks."

She let out a breath and did as she was told. Deep inside, she had a new darkness, a new part of her she hadn't been able to name.

"I want you to picture it as a rope or a thread. Once you do that, tug on it. It's going to hurt, but keep tugging and let the newness wash over you."

He kept his hand on her back and whispered words of encouragement to her, the deep timbre of his voice soothing her in a way she never thought possible. She pictured a rope she could grasp while the other end wrapped around the darkness. When she tugged, she groaned. It felt as if there were a hundred tiny needles dragging over her skin. She tugged again, wanting to see her wolf, wanting to be part of something far greater than herself. This time, the pain lashed at her, breaking bones, tearing at tendons. It reminded her of the torture at the hands of the doctors who had once sworn to care for her.

She screamed, her voice high and panicked.

In the distance, she could hear Holden shouting at her to keep going, to find him. She couldn't breathe, couldn't think. Her body broke out into a sweat and she screamed again.

Only this time, it wasn't a scream.

It was a howl.

"Oh fuck, baby, you're beautiful." Holden ran his hands through her fur and she blinked up at him, her eyes finally not hazy.

She tried to speak, but a yip came out instead. Oh yeah, she was a wolf. A freaking shifter.

It had *worked.*

Holden lifted her muzzle, pride in his gaze. "You're pure white wolf, siren. So gorgeous. It's going to take you a minute to get your bearings, so I want you to stay where you are and try to get used to your new senses. I'm going to shift while you do, and then, we can run. Do you want that? Do you want to run?"

She rolled her eyes at him. Did he have to sound like he spoke to a dog?

He snorted then kissed her nose. "That came out wrong, but you know what I mean. You made it, baby. You're a wolf."

She didn't cry, but her heart ached at the thought of what would have happened to Holden if she hadn't made it through the shift. The pain had been horrible, but there had been a chance she wouldn't have made it. Claire had said as much and has spoken of what would have happened to Holden. They wouldn't have to deal with that now, thank God. He wouldn't lose it now—wouldn't lose her.

Holden kneeled in front of her and shifted, his process much more graceful than hers. In fact, every other wolf had shifted quicker and with less screaming—practically none. She knew that born shifters didn't have as much of a problem with the change as those who had been bitten. The first change was also the hardest. Hopefully, soon it wouldn't be as bad, and she wouldn't want to vomit during it.

Holden finished changing and soon stood tall as a larger than normal, black wolf with an adorable white stripe down his nose. She'd have to tell him that once they were back in their human form. The big, bad Alpha was so stinking cute.

He nipped at her ear, and she had a feeling he'd read her thoughts in her gaze. Whatever. He was *hers*. He licked at her muzzle, cuddling her close before biting down on her neck. Her legs shook and she bowed her head, giving in to his dominance. They were wolves, pure and free in this form. It didn't matter they still wore their collars, and they had walls around them. In this moment, they were free in their hearts and souls.

This was why they ran, why they hunted as they did.

Holden walked backwards in front of her and nodded his head. She took a step and fell on her face. Well then. Graceful she was not.

He huffed, but it didn't sound like a laugh. Good for him. She stood up again, aware others were watching her. She was the Alpha's mate, after all; they needed to see that she was strong and capable.

Walking on her own four paws would probably go a long way in helping that.

This time she let her wolf forward, a gentle presence she'd known had been there but now could feel fully. Her wolf held a strength she hadn't possessed before and the need to care for those under her charge.

Ariel would be able to do this with her wolf at her side. She knew it.

With her wolf's help, she took a step then another. Holden let out a yip and licked her muzzle before turning on his heel. She followed him, gaining speed and confidence with each step. Soon the two of them were running in the forest, their paws digging into the soil. The others joined them, matching their pace but still giving them space.

She let her wolf roam, her soul feeling as though it had found another half she hadn't known was missing. This was her new life, her new presence, her new destiny.

This was *her*.

She followed Holden, staying close so she could find her way. When they reached the top of the rise, Holden slowed and waited for the other wolves to join them. With the way the compound was situated, there wasn't a lot of room to roam, but they at least had a place to gather. Holden stood the tallest with Ariel by his side. Soren stood on Holden's other side while the rest of the wolves moved so they were in order of dominance circling them.

She'd been so afraid they'd push her away and reject her, but right then, those who had hunted that night did not shun her. Instead, they lowered their gazes—even Soren—conceding that she was the dominant female, the Alpha's mate.

Pride and awe swelled deep inside, and she let out a howl. She hadn't known she could make that sound, but it was instinct. The others joined her, Holden's deep growl providing a perfect harmony to her melody. When they were through, the others slowly started to go their own way, either to go home or continue the run. Holden nipped at her flank then shot off toward the trees. She followed him without question, wanting her mate.

When they were finally alone, he turned to her and shifted back. He stood naked, sweaty, and erect, his heated gaze on hers.

"Shift back, siren."

His voice sent shivers down her body and she closed her eyes to try and tug on that rope again. This time, when she did so, it didn't hurt as much. Instead, it was a quick burst of pain before a blessed newness.

Before she could catch her breath, Holden crushed his mouth to hers, his taste heady. She raked her nails down his back, pressing her breasts against his chest.

She ripped her mouth from his, needing air. "I need you," she panted.

"Fuck. You're mine, Ariel. Anything you need. Anything you want. You got it. Let me fuck you hard tonight then we can make love in the moonlight. How does that sound?"

She reached between them and gripped his cock. "I think I like that idea. Anything I want, you say?" She pumped him once, twice and he groaned.

"Anything," he bit out, his jaw tight.

She grinned then bent forward, taking him in her mouth. He growled, fisting his hand in her hair. When he tried to pull her back, she dug her nails into his hips and sucked hard.

"Fuck, Ariel. You don't have to do this."

She pulled back, releasing him with an audible pop. "You said I could do anything I want. I want this. I want you to come down my throat as I swallow you whole. Let me have this control, this part of you."

He brushed her cheek with his thumb then pushed gently at her head. "Go for it. I love the sight of your lips wrapped around my cock."

She hummed against him, licking up his shaft before squeezing the base. She rolled his balls in her hand while hollowing her cheeks, bobbing her head up and down. She loved the salty taste of him. When he groaned once more and his hand tightened in her hair, she relaxed her throat even as she kept her the motions going.

The first spurt of come splashed on her tongue and she swallowed. He threw his head back and howled, coming full-on down her throat, hot and heady. As soon as she swallowed the last drop, Holden had her pressed against his body, his tongue sliding across her lips.

She wrapped her arms around his neck, pulling him closer. His cock hadn't softened in the slightest and pressed hard into her belly.

"Want you," he growled. "Inside. Now."

He sounded more animal than man. All Alpha, and all hers. She tightened her arms around his neck and let out a gasp as he gripped her ass in both his hands, lifted her up then slammed her down on his cock.

They both froze a moment, his length filling her up so full she could barely breathe. He was still on his knees holding her up with his strength. Damn, he was so fucking sexy.

Before she could say a word, he slid her off his cock slowly so only the tip remained inside, teasing her.

"Holden," she moaned.

"Mine," he growled then pulled back down on him. She threw her had back, taking him all in, and he fucked her hard, his muscles straining, the veins in his arms standing out and looking so damn hot. He kept up the pace before he pulled her even closer and pressed her into the hard ground. With one hand, he pulled one knee up by her ear and slid in and out of her in fast strokes.

Her nipples pebbled, and he used his free hand to cup one then the other. "Come, Ariel. Show your Alpha you want him. Come on his cock."

She gave him a wicked grin then slid her hand between them. Her fingers swept over her clit, already hard and peeking out of the hood. At the first touch, her body stiffened and she came, her pussy clenching around his cock.

Holden roared and slammed into her once more, coming deep inside her—this time without a condom. They hadn't even talked about it, and she didn't care. She was his now, part of his life, part of this world.

It didn't matter she hadn't been born into it, didn't wear the ink of his mating.

She was his.

And as long as she remained hidden from those who had harmed her, she would rejoice in her new life, her new strength.

For she was wolf, Pack, and so much more.

She was Ariel.

CHAPTER 9

Holden gripped his mate's hips and thrust deep inside of her, craving her touch, her taste. If this were how he would wake up until the end of his days, then he'd be one happy fucking wolf. Ariel had her ass in the air, her face down on the bed, and her hands gripping the sheets hard as he fucked her from behind.

She felt so tight, so fucking hot around his dick that he never wanted to leave. Call it a dominant male thing, but he couldn't help it.

"Harder!" Ariel panted.

Holden dug his fingers into her hips and grinned. "Think you can take it?"

She turned her head so she could see him even with her cheek pressed to the mattress. "You know it. Now fuck me harder."

He gave her a feral grin and slammed back into her, pistoning his hips until they both called out, screaming each other's names as they came. His arms shook, so he brought her back to his front then lay down on his side so they spooned.

"Good morning," he said roughly.

Ariel let out a snort. "Good morning, indeed. Can we do that every morning?"

"Hell, yeah. And at night. And maybe during the day if we can get away."

"I'll be pretty sore if we keep that up."

Holden kissed her shoulder then ran his hand down her stomach to cup her intimately. "Then I'll just eat you out and fuck you with my tongue."

She groaned and went limp in his arms. He kissed her shoulder again, not wanting to ever leave this bed. Things had been going well since the hunt. Ariel had begun her role as Alpha's mate by going from station to station and learning how the Pack functioned within the compound walls. Others started to come up to her and not act like she could out their secrets by her mere existence. His wolf had his mate, and Ariel could shift without losing her life.

Things were *finally* working out on some front.

Soon he'd tell her he loved her because, damn it, he couldn't hold it back much longer. He wasn't one for expressing feelings, but with Ariel, it was different. He wanted her to know she would always have a place in his life, despite how things had started. At first, he'd been afraid things were going too fast for her since they'd mated in the ways of wolves and not how humans married. But now things were different. Things were good.

He scented Soren before he heard him.

Holden quickly threw a sheet over Ariel and sat up as his Beta stormed into their bedroom.

"You better have a fucking good excuse for barging into our room," Holden growled.

Soren kept his eyes averted, but Holden could see the anger in the other man's shoulders...and the slight edge of fear on his scent that had Holden standing and reaching for his jeans.

"Claire fucked up big, Alpha. Like really fucking big."

Ariel scurried off the bed and slipped on her pants and bra. Holden knew Soren's gaze remained on Holden's in respect to Holden's wolf, but shit. This couldn't be good.

"What did she do?" Holden asked, slipping into his boots.

"She told the guards that she found Ariel, and that she's a shifter."

Bile filled Holden's throat as Ariel let out a shocked gasp.

"Why would she do that?" Ariel asked, her voice shaking.

Holden couldn't speak, pure rage jolting through his system. That fucking bitch. And he didn't use that word lightly. What had she being thinking? Why would she risk *everything* for something as petty as jealousy?

"I don't fucking know," Soren spat. "She's outside on her knees waiting for you. Theo and Ana are guarding her. I don't think she thought of the consequences of her actions, Holden. I think she's just that stupid."

Holden shook his head. "It doesn't matter if she did it on purpose to kill her people or to just get Ariel out of the picture. Either way, she just sentenced us to death."

With that, he stormed out of the room, Ariel and Soren on his tail. He forced his wolf back, not wanting to shift and kill the woman who he'd once cared for. She'd graced his bed but had never been in his heart, never been his mate.

She'd known the score and yet hadn't followed through with her promises.

Now she'd risked the lives of not only is Pack, but those of every shifter in the world under SAU control. If the humans knew what it took to create a shifter, then they'd torment who they could to further their own armies and sciences. They'd been trying to find a connection for twenty-five years, and with one bite from Holden and one woman who hadn't thought enough about the future, the humans would now know everything.

When he got outside, he searched the perimeter for guards before he looked down at Claire. He couldn't scent humans yet, but they would come. There was no other possible outcome.

Holden would have to fight for his people or play a hell of a game of politics. He honestly didn't know what he would do, but he knew he'd do everything to protect the Pack. There wasn't another option.

"What the fuck were you thinking?" Holden shouted.

Claire looked up at him with tears running down her face before lowering her gaze. Good. She wasn't worth the rank in the Pack she'd fought so hard for. She didn't deserve to meet his gaze.

"Answer me, Claire," he bit out. "We might not have enough time to get your answer before the humans sweep down on us for Ariel. Wait. That's what you wanted, right? You wanted her out of my life, out of the Pack? Well fuck that. You killed us, Claire."

Claire let out a small whimper. "You killed us," she whispered.

Holden froze, his wolf deadly quiet. "Excuse me?" he asked then prowled closer. He stood in front of her but didn't bend down. He wouldn't go to her level. Never again.

"You are the one who bit her, made her into what she is. You're the selfish one who risked our lives."

If she'd been a man, he would have hit her then. But she wasn't. Instead she was a woman who had once been in his bed and his life. He couldn't let himself break that far.

That didn't mean her words didn't ring true, however.

"Yes, I risked our Pack. I will *always* know that. I was ready to take that blame, fall on the sword if the humans found her. But I didn't bring the SAU to our fucking door!"

Claire winced as he yelled. No doubt the rest of the den could hear him shouting, but he couldn't stop. He honestly had no idea what the fuck they were going to do right then. They didn't have a plan for this, not for this kind of betrayal.

Ariel came to his side and put her hand on top of his fist. He immediately opened his hand to thread his fingers with hers.

"I know you hate me because of what I could have done to Holden, what I could still do," Ariel said softly, much calmer than him. "But I don't understand how you can hate your people? How could you risk them?"

"I didn't think," Claire whispered. "I just wanted the threat away so we could go back to how we were. I...I am so sorry. I didn't *think*."

Holden blinked. "Seriously? That's your excuse? That you didn't think?" There might not be a war this very second, but everything had changed. He hoped to God she understood that, because she clearly hadn't when she'd told that guard. It didn't matter that no one was there to take them from their homes right away. They would come. There was no other way.

Claire looked up at both of them, her face pale, her eyes lacking anything but remorse. "It's all I have to give."

Holden shook his head in disgust. "We need to rally the den for the guards," he said to Soren. "As for you, Claire? If we survive what is coming, then I will leave your fate to Ariel. I can't even look at you right now."

Ariel tugged on his hand, her face pale. "Me?"

Holden held back a growl and pulled her away from the others. "You. She's the one who risked *your* life. So yes, you get to decide if she dies by our hands or if she lives by your mercy. You're the Alpha's mate. It's a decision for you."

Ariel thinned her lips and shook her head. "We're going to have to talk about this later. I get where you're coming from, but you can't just hand off someone's fate to me. You say I'm your mate, yet you keep dictating to me. We're going to have to find a balance Holden, because right now? It's not working."

He felt as if he'd been punched in the chest for the second time that morning, but he couldn't say anything about it. Instead, he gave her a tight nod. "We need get ready for the guards."

Ariel searched his face. "Of course. The Pack is more important." She didn't reach for him, and he ached for her touch. "I get that. They took me in, Holden. They're mine now. I'm not going to let them get hurt because of me."

He froze. "You're not giving yourself up to them, Ariel. Not only will I track you down and find you, but even if you give yourself to them, it won't stop them from finding a way to use this new knowledge to hurt shifters as a whole."

"If I can help *our* Pack, I will."

Despite the fact that the humans could be there any moment with their guns and their laws, it wasn't lost on him that she'd said *our* Pack. She'd finally become one of them, finally given in and found her place at his side.

And it could all be lost.

"Holden, we've got company at the gates," Soren called out. "There's a group of humans including a doctor out there. They aren't coming inside, but apparently, they demanded to see the Alpha and Test Subject A."

Ariel flinched and Holden let out a growl. "We aren't letting them take her, Soren."

Soren look offended that Holden would even say that. "Of course not. She's my Alpha. She's one of us. Even if we gave her up, it's not going to stop them from trying to find a way to use us to make shifters of their own that they can control for their own ends."

"We're fucked," Theo said from Claire's side.

Claire let out another whimper, but Holden ignored it. "Fuck. Okay, Theo and Ana, bring Claire. We're going to the gates as a unit in case it turns into a fight. We have strength and our wolves, which will have to be enough." Holden took a deep breath and faced the men and woman of his inner circle. Ariel put her hand in his and his wolf centered. "We can't let them take us," Holden began. "We've rolled over for so long because we've been protecting those weaker than us, but at some point, we need to remind the humans that we are strong, that we are wolves. I won't ask you to fight if you feel you need to stay behind and protect the submissives, but if you stand by me today at the gate, then I ask for your strength, your loyalty."

Soren bowed his head. "You have always had it, Alpha."

The others followed, bowing their heads in submission. Holden's wolf howled, the strength of their Pack bonds far greater than anything the humans could hope to come up with.

They made their way as a unit toward the gates, tension rising with each step. Others joined them, and he knew even more would be protecting them in hiding, as well as caring for those who could not care for themselves. Holden had no idea what they would face, but he knew they would do it as a Pack. He might not be able to free his people from the walls, but he could protect them from further prosecution.

At least he hoped he could.

Ariel stood by his side, her hand still in his. Oh, he might have wanted to keep her locked away and hidden from prying human eyes, but they were beyond that point. The humans had heard she was alive, and keeping her away wouldn't help the situation but make it worse.

At the gate, at least ten guards stood on the human side, batons and Tasers in their hands. He couldn't see a single gun, but that didn't mean they weren't there. In fact, he wouldn't put it past the SAU to keep snipers on hand in case of shifter unruliness.

Holden stood in the center of the gate opening with Ariel on his right but slightly behind him. Soren did the same, but on his left. The others got into position with Claire on shaky legs between Theo and Ana.

Holden didn't say anything. Instead he stared at the doctor who stood in the center. There was something...off about this man. There was a manic curiosity in his eyes that set Holden on edge.

"It's him," Ariel whispered, her voice stark with fear. "The doctor. It's him."

Her hand on his hip tightened and Holden had to hold himself back from howling with rage. This little fucker was the one to hurt his mate? To make her bleed?

Soren let out a curse at his side. "We'll back you, Holden. This man doesn't get to live."

Holden gave his Beta a tight nod. No matter what happened today, he'd make sure the man who had hurt Ariel, who had tied her down to a table to watch her bleed would not walk away from this.

"I see the rumors were true," the doctor said, breaking the tense silence. "Subject A, you look well." He grinned. "Alive. Interesting, as the last time I saw you, you were on your way to death's door. I wonder how that happened? I can't wait to cut you open again to see how everything works. You'll be a true gift to science like you never were before."

Holden let out a low growl. Soren. Ariel, and the others joined in, a perfect harmony of wolves, anger and vengeance.

The doctor's eyes widened ever so slightly in panic.

Good.

"What is your name?" Holden bit out.

"Henry," the doctor stammered. Looks like the doctor wasn't all that used to shifters not drugged and helpless. Too bad he wouldn't live long to learn all aspects of that fear. "Why?"

"Because I want to know the name of the man who I am about to end because he dared to torture my mate. And now you come here to what? Take more of us? Take my mate so you can study her some more? I'm sorry, but that is not going to happen. You might have us in cages, but you all need to remember that we are stronger than you when we're fighting. We can kill you before you even call out for help for so many other humans. We are in these cages because *we* choose not to fight. Yet."

It was time to remind the humans who they'd put in cages.

Henry moved through the guards so he stood only a few feet away from Holden. "Do you know why we chose her? Why we tried so hard to turn her into one of you using all the science and technology we had?"

Holden let out a growl once more.

"I'll take that animal noise of yours as a yes. You see, she was the perfect specimen. We've watched her since before she was born."

"What?" Ariel gasped. "That can't be possible."

"Of course, it is. The SAU had been in its infancy when your mother was pregnant with you. Both she and your father caught the Verona Virus. They were both dying like much of our population."

Holden stiffened, his mind going down a path he wasn't sure he wanted to go.

"The shifters had just come out and we found a vaccine. Your mother used it while she was pregnant with you."

"What does this have to do with why you kidnapped and tortured me?"

"Don't you see? We used shifter blood to come up with the virus since they were somehow immune to the disease. Since your mother had been pregnant with you when we cured her, that same blood runs through your veins. You weren't the only baby born under this situation, but you were the closest to me. I needed you as Test Subject A. Don't you understand that? I *needed* to see what would happen when you grew up."

"So you're a sick fuck, fine. This is getting tedious," Holden spat.

"Your parents didn't want to let me have you though," Henry continued as if he hadn't heard the threat in Holden's tone. "So I took care of the matter once you were born. It was easy really. No one truly paid attention to each and every survivor in the wake of the virus. Once they were out of the way, I could watch you in the orphanage."

Ariel leaned into Holden, her body stiff with rage. "You killed my parents so you could *watch* me? You let me grow up alone so you could see if I learned to shift? You're fucking crazy."

"You see? That's why I needed to study you. We need shifters. We need their strength and their ability to heal. Imagine how incredible the human race could be if we could harness the shifters' powers. I had hoped you would be able to aid me in this endeavor; you failed. When your body gave out, we threw you to the wolves. Literally. I wanted to blame your death on the wolves so I could easily ask for another wolf of my own to study. You see, it's getting harder and harder to take you beasts into my custody for research. It seems you have friends in high places." Henry smiled and the hair on the back of Holden's neck stood on end. "Imagine my surprise when I hear from one of the guards that you are alive and well...and a shifter. Now, if I hadn't heard it from one of your own, I would have assumed that you'd *finally* found your true calling and the vaccine had something to do with it. However, it seems that it was a bite that changed you." He grinned. "Interesting."

"Enough," Holden said. "We're done. You can't hurt her anymore."

Henry met Holden's eyes. "We tried biting before, you know. But it never worked. Now I think it must have been the wrong wolf and perhaps the wrong human. Maybe it was the blood in her veins and the vaccine aided her transition. We will have to try that out in the future. But perhaps it was also the fact that you are the Alpha and Test Subject A is your mate. Hmm? Interesting isn't it. I can't wait to dissect her again to see what I find out."

Holden took two steps forward but Soren's growl held him back. He stopped but didn't keep his gaze off the doctor.

"You know you can't kill me," Henry continued. "You are nothing. Just a wolf with no power. The guards here will protect me. And when I am through with Test Subject A, I will find more of you to study. We *will* make shifters of our own. You can't fight back because you are scared. Little wolves with your tails tucked between your legs."

Holden threw his head back and howled. Before the humans could react, he jumped, his hands turning into in claws. The doctor jerked once as Holden sliced through the man's neck. Henry gurgled before he fell to his knees, not even allowed to take one last breath. Holden rolled to the side and knocked a guard on his ass, taking his Taser and throwing it toward Ariel. His mate caught it easily, arming herself. The rest could fight as wolves, but she wasn't ready for that yet.

"Stop!" one guard yelled, his arms up.

Blood dripped from Holden's hands, and his chest heaved. He could kill each one of these guards now and get his people out. He'd find a why to hide them all and try to keep them alive. But the countless other shifters in the world would pay the price. It wasn't time their plan.

Yet.

"We let you kill him because he tortured a human," the guard said, his face pale. Holden remembered him. This was the one from before that hadn't wanted to hurt the wolves. No, this was one who merely did a job. A horrific one, but he didn't enjoy it. "We can't let you go if you keep fighting. We can say the doctor had an accident, but if you don't get back behind the gate, we will have to fight back." The guard let out a breath. "I know you have extra senses. Use them and find the guns we have on you."

Holden inhaled deeply and cursed at the tang of metal, gun oil and gunpowder too close for comfort.

"We'll take care of the doc, but you need to get back. You hear me?"

Holden could hear the fear in the man's voice, but understood the chance they had here. No more bloodshed—at least for the time being. The man who had hurt Ariel had died by his hand. It would have to do. For now.

"Keep your men away from us," Holden said. "We won't be lying back anymore."

The guard lifted his chin, and Holden slowly backed away so he stood behind the gate. Ariel came up to his side, her body tense but her gaze on the ones that had threatened to hurt them. The metal fence closed in front of them, locking them in once more. But things had changed ever so slightly, and they all knew it.

No matter what happened next, they had stood up for themselves, shown the humans that they would no longer merely lie down and take it.

The guards backed away with the doctor's body in tow, leaving the wolves behind the fence.

"Do you think I'm a monster for killing him?" Holden asked.

"I'm only pissed I couldn't do it myself," Ariel answered. "You'll have to teach me that claw trick."

Soren let out a snort beside them. "It's not over, you know. They'll come back to find out more about the change."

"And I have a feeling they might still punish us for what happened to that douchebag doctor," Theo put in.

Holden nodded. "I know. It's far from over, but damn, it felt good to use my claws again."

"Next time let the rest of us join in," Soren said softly. "We were all set until that guard backed off."

Holden brought Ariel into his arms, needing her body pressed close to his. "I know. And I thank you for that. Now let's get back to the den center and make sure everyone is aware of what just happened. It's only the beginning."

"Only the beginning," Ariel repeated softly. "But we won't back down."

He kissed her once, hard and fast. "Never."

The River Pack was just one of many thought lost to a world of terror and pain. But soon the humans would remember who saved them. Soon there would be vengeance.

And as long as Holden had his mate by his side, he could face the future. Because without her, there wasn't a future worth living.

CHAPTER 10

A riel fingered the mating tattoo on her arm, freshly inked and yet not painful at all. In fact, the buzz of the needle pressed against her skin had only turned her on. Okay, so maybe it had been Holden's cock firmly pressed against her ass while she'd gotten her mating tattoo that had turned her on. He'd made her sit on his lap while Gibson finished up the ink, and she hadn't put up much of a fight.

Or any fight, really.

"If you keep doing that, I'm going to bend you over the table and fuck you before we head back to the center of the den."

Ariel rolled her eyes at her mate's warning, even as her nipples hardened at his words.

"We are already running late as it is. I promised Mandy I'd be there to help set up the food tables for the bonfire."

The wolves would have their annual bonfire to celebrate the lives of those lost, and the lives of those still with them. It had been three weeks since they'd seen or heard a guard. Ariel wasn't sure what that meant, but it had kept everyone on edge. The consequences of Claire's betrayal—as well as Holden's and Ariel's—would soon come to light. However, for that night, they would do their best to push that form their minds and be who they were.

Shifters.

She kissed him quickly then tried to make her way to the door, only to have Holden wrap his arms around her waist.

"Not so fast, siren." He kissed her temple and she shivered. She turned in his arms and leaned into him, craving him more now than she had the first time he'd held her. "I love you, my Ariel, my mate. I should have said that before, but I didn't. And for that, I am sorry. I love you so fucking much. No matter what happens with the Pack and with the ones around us, I want you to know that you will always be in my heart and my soul."

Tears filled her eyes and she lifted onto her toes to kiss him softly, her heart so full she could barely breathe. "I love you, too. You're everything to me. You're my mate, my Alpha, and my soul. I know we came together in the worst way possible, but I don't regret my love for you and our chance at a future one bit. I know that the future won't be easy, but I will never leave your side. You're everything to me. You're mine as I am yours."

Holden growled and crushed his mouth to hers. She moaned into him, her wolf brushing along her skin, wanting contact as well. Holden backed her to the wall, his hard cock pressed against her belly. With a sigh, she pulled away from his mouth, trying to catch her breath.

"We can't be late, Holden."

He growled softly then pressed a kiss to her mouth once more. "Fine. But when we get back, I'm fucking you hard into the bed. It's only fair."

She snorted. "Okay, if that's what you want." She let out a put-on sigh. He slapped her ass and she jumped. "Dude."

"Dude." He wiggled his eyebrows, forcing a laugh from her. She loved when he showed his playful side. He didn't let it out often, and she had a feeling he wouldn't be able to that many more times in the near future, but she'd take what she could get now.

They tangled their fingers together and made their way to the den center. People gathered around, saying their greetings and working on setting up the event. Out of the corner of her eye, she saw Claire lurking around.

In the end, the other woman's fate had been on Ariel's shoulders. While some might have killed her since it was the way of wolves, Ariel hadn't been able to do it. Instead, she forced the woman to live in a world where she was part of the cause of what would come. She would be forced to watch the pain and death if that was what the humans decided. If the humans rebelled and found a way to use this newfound knowledge for their own gain, Claire's fate would be worse than death.

As it was, the Pack had shunned her. Claire lost her rank as a dominant and now tried to be part of a Pack that didn't want her.

Ariel didn't envy her in the slightest, but she did pity her.

Holden let out a small grow. "Stop it. You made your choice, and so did she."

"I understand that, but it doesn't make it any easier. Seeing her reminds me of the role I played."

"The role you played was to survive. What's done is done. Now let's celebrate with our Pack." He kissed her once more, and she moaned. That man could make her drunk on his taste alone. He broke off the kiss and left her with Mandy while he went to help Soren prepare the bonfire.

As they set up the food area, Ariel and Mandy talked of trivial things, their focus on that night rather than the future. As the sun began to set, the hairs on the back of Ariel's neck stood on end.

She lifted her head, her wolf on edge. Five guards strolled in, guns at the ready and their faces set. Ariel didn't see the guard who had helped them before.

She quickly moved to Holden's side. Her mate stood in front of her, but didn't push her back. That he valued her presence spoke volumes of both of their dominances.

"Holden," a new guard she hadn't seen before called out. "We have a letter for you from the leader of the SAU."

Ariel frowned as Holden moved forward and took the letter from the human.

"You'll have a month to set up. Don't waste time." With that, the humans fell back, leaving the wolves alone and confused as ever.

"What does it say?" she asked as Holden ripped open the envelope.

He let out a curse, his hands fisting. "They found their punishment."

"What?" Soren asked.

Holden met Soren's gaze and Ariel saw a look pass over her mate's face she didn't understand. "They're moving the Feline Pack into our compound. It seems we're going to share the space."

Soren paled, his hands fisted at his side.

Ariel blinked. "What does that mean?" she asked. She was still so new to the shifter world; she didn't understand all the dynamics that came with it.

"It means the SAU changed the game. The Felines have never been our enemy, nor have they been our friends. They have an Alpha of their own, a culture of their own." Holden took a breath, and Ariel put her hand on his hip, knowing he needed her touch to calm down. "There was a reason the SAU separated us in the first place. Felines and Canines together has never ended well."

Ariel sucked in a breath. "And now they will live with us. For good."

"The humans found the perfect punishment. And they don't even have to lift a weapon to carry it out."

Two Packs. One den. A change had come, all right. And Ariel wasn't sure she knew who would come out on top. Yet, no matter what, she would be by Holden's side. Her mate kissed her temple, and she let out a sigh. They would survive, they always had.

The future might be uncertain, but they had one thing on their side.

Each other.

Forgiven

Prologue

The wolf slid through the wooded darkness, careful to avoid the man-lights that turned the night to day in the middle of the compound. The communal area where the River Pack publicly gathered to meet was always bathed in the harsh glow of lanterns.

Thankfully, this part of the compound was thick with pines and moss, hiding him from view. He was alone, surrounded only by the rich gifts offered by Mother Earth.

He might be a Pack animal at heart, but on this eve, he had no desire to run with his brothers.

No. This was not an excursion to celebrate life and the joy of the hunt. Or to ponder the growing danger from the humans after his Alpha had sliced his claws through the throat of the doctor trying to take away his mate.

This was an attempt to exorcise the demons of his past.

Almost as if to mock his efforts, his large silver and black fur-covered body came to a sharp halt as he caught the unmistakable scent of feline.

Tiger.

He'd known the Golden Pack had arrived earlier in the day, spreading among the precious few cabins that were scattered throughout the outer part of the den. But he hadn't expected to pick up *her* scent so swiftly.

A dangerous yearning curled through his belly.

Something that was a mixture of hunger and lust and need.

Tilting back his head, the wolf howled at the moon.

CHAPTER 1

Seated in front of her bedroom mirror, Cora Wilder pulled a brush through her long curls that shimmered with red and gold highlights in the muted glow of the nearby lamp.

She ignored her own reflection. She was too familiar with her thin, feline face and slanted emerald-green eyes rimmed with pure gold to see the beauty. Nor did she care that her sleek, well-toned body with a hint of copper in her satin-smooth skin featured in the wet dreams of most males who crossed her path.

But the large tiger shifter standing behind her was aware of Cora's ability to daze and befuddle the opposite sex. And as her father, and Alpha of the Golden Pack, Jonah Wilder was prepared to use her as a weapon when necessary.

"I don't know why you have to be so stubborn," he growled. Although well into his fifties, Jonah was still a handsome male with a lean, arrogant face and dark red hair that was cut short. His body was spare, but there was no mistaking the strength in his fluid muscles.

He wasn't Alpha because of his ability to win friends and influence people.

He was the meanest, baddest cat around.

Cora, however, wasn't about to be intimidated, manipulated, or bullied.

The dominance structure among the feline Pack wasn't nearly as structured as the wolves, and while she respected her father's authority, she was too independent to be told what to do.

"Probably because I'm your daughter," she told him.

"Ha." The male's emerald eyes narrowed in triumph. "So you do accept your position as the Alpha's eldest child." He planted his hands on his hips, stretching the crisp white shirt that he'd matched with a pair of black slacks tightly across his chest. "Which means your place is at my side as I greet our newest neighbors."

She shrugged, keeping her voice light. "Trust me, the wolves have no interest in a spoiled tiger princess."

"I assume you speak of one wolf in particular?" her father challenged.

Her delicate features hardened. Oh, no. He did *not* go there.

"I don't know what you mean."

"Cora, I'm not stupid, and I'm certainly not blind." Something that might have been regret darkened his eyes. "I was well aware of your fascination with Soren."

Cora dropped the brush on her dresser. She didn't want her father to see her hand tremble. She may not have much after Soren Slater had crushed her soul, but she did have her pride.

"I was young and stupid." Golden sparks glowed in her eyes, warning the older male that her ready temper was about to explode. "I was fascinated by a lot of different males." *Lie, lie, lie.*

"Maybe, but not all of them broke your heart."

With a sharp motion, Cora surged to her feet, her hands clenched at her sides as she moved toward the suitcase that she'd left on a chair.

Like most cats, Cora was not only fastidious in her grooming; she was a neat freak. Something that used to drive Soren nuts...

A low growl rumbled in her throat.

Dammit. She'd promised herself that she wasn't going to allow this forced move into the wolves' den to catapult her into the past. She'd wasted enough time mourning the loss of the mate her cat had chosen. She wasn't going to give the bastard one more tear.

"It doesn't matter."

"It did." Her father grimaced. "And I would have neutered the dog if I'd thought he'd deliberately tried to hurt you."

She kept her face averted, absently pulling out a shirt before she moved across the small bedroom to hang it in the closet.

"What makes you think he didn't?"

"I, better than anyone, understand the burden of duty." Jonah's voice was rough. No surprise. As Alpha, Jonah was taking the forced move of his people as a personal insult. "There are times when we all have to put our Pack before our own desires."

Cora's cat pressed against her skin, agitated by talk of the male that had denied her attempt to form a permanent bond.

"It was a long time ago."

There was an awkward hesitation as her father watched her unpack the last of her clothing into the closet that was far too small to contain even a quarter of her wardrobe. Not that Cora was about to complain. She was one of the few who actually had her own space. Now that they were squashed into the same area as the dogs, they barely had room to breathe.

"You know, his mate died," Jonah abruptly broke the silence.

She stilled, her hands crushing the silk shirt in her hands. "Father, I'm not interested in Soren."

"Then prove it," he commanded. "Come with me."

And have her first meeting with Soren in over seven years be in front of an audience? Not a chance in hell.

"I have nothing to prove."

"If that were true, you wouldn't be hiding in your room."

Heaving an aggravated sigh, she turned to glare at her father.

"Don't you have a welcoming ceremony to attend?"

"Welcoming ceremony?" There was a glimpse of Jonah's tiger in his eyes as he battled back his surge of frustration. If they'd been in their previous home, the male would already be shifted and hunting down something to kill. "More like a clusterfuck waiting to happen. Dogs and cats weren't meant to live together. If I were a betting man, I'd lay odds we won't make it through the first meal without bloodshed."

Cora dropped her shirt and crossed the floor to lay a hand on her father's arm. She, better than anyone, understood the stress he was under.

It'd been hell when they'd been penned in a fenced compound, not to mention collared and branded like they were rabid animals. But Jonah had lost his beloved mate, Caroline, the mother of his children, during the initial roundup.

Now they were once again being punished, and her father was being squeezed between a rock and a hard place.

"It's up to you to make sure that you find some way to create peace with the wolves, Father," she reminded him. "The humans want us at each other's throats." Her hand lifted from his arm to touch the collar around his neck. At the same time, the overhead light picked up the stylized cat tattoo on her forearm that partially hid the ugly brand. Reminders of the cost of failure. "The SAU know we could break free of this prison if we ever find a way to work together."

"You see." A wry smile touched Jonah's lips, softening his grim expression. "You have the voice of reason. I need you at my side."

With a shake of her head, she gave her father a gentle push. "Go. Do your thing. I need to finish unpacking."

"Stubborn," the older man muttered, reluctantly heading toward the door.

"I love you, too," she called out behind him.

Waiting for her father to leave along with her three younger brothers, Cora finished stowing away their belongings then headed into the shower. There was a limited amount of hot water. Why not indulge while everyone else was occupied?

It was nearly an hour later when she pulled on a tiny tee and matching boxers. Then, ignoring the sharp chill of the late October air, she stepped out the back door and sucked in a deep breath.

Instantly, she was surrounded by the tangy scent of pines, and the sweet hint of aster that was planted beneath the kitchen window. And...something else.

Something she recognized instantly.

Wolf musk.

She stiffened, her heart pounding. But not with fear. Instead, it was pure excitement that made her pulse leap and her palms sweat.

"Show yourself," she commanded.

There was a rustle in the undergrowth before a tall male wearing nothing more than a faded pair of jeans stepped from the shadows.

Soren Slater.

Cora released a low hiss. The sight of him was like a punch to the gut.

Against her will, her gaze hungrily drank in the sight of the male she hadn't seen for what felt like an eternity.

His shoulders were broad, and his bare chest was smoothly muscled as it tapered down to a narrow waist. The jeans that hung low on his hips emphasized his long legs.

He had tousled curls that were as dark and glossy as polished ebony, while his eyes were the color of cognac. He had a thin nose and sharply chiseled cheekbones a woman would kill to possess.

Over the years, she'd tried to tell herself that his finely carved features couldn't be as impossibly beautiful as she remembered. Now, she couldn't deny the impact of his male perfection.

Cora clenched her hands, her gut twisting with apprehension.

It wasn't the shattering pain exploding through her that troubled her. She'd always known that this reunion would be agonizing. Even after all these years. No. Her unease was a direct response to her cat's piercing joy at the sight of Soren.

The animal didn't care that this male had used her as just another meaningless body in his bed. Or that he'd chosen another female to share his life.

It only knew that her mate had returned, and was

purring with a contentment that scared the hell out of Cora.

Time seemed to stand still as they simply stared at one another.

Heat. Need. And something far more dangerous smoldered in the air, threatening to stir old feelings that Cora had thought she'd banished years ago.

"Why aren't you at the ceremony?" She abruptly broke the silence, wrapping her arms around her waist as she battled the urge to flee into the house and slam the door shut.

She wasn't going to give the son of a bitch the satisfaction of knowing he could still disturb her.

Soren strolled forward, his gaze skimming over her scantily clad body with blatant appreciation. Briefly, she considered the pleasure of kicking him in the nads.

"I could ask you the same thing," he said, at last turning his attention to her flushed face.

She shrugged. "I don't have a formal position among the Pack."

He gave a short laugh. "No one familiar with the tigers would ever underestimate your power, princess."

"Power?"

He halted directly in front of her, wrapping her in his warm musk.

"Your father and brothers adore you. It's well known that they listen to your council," he murmured. "It's also known that your father isn't above using your beauty to dazzle unsuspecting males during difficult negotiations."

It actually wasn't well known. Her father laughingly called her his 'secret weapon.' But Soren had covertly traveled to the tiger compound as Holden's prime diplomat, seeking to build an open channel of communication between the Packs. Which meant he knew far more about them than any other wolf.

"As charming as ever, Soren." She offered a meaningless smile. "Unfortunately, it's a wasted effort on me. Why don't you run along to the ceremony? I'm sure there are a lot of females eager to hear your sweet lies."

Soren went predatory still, his eyes narrowing. "Are you claiming that I lied to you, princess?"

Of course, he hadn't. He was too cunning to make promises he couldn't keep.

Which only pissed her off more.

"I'm not claiming anything, I'm telling you that I want you to go away," she said.

Something that might have been regret flared through his eyes. "We need to talk."

"Yeah, I don't think so."

"Cora."

He reached out as if he intended to grab her arm. Instinctively, she slapped his hand away.

"Don't. Touch. Me," she said between clenched teeth.

He studied her with shadowed eyes, the air so thick it was difficult to breathe.

"Whether you like it or not, we're about to become one big, messy Pack," he finally said.

"I don't like it."

His lips flattened. "Peace is going to be difficult enough without open tension between the Tiger Princess and the Beta of River Pack."

"There doesn't need to be any tension." She nodded her head toward the nearby trees that ringed the area designated for the felines. "Just stay the hell away from me."

He made a sound of frustration. "The space is too

small for us to completely avoid one another."

"Not if we both make an effort."

"Princess-"

Once again, he stretched his hand toward her, and once again, she smacked it away.

"I told you not to touch me," she snapped.

Cognac eyes suddenly smoldered with the heat of his wolf, his musk teasing at her senses as he took a deliberate step forward.

"That's not what you used to say," he growled, leaning down until they were nose to nose. "Once you begged for my touch. My kisses."

She didn't think...she just reacted. Spectacularly.

Lifting her hand, she slapped him across his too-handsome face.

"You bastard."

****

Soren flinched. Not from the pain of her slap. But with the realization that he was behaving like a bastard.

Which was the last thing he wanted.

When he'd seen her standing in the moonlight, his entire being had ignited with pleasure.

It was like he'd been sleepwalking through his life for the past seven years, only to be reawakened by the sight of the female with the glorious mane of reddish-gold curls and stunning emerald eyes.

Everything was more acute. The crisp breeze. The tang of the autumn air. The silver of the moonlight as it glided over Cora's half-naked body.

A longing so urgent it'd nearly sent him to his knees blasted through him, even as he watched Cora's expression harden with dislike.

Shit. He desperately wanted to erase that look of loathing. To see her features soften with delight at the mere sight of him.

Which was why he was bungling this first meeting on an epic scale.

Forcing himself to take a step back, he drew in a deep, steadying breath.

"My mother would argue with the term bastard, but I'll agree, I deserved the slap," he said in rueful tones.

"Good." She pointed toward the trees. "Now, go away."

He leashed his wolf that snarled with impatience. His animal wasn't politically correct.

It wanted this woman beneath him as he pounded them both to paradise.

"Would you believe me if I told you that I never meant to hurt you?"

"No."

He grimaced. He hadn't expected her to welcome him with open arms, but this...

"It's true, princess," he insisted, his fingers itching to reach out and touch her.

He fiercely needed to know that she was real and not just another fantasy that tormented his nights.

She gave a feline toss of her head. "You seduced me and then walked away to mate with a wolf."

He flinched but held her gaze. "I was young. I never expected our flirtation to become so serious."

She rolled her eyes. Not really subtle, but he wasn't surprised by her lack of mercy. He'd been recklessly addicted to her, allowing his selfish desire to play with fire to wound her deeply.

It didn't help that she hadn't been the only one burned by his dangerous games.

"I have one question," she said.

"What?"

"Were you already promised to the female wolf when you were with me?"

He jerked in pain at the realization of just how low he'd sunk in her estimation.

"No." Blunt. Unmistakably honest.

Of course, Cora wasn't satisfied.

"But you knew that you would choose a mate from your Pack?" she pressed.

Another flinch. More pain.

"I had no choice," he growled. "Holden hadn't mated, and there was a growing insecurity that threatened to undermine my people when they needed to be united against the humans. The Pack needed the stability of a mated Beta, who could assume leadership when Holden's wolf was lost to his dark moods and in need of the time and space to run off his aggression."

Her lips flattened. "Right."

"It's the truth, Cora."

"If you were so dedicated to duty, then why the hell were you flirting with me?"

His shoved his fingers through his hair that was tangled from his recent run through the woods.

"You know why."

She narrowed her eyes. "Say it."

She needed to hear the words? Fine.

"I wanted you."

"And what Soren wants he has to have?" she taunted.

"Yes." He'd seen her standing in a sunlit glade, the long strands of her hair shimmering like fire, her eyes dancing with amusement. Between one beat of his heart and the next, he'd known that he would move heaven and earth to have her in his arms. "It was that simple. And that tragic."

"Tragic?"

He shrugged, knowing she wasn't ready to hear the full truth. Or maybe he just wasn't ready to reveal that he was even more of an ass than she already assumed.

"Why haven't you mated?" he instead asked.

Her expression tightened to an unreadable mask. "I learned a lesson from you. I take my fun where I want and then move on to the next."

"Don't say that," he rasped, unwilling to believe that his sweet, playful kitten had become a hardened cynic.

She shrugged. "Why not?"

"Because I carry enough guilt."

"There's no need for guilt," she assured him with a smile that didn't reach her eyes. "I'll eventually settle down with a nice, steady male who knows how to treat a female."

His jaw clenched. "I suppose your father is still trying to shove you into the arms of Max Leskov?" Holden demanded, recalling the golden-haired, too pretty Beta of Golden Pack.

The male had always played the role of trusted friend, even as Soren had sensed he was more than prepared to take Cora as his mate.

"At least Max wouldn't bed me while he was looking for another mate."

"Shit." He lifted a hand to press it against his chest. Inside, his heart felt as if it were being ripped in half. "You really know how to twist the knife, don't you?"

She lowered her lashes, hiding her eyes from him. "What do you want from me?"

Now that was a loaded question, wasn't it?

"For tonight?" he asked in low tones. "Peace."

CHAPTER 2

The high-tech medical facility that was built on the western edge of Boulder was nearly invisible to the public. With the back of the four-storied structure overlooking the vast natural parkland, the front and sides were well hidden behind a ten-foot fence that was guarded 24/7. No one was allowed to enter without proper credentials.

Inside, it was a combination of laboratories with cutting-edge equipment, meeting rooms that were filled with sleek furniture, and large offices. Exactly what was expected.

It was only deep in the basement that it became evident that this was no normal facility. Not only were there a dozen cages with thick metal bars and shackles hanging from the ceiling, but also a hidden room for the fighting pit, complete with bleachers for the guests of the SAU who paid to watch the animals fight.

Dawn was barely brushing the sky with hints of pink when Dr. Frank Talbot put away the last of his files and straightened the nameplate he'd placed on the edge of the mahogany desk.

A tall man with thick chestnut hair he kept carefully brushed back to emphasize his tanned face and pale blue eyes, Frank had been working for hours to clear the office of the previous owner's belongings. Now, at last, he could claim it as his own.

Running a satisfied hand over the leather seat he'd ordered just minutes after learning his predecessor had had his throat ripped out by the Alpha of the River Pack, Frank was interrupted when the door was rudely shoved open.

"Director Markham," he forced himself to murmur as the large man with short, iron-gray hair attired in a crisp blue suit strolled into the office.

Frank stiffened as the head of the Denver division of the SAU studied him with a mocking smile. Unlike him, Markham had risen through the ranks of the military before becoming a part of the secret organization.

A trained monkey in a suit, Frank silently told himself.

He, on the other hand, had graduated top of his class from Harvard Medical School, and had been one of the most promising researchers in the field of virology until he'd been fired for using the homeless as his test subjects. Ridiculous laws.

Thankfully, the fact that the Verona Virus had nearly wiped out humanity had prevented him from being tossed into jail. Instead, he'd been transferred from his prestigious position to this shadowy agency that wasn't nearly so concerned with pesky details like morals and ethics.

"Talbot," the older man drawled.

Frank narrowed his eyes. "Doctor."

"Excuse me?"

"It's Dr. Talbot."

The Director snorted, glancing around the

paneled walls that were now decorated with Frank's framed diplomas and a picture of his mother who'd died during the Verona outbreak.

"I see you've made yourself at home."

Frank shrugged. The dead doctor had been an idiot. Frank was far more deserving of the position as head of research. Why pretend otherwise?

"There didn't seem any point in allowing a perfectly good office to sit empty," he said.

"The previous owner is barely cold in his grave."

Frank shrugged, increasingly annoyed by the interruption. Didn't Markham have better things to do than worry about proper etiquette for taking over for a colleague who'd recently had his throat ripped out?

"We all mourn in our own way," Frank snapped.

The Director held up a beefy hand. "Don't get your panties in a bunch, doc. I prefer a man who sets his sights on the finish line and refuses to let anyone or anything stand in his way."

"Then we should work well together."

"Time will tell." Markham folded his arms over his chest, his square face hardening as he got down to business. "What are your plans now that you've claimed the position of head researcher?"

Frank smoothed his hands down the white lab jacket that he wore over his pale blue shirt and black slacks.

"It's obvious that we need to discover more about the process of mutating a human into a shifter."

The older man nodded. Since the wolf traitor had revealed that a shifter didn't have to be born, but could actually be created by the bite of an Alpha or a true mate, the SAU had been foaming at the mouth to see if they could discover the exact details of how it worked.

They claimed it was merely to better understand the enemy. Frank, however, knew that wasn't the entire truth. The Board of Directors had every intention of trying to create their own shifters that they could control.

"Easier said than done," Markham muttered.

"True," Frank agreed. "The best-case scenario would be to bring the Alphas to the lab, where I could have the shifters—as well as the humans—hooked up to my equipment so I could scientifically monitor each step of the process."

"Impossible." The Director gave a firm shake of his head. "After the previous doctor's bungled attempt to get his hands on the wolf's human mate, the Packs are on edge. If we try to take their leaders, they'll explode into a full-out riot." Markham grimaced. "The SAU can't afford that sort of unwanted attention. Not now."

Frank hid a smile. The SAU liked to pretend that they were a powerful force in the government, but the truth was, there were many members of the Congress and a few judges on the Supreme Court who thought they were going too far in containing the shifters. And there had been more than one attempt to close them down.

If they knew what truly happened behind the fences...

Well, it would be a sad day for Markham and his cronies.

"Fine," Frank said. "Then we need to encourage one of the Alphas to willingly participate in our experiments."

Markham widened his eyes before he released a sharp laugh. "Yeah, right. And why don't you teach him how to shit gold while you're at it?"

Frank wasn't amused. "It's all a matter of

leverage."

"Leverage?"

"They have something we want, so we must discover something they want."

The older man continued to study him with barely concealed disdain. "There's nothing that would force them to teach us how they create shifters."

Leaning to the side, Frank grabbed a file off his desk, holding it toward his companion.

"She would."

Taking the folder, Markham flipped it open, his heavy brow wrinkled as he studied the picture inside.

"Why does she look so familiar?"

"Cora Wilder," Frank said in smooth tones. "From all reports, the Alpha of the Golden Pack adores his only daughter. Which means he would do anything to protect her." He deliberately paused. "Anything."

The Director jerked his head up, clearly caught off guard by Frank's daring plot.

"Exactly what are you suggesting?"

Frank didn't hesitate. "It's simple. You need to kidnap-"

"The SAU doesn't kidnap," Markham corrected in stern tones. "We detain hostiles."

"Very well." Frank forced himself not to react to the idiotic interruption. "You need to *detain* Cora and bring her to me."

Markham once again studied the picture, clearly considering the various implications of capturing the pretty young shifter.

"It would cause a rebellion among the Felines," he at last pronounced with blatant regret.

"Not if you managed to extract her from the den before anyone knew that she was missing," Frank said, inwardly wondering how the stupid fool had ever risen to the role of Director. Certainly it wasn't because of his limited brains. "Once she is here, you could use her continued good health to ensure the cats' good behavior."

"It might work," Markham slowly admitted.

"Then you'll retrieve her for me?"

Without warning, the older man stepped forward, poking his finger into the center of Frank's chest.

"No. I'll retrieve her for the SAU." Another poke that was certain to leave a bruise. "Perhaps you need to be reminded that despite your new office, you are a mere tool for our greater purpose, Talbot."

Frank clenched his teeth, briefly considered the pleasure of reaching for the syringe he kept hidden in his pocket. It was loaded with a potent poison that would kill Markham in less than thirty seconds.

Then, with effort, he restrained his homicidal fury. For now, he needed the stupid bastard and the SAU.

Soon...

"Of course." He pasted a stiff smile on his lips. "I am here to serve."

"Hmm." Markham looked as if he wanted to say more, but perhaps realizing that Frank was his best researcher, the Director pulled a phone from his pocket and pressed it to his ear. "Paulson, I need you to choose six of your best soldiers. I have a mission that demands the utmost discretion," he barked into the speaker as he turned and headed out of the office.

Frank waited for the door to close before he gave a roll of his eyes. Pompous prick. Did the fool truly imagine that having an Alpha bite one human at a time would do any good? They had no idea the survival rate of humans undergoing the transformation. It might be one in a million. And they didn't even know how often the Alpha could use his bite to create a shifter. Nightly? Weekly? Yearly?

Frank, however, had far loftier goals.

He smiled with anticipation.

Once he understood how the actual process worked, he intended to create a virus that would infect thousands of humans at the same time.

Let the SAU think small, he was meant for far bigger things.

****

Soren shuddered as he shifted from wolf to human, the agonizing pleasure wrenching a groan from his throat.

He'd intended to head straight to the shower before seeking his bed after a night of running in his animal form, but he'd caught the smell of his Alpha before he ever made it to his small cabin.

With a resigned sigh, he reached for the pair of jeans he kept stashed in a small cubby at the edge of the woods. All shifters learned to stockpile clothing in various locations in case they needed a quick change.

Scrubbing his hands over his face that was in dire need of a shave, he headed around the edge of the cabin to discover Holden leaning against the front door.

The lean male with brown hair and blue eyes watched his approach with an intensity that made his wolf give a low growl. His Alpha would always be dominant, but as the Beta of the Pack, Soren refused to take any shit.

"Trouble sleeping?" Holden demanded, glancing toward the crisp blue sky.

"These are difficult times."

"No crap." The fierce gaze never wavered. "But I suspect your restless night had more to do with a beautiful cat."

Dammit. He'd known his absence would be noticed, but he'd hoped that Holden wouldn't so easily suspect that it was Cora's arrival that had lured him away from his duties.

"You're my Alpha," he growled. "Not my father."

"Thank God."

Soren rolled his eyes. "How did the ceremony go?"

For a minute, Soren feared his companion would press for details about the reunion. Not that Soren had anything to share. He'd seen Cora. She'd reinforced her opinion that he was a heartless pig. And he'd crawled away with his tail between his legs.

Badda-bing, badda-boom.

"As well as could be expected." Holden at last allowed himself to be diverted. "In the short-term, we know that we have no choice but to try and share the same territory, and fighting between the Packs only helps the SAU convince the world that we're dangerous beasts who need to be caged."

Soren nodded. "And long-term?"

"We have to do whatever it takes to make sure there is no long-term."

Holden didn't have to point out the obvious. They all knew that two predatory Packs couldn't live in the same territory. Not without open warfare.

"Have the tigers made any connections with the officials that might help our cause?" he asked.

"They have a diplomat, but they're told the same lies that we keep getting shoved down our throats," Holden said, his voice thick with disgust. "That the humans are still traumatized by the virus. Once they accept our presence, we'll be free to live wherever we want. Yadda, yadda, yadda."

Soren folded his arms over his chest. As the Beta, his wolf was deeply connected to his Alpha. He could sense the older male's emotions, and while he couldn't actually read his mind, he always knew what he was thinking. Which meant he knew when Holden was holding something back.

"What aren't you telling me?" he demanded.

Holden's gaze moved toward the narrow band of trees that was now all that separated the two Packs.

"I didn't get a straight answer, but I sense the cats have a spy on the inside."

Soren cocked a brow. "Inside of what?"

Holden paused before returning his attention to Soren. "I'm not entirely sure, you know the cats love to be secretive, annoying bastards. But Jonah Wilder had information that could only come from a source with ties to the human government."

Soren wasn't surprised. Every Alpha would be anxious to create allies among the enemy camp. And if they could find a sympathetic individual willing to act as a spy, then so much the better.

"We have a few of our own sources," he said, referring to the congressmen who were willing to hear Holden's grievances and pass along information.

"True, but it would help to know who the cats have as their spy."

Soren shrugged. "Then ask."

"I prefer to be a little more..."

"Sneaky?" Soren offered as Holden hesitated.

"Something like that."

Soren abruptly frowned, planting his hands on his hip. Okay. He recognized that expression on his companion's face.

It meant that he was about to bully Soren into something he didn't want to do.

"What do you want from me, Holden?" he bluntly asked.

"There's more than one way to skin a cat. Figuratively speaking," Holden informed him. "Your princess is close to her father-"

"No," he snapped, his beast lunging beneath his skin in fury.

"No?"

It was the first time Soren had ever directly denied a request from his Alpha.

"I'm not playing games with Cora," Soren warned, knowing his eyes had shifted to wolf. "Not again."

Holden narrowed he gaze. "Don't tell me you don't intend to seduce the female. You've been prowling around their compound since they arrived."

Soren stepped forward, his expression hard with an unspoken threat.

There would be no compromise. No negotiations.

"What happens between us is private."

Holden allowed his power to thunder through the air between them.

"Even if it could help your Pack?"

Soren refused to back down. Not this time.

"I allowed my duty to hurt Cora before," he said, regret scouring through him like acid. "I won't sacrifice her again."

Holden folded his arms over his chest, studying Soren with blatant curiosity.

"If you feel so strongly about the female, why didn't you go after her before now?"

Soren felt a chill inch down his spine, even as the morning sunlight brushed over the bare skin of his back and the heat of his wolf warmed him from the inside.

It was always the same.

Any time he was forced to recall his first mating

and the female he'd been unable to love.

Her name came out as a croak. "Leah."

Holden's brows snapped together. "You can't mourn forever, Soren. Leah passed two years ago."

He grimaced. "Leah may have passed, but not my guilt."

"I don't understand."

Of course, the Alpha didn't understand. No one did. Hell, Soren wasn't sure *he* fully grasped the toxic mixture of regret and guilt and sadness that consumed him.

"I...cared for Leah," he forced himself to try and explain. "And I did my best to make her happy."

"It wasn't your fault she couldn't get pregnant," Holden assured him.

It was well known that Leah had been desperate to have a child. She'd tried every method available to become pregnant, from human technology to mystical ceremonies that promised fertility.

And, as the final tragedy, she'd been traveling in secret to yet another clinic when the small, private airplane had gone down during a storm.

"No, but it was my fault that she became so obsessed with trying to give me a son," he said in a strained voice.

"Why?"

"She knew I had someone else in my heart." Soren pressed a hand to his chest that always felt too tight when he thought of his dead mate. "She thought a child would bind us together."

Sensing the pain that Soren had kept bottled up for the past two years, Holden reached out to lay a hand on his shoulder.

"I'm sorry."

"It's not your fault."

"It is," Holden insisted, genuine regret twisting

his features. "If I had mated sooner, you wouldn't have been expected to bond with Leah."

Soren shook his head. He'd never blamed his Alpha. Never. They both sacrificed for the Pack. It's what leaders did.

"And you wouldn't have found Ariel," he murmured.

Holden remained troubled. "So I found my heart while you-"

"Don't." Soren stepped back, dislodging his friend's hand. There was no way in hell he was going to allow Holden's relationship with his beautiful mate to be tainted with guilt. "The second I caught Cora's scent I accepted that the past is behind us. It's time to move forward."

There was a long pause before Holden gave a nod of his head, accepting Soren's request to concentrate on the future.

"The question is...move forward into what?" he asked with a grimace.

Soren's gaze drifted toward the fence he could see in the distance. A tangible sign of their imprisonment.

"These dark days won't last forever," he murmured.

"No, they won't," Holden agreed, his expression suddenly grim. "And I swear I'll do whatever is necessary to make sure we survive to enjoy a life where we can live without fear."

Soren nodded. "I have full faith."

They shared a moment of silent determination, both dedicated to seeing the day they would live without fences. Then, Holden narrowed his gaze.

"In the meantime, I need to you to be careful," the older man said. "If you piss off your cat, it could strike a spark that sets off the powder keg beneath our feet."

With his warning delivered, Holden headed down the narrow path that led toward the communal area. Soren turned in the opposite direction, his earlier plan of a shower and a few hours of shut-eye forgotten as he was overwhelmed by a sudden need to finish what he'd started.

Jogging through the undergrowth, he made his way to the young aspen tree he'd planted in Leah's favorite spot next to the lake. Then, dropping to his knees, he bent his head and released the ghost that had haunted him for so long.

"Rest in peace, Leah," he whispered.

****

Cora stood in the small back garden of her new home and sipped her coffee. After a night of tossing and turning, it felt good to get out, feel the sun against her skin and allow the crisp air to clear the fog from her brain.

She hadn't expected to sleep. Not after her encounter with Soren. But she'd assumed it would be anger that kept her awake. And perhaps a need to plot the wolf's slow, painful death.

The last thing she'd expected was the savage hunger that had clenched her muscles until she wanted to scream.

She wanted Soren. No. It was more than that. She *ached* for Soren.

Memories of having him in her bed with her legs wrapped around his hips as he pounded deep inside of her had tormented her for hours. Even worse were the vivid images of having her head pillowed on his chest as they slept in sated exhaustion, and his lips tickling her ear as he woke her to begin their day together.

At last crawling from her bed, she'd released her cat to go for a long run, hoping to work off her seething frustrations. It'd helped until her animal had caught the scent of Soren near a small lake. Cora had instantly shifted back to human, ignoring her urgent need to be close to her mate.

Instead, she'd returned home and tried to convince herself that she'd become used to having Soren around. That eventually, his mere scent wouldn't send her cat into a frenzy of longing.

Thankfully, she didn't have to dwell on the futile effort. She'd barely finished her coffee when a handsome male stepped through the bushes to join her.

Max Leskov was her father's Beta and current heartthrob of the Golden Pack.

Her lips twitched as she took in the thick blond hair streaked with gold that he wore long enough to brush his broad shoulders and fall across his piercing green eyes. His father was a Siberian tiger, which meant that he was larger than most males in the Pack, with thick muscles and a strength few could match. But it was his deep dimples and his breathtaking beauty that were his greatest weapons.

And he wielded them without mercy.

"A beautiful morning, kitten," he murmured, his gaze taking a slow survey of her faded jeans and tight jade sweater. She'd pulled her hair into a high ponytail to keep it tamed in the brisk breeze.

"Max." She cocked a brow, doing a mutual inspection of his jeans and loose Denver Broncos sweatshirt. Not that she thought of this male as anything other than a surrogate brother. Despite her father's best attempts, she couldn't seriously consider Max as a mate. "Isn't it a little early for you to be out and about?" She tilted her head to the side. "What's her name?"

He moved to stand at her side, his dimples flashing. "Would you believe me if I said...Cora?"

She rolled her eyes. "No."

"You never take me seriously."

"You would flee in horror the second I did."

His tiger suddenly lurked in the back of his eyes. Quiet, intent, ever patient.

"Try me."

Cora stiffened. "Max-"

"I could smell the dog when I returned last night," the male abruptly interrupted. "What did he want?"

Cora's heart clenched, her hands tightening on her coffee cup.

"Nothing important."

Max wasn't fooled. He might play at being man-candy, but beneath the good looks and charm he was a cunning, calculated hunter.

"Do you intend to return him to your bed?"

Cora blinked at the blunt question. "I didn't realize I had to discuss my lovers with you."

He continued to study her with his tiger peering from his eyes. "I prefer not to share."

Cora frowned. Max always flirted. Hell, she was fairly certain his balls would explode if he weren't trying to charm the pants off of whatever woman was nearby. But until this morning, it'd never been anything more than a game.

"Have you been into the catnip?" she demanded.

Max shrugged. "It's been expected that we would eventually mate."

"Hoped for by my father, but never expected," she corrected.

"Why not?" he unexpectedly pressed. "Our mating would strengthen the Pack and give our people a reason to celebrate." His charming expression briefly faltered, revealing the stark concern beneath. "Something they desperately need."

She reached out to lightly touch his arm. Sometimes she let herself forget that he was as fiercely devoted as her father was to protecting their Pack.

"So you're willing to martyr your future so our people can have a big party?" she lightly teased.

His fingers brushed down the side of her throat, tracing the collar that he intended to see removed from her neck before he died.

"Trust me, babe, I don't feel like a martyr when I think about taking you as my mate."

"No doubt because you have an entire harem to keep you happy."

"Not quite a harem."

Her lips twisted. She understood. She truly did. He was willing to do his best for the Pack. Even if it meant bonding his life with a female who wasn't the love of his life.

She even admired him for it.

But she wasn't going to enter into a relationship that would make them both miserable in the end.

"I'm like you, Max," she said in soft tones. "I don't share."

"Say the word and they're gone."

She shook her head. "We both know..."

Her words trailed away, her head jerking to the side as she caught the distinct scent of wolf.

Shit.

Clenching her hands, she watched Soren walk around the edge of the house wearing nothing more than a pair of faded jeans.

Instant heat exploded through her. Christ, he was

gorgeous with his dark curls tangled and a hint of whiskers darkening his strong jaw. He was raw, and primitive, and so uncompromisingly male her cat wanted to lick him from head to toe. And all the yummy places in between.

His eyes narrowed as he studied Max. "Am I interrupting?"

"Yes," Max answered before Cora could speak. "Go away, dog."

"Never." Soren halted close enough to Cora that she could feel the heat of his body stroke her like an intimate caress. "Like it or not, I'm here to stay."

"Ah." Max offered a dimpled smile, his eyes glowing with the power of his cat. "Do you want to play?"

Aggression filled the air until it was so thick Cora could barely breathe. With a muttered curse, she moved to stand between the two males.

"Enough," she snapped, sending Max a warning glare. "We'll speak later."

Max's gaze never strayed from Soren. "I'll be waiting."

Soren tensed, but thankfully, Max turned to stroll away from the cabin, bringing an end to potential disaster. Once he was out of sight, Cora spun around to glare at the male who was the direct cause of her sleepless night.

"What's wrong with you?"

Without warning, he was crowding into her personal space, herding her until her back was pressed against a shed, well out of sight of the kitchen window.

Then, lowering his head, he whispered directly in her ear.

"Don't let him touch you again."

She pressed her hands against his chest, wanting

to be pissed off, but instead, shuddering with excitement at the feel of his thick erection pressing against her stomach.

She needed her head examined.

"Excuse me?" she forced herself to mutter.

"I won't repeat myself." He gave the lobe of her ear a sharp nip. "If you don't want your kitty to get hurt then you'll warn him to stay the hell away."

A melting pleasure poured through her, pooling in the pit of her stomach with a delicious quiver of need.

Angered by her eager arousal, she released her claws, allowing the sharp tips to press against his skin. Just a warning that she wasn't ruled by her treacherous desires.

"Careful, Soren," she said in a husky voice.

He dragged his tongue down the length of her jaw, the musk of his wolf saturating the air with his scent.

"Too late for careful."

CHAPTER 3

Soren had fully intended to return to Cora's cabin and play the role of the perfect gentleman. He would approach her like any other male interested in a female, and begin a slow, utterly irresistible seduction that would win her wary heart.

Instead, he'd approached the house only to discover the scent of a male cat. A red mist had clouded his mind as he stalked into the backyard, discovering the bastard standing only inches from Cora.

Any hope of playing the civilized lover was smashed by the explosive reaction of his wolf.

No male was allowed near his female.

Not unless he had a death wish.

Now he buried his face in Cora's neck, ignoring the damn collar as he breathed deeply of her scent. Anything to try and ease his snarling beast.

He felt her revealing tremors even as her nails pressed into his skin, the kiss of pain nearly making his cock explode.

Shit. He'd already scratched being a gentleman off the list. It looked like the whole 'going slow' thing was fucked, as well.

"I thought we agreed that we would try to avoid each other?" she asked, her voice not entirely steady.

His hands slid down her arms, savoring the brush of cashmere beneath his palms. Not that he wouldn't have preferred her bare skin.

One step at a time.

"Just think how disappointed you'd be if I gave you what you wanted," he murmured, nuzzling the pulse that pounded at the base of her throat just below the collar.

"Disappointed?"

"How can you make me suffer for the past if we're never together?"

"If I wanted you to suffer, I would have sliced off your dick," she said.

He chuckled, as always delighted by her fierce spirit. His wolf needed a female who wasn't afraid to stand up to him.

"I'm sincerely glad you resisted that particular form of retaliation," he said, pressing his rock-hard erection against her hip.

A groan was wrenched from his throat. Oh...hell. He needed to be inside of her.

Deep, deep inside.

"Why are you here?"

He licked her pulse point, delighted when he felt her heart skip a beat.

"Do you love the cat?"

She stilled, no doubt considering whether or not she could use the other male as a way to keep him at a distance. But Cora wasn't a female who needed to hide behind lies and deceit. If she decided she didn't want him around, she'd kick his ass out the door.

"No, but he's a sensible choice for a partner," she at last muttered.

"Don't." He lifted his head to study her with a pained expression. "Never settle for less than a true mate."

Their gazes locked, her body softening against him as she briefly allowed herself to forget he was the enemy. But even as his hands spanned her waist, intending to haul her against his aching body, she was giving him a rough shove so she could step away.

"What I decide about my mate is none of your business," she told him, bristling with annoyance.

With him? Or herself for nearly giving in to temptation?

His wolf snarled, pressing against his skin. His beast didn't understand man-games. It didn't want to deny the mutual arousal that simmered between them. Not when he'd waited so long to claim this female.

Thankfully, his wolf did comprehend the need for patience when hunting his prey.

"Fine." He managed to leash his raging lust. Barely. "Then perhaps I can interest you in something that is my business."

She eyed him with a frown. "What?"

He held out his hand. "Come with me."

"Where?"

"I need to show you." He deliberately held her gaze, silently challenging her.

Tension hummed around her. He got it. She didn't trust him.

That didn't mean he liked it.

Not. At. All.

At last, she heaved a resigned sigh and placed her hand in his. No doubt she sensed he wasn't leaving until she'd given in to his request.

Smart enough not to give her time to change her mind, Soren tugged her toward the trees and across the compound to his secluded home.

He'd moved into the four-room cabin shortly after Leah's death, giving up his larger house to a mated couple with children. As long as he had a bed and a roof over his head, he was content.

Now, as he pulled a reluctant Cora through the front door, he didn't miss her quick glance around the small living room that held a worn sofa and matching chair. There were no pictures on the wall, no shelves or pretty doo-dads that women loved to clutter up a space.

It was starkly masculine, with books stacked haphazardly on the floor, and a backpack filled with his dirty laundry tossed in the corner.

Seeming to realize the intimacy of being alone in his home, she gave a tug of her hand, trying to free her fingers.

"Soren."

"I genuinely need your advice," he overrode her protest, continuing to pull her through a doorway on the other side of the living room into the narrow kitchen at the back of the cabin.

"If this is a trick," she muttered.

"Have a seat," he softly commanded, urging her into one of the high bar chairs set next to the island in the center of the room.

The space was too small for a dining table, but it did have a row of windows that overlooked the garden. And, thankfully, he'd cleaned the night before. His fastidious cat could be a little whacko when it came to his casual approach to neatness.

His lips twitched as he moved to the refrigerator. He vividly remembered having Cora constantly tidying whenever he'd stayed the night.

"What are you doing?" she asked.

Pulling out the necessary ingredients, Soren

moved to the stove. He may not be a neat freak, but he was one hell of a chef.

"Cooking you breakfast."

"What makes you think I'm hungry?"

"I heard your stomach growling earlier," he said, moving with ease to the counter to slice the bread he'd baked the day before. "Do you still like your eggs over easy and strawberry jam on your toast?"

He heard her tiny sound of surprise. Did she think he'd forgotten? That he didn't remember every single thing about her?

"Is that why you brought me here?" she asked in a husky voice. "To make me breakfast?"

"Not entirely." With the bacon and eggs cooking, and the bread being toasted, he turned to study his companion. Instantly, his heart clenched with a sharp-edged longing. Christ. She looked so perfect sitting in his house. It didn't matter that her gorgeous hair was tied back, or that her face was scrubbed free of makeup. There was a sense of 'rightness' that settled deep inside of him. "I have a favor to ask."

She regarded him with a wary scowl. "What favor?"

He grimaced. Someday she was going to look at him with joy, not that aggravating suspicion.

"Despite the efforts of our two Alphas, the melding of our Packs is bound to be difficult."

She wrinkled her nose. "Yeah, understatement of the year."

"I hoped you would help me keep the peace."

"Peace?"

He gave a lift of his shoulder. During his long nighttime run, he'd given considerable thought to how he could ease the burden carried by his Alpha. There were some duties only Holden could deal with, but it was possible Soren could help prevent the brewing battle between the two Packs.

"Right now, we're all on edge and waiting for an opportunity to strike out," he said, watching as she gave a small shiver. He didn't blame her. The very air in the enclosed compound seethed with the promise of violence. "I hoped we could find a casual means to provide interaction."

"What sort of interaction?" she asked.

"Casual competitions."

"Competitions?" She blinked in confusion. "Wouldn't that just ramp up the sense of wolf versus cat?"

"Not if we mix the teams," he explained. "We could divide up the more aggressive members of the River and Golden Packs and add in the submissives to tone down the urge for violence."

He sensed her wariness fade as she leaned her elbows on the island, her expression one of feline curiosity.

"What would the competitions entail?"

Ah. He knew she wouldn't be able to resist the idea of helping ease the tension between the Packs. She might be a princess, but she was utterly devoted to her people.

"We should switch them up so everyone can be involved," he said. "Some could be organized sports like softball and football. And others would be less structured. Maybe races or an obstacle course."

Cora's emerald eyes sparkled with anticipation. The cats were bound to excel at anything that included climbing.

"Like American Ninja Warriors?"

"Exactly." His fingers itched to reach up and stroke the hint of color that bloomed beneath the satin softness of her cheek. Would she purr or scratch? The fact he couldn't be sure kept him from trying.

"Afterward, we could have a picnic to celebrate the winners."

She gave a nod, clearly approving his suggestion even as she hesitated to agree. No doubt she understood they'd have to spend a considerable amount of time together planning the various events.

"Isn't this a discussion you should be having with Max?" she asked. "He's our Beta."

Soren shook his head. "As soon as I go to him, any suggestions I make will become a part of formal mediations that have to go straight to your father."

She instantly bristled. She was overly protective of her father since her mother's death.

"Would that be a bad thing?"

"It's not a bad thing," he instantly assured her, "but I don't want the Alphas making this a mandatory get-together. No one's more bullheaded than a shifter, and once it gets turned into a duty, everyone will resent having to do it. If we keep it spontaneous, then it has a better chance of getting people involved."

She considered his words before giving a slow nod. "True."

"Then you'll help?" he asked.

She bit her bottom lip. "I'm not sure."

"Cora, you know that your people adore you." He shamelessly manipulated her by bringing up her loyalty to her Pack. "If you put your full energy into the events, then the cats will come."

No doubt sensing she'd just been lured into a well-planned trap, Cora narrowed her gaze. She wanted to tell him to go to hell. He could read it in her eyes. But even as he prepared himself for a fight, she heaved a small sigh of resignation.

"Fine. I'll help."

His wolf howled in silent triumph.

****

A week later, Cora stood at the edge of the communal gathering area and tried to look interested in the assorted activities that were spread around the large opening.

The "Pack Games," as Soren had labeled them, had been a roaring success.

Around the edges of the clearing, Soren had constructed an obstacle course that consisted of narrow tunnels built of barbed wire, six-foot-high walls that had to be jumped, a mud pit, and a three-hundred-pound weight that had to be carried over a narrow bridge.

Cora had been in charge of the cats, designing a devilish course that consisted of thin ropes they had to balance on to cross from tree to tree, and massive leaps over wide pools of water. At the end was a fifty-foot pole they had to climb to ring a bell at the top.

Beyond the obstacle courses, there were volleyball courts, and a grassy area that was reserved for flag football—that more often than not turned into a full contact sport.

And a central sandpit where two combatants could beat the crap out of each other without using claws or fangs.

Currently, a gorgeous male panther, Cole, was battling Theo, a dominant wolf. Theo was brutally strong with fighting skills that made him a formidable warrior. But Cole was wicked quick with a cunning ability to avoid a direct blow from Theo's massive fist.

Even as she watched, the agile panther dodged a punch that would have broken his jaw. Then, with a liquid grace, he leaped high into the air and did a spinning kick that connected squarely with the side of Theo's head and dropped him to the sand.

There was a roar of cheers—not only from the felines—and more than one female crowded forward, anxious to congratulate Cole in a more private setting.

The Pack Games didn't ease all the tension between the two predatory shifter groups, or even avoid the occasional bloodshed. But it had helped to build a sense of community that might eventually lead to the ability to work together against the humans.

Cora should feel delighted.

They'd done the impossible.

Unfortunately, there was a restless itch deep inside of her that refused to be eased.

An itch that was directly related to the gorgeous male wolf, who was slowly and methodically breaking down her defenses.

Her lips twitched as she glanced down at the box of her favorite chocolates that Soren had covertly pressed into her hands before he'd headed off to get the afternoon contests organized.

It was more than the fact that he'd remembered she loved cashews in her chocolates, it was the knowledge that he must have used an appalling amount of his limited rations to acquire them.

And this wasn't the first gift. Not even close.

He'd left her flowers on her doorstep, a lovely painted scarf tied to a branch outside her window, and her favorite banana bread he'd baked and wrapped with a bow.

Then there'd been the touches.

Nothing blatant.

A warm hand at the base of her spine when they were walking together. A brush of his fingers across her cheek, gone before she could protest...

It had all combined to stir her to a fever pitch that

was making it increasingly difficult to think of anything but getting the damned male in the nearest bed.

"From Soren?"

Lost in her seething frustration, Cora gave a small jerk when Max abruptly appeared at her side, a wry smile on his lips.

"He's very...persistent," she said, glancing at the chocolates in her hand.

Max snorted. "He's a stubborn, pig-headed, mangy hound."

Cora gave a shake of her head. She'd expected to be constantly pulling Max and Soren apart. They were both aggressive males who claimed to want her as their mate.

But while they thoroughly enjoyed sniping at one another, Cora had watched in shock as the two had put aside their natural aversion to work together.

"You like him," she teased.

"Not as much as you." He waggled his brows, only to wince when she reached up to punch him in the arm. "Hey, the truth hurts." He rubbed his arm. "Damn. And so do you." Lowering his hand, he allowed his dimpled smile to fade. "Why don't you put him out of his misery?"

Her jaw tightened, her heart flinching at the blunt question.

"Because he abandoned me."

Max snorted. "You're old enough to know that shit happens, Cora," he said. "Especially for those of us who have a responsibility to Pack."

She grimaced. Over the past days, she'd been forced to accept that a portion of her fury toward Soren was embarrassingly close to the reaction of a petulant child denied her favorite toy. True, he'd broken her heart and deeply wounded her cat, but it was duty that had forced him to walk away.

Something she'd refused to admit. Even to herself.

Watching Soren with his people, however, had revealed just how deeply he cared. It was painfully obvious that he would lay down his life if it meant keeping his Pack safe.

And ironically, it was that loyalty that her cat most admired.

But, while she might be prepared to accept that his mating to another female had been inevitable, there was still a small part of her that couldn't entirely put the past behind her.

"I've accepted he had to do what he had to do," she said in low tones.

"But?" Max prompted.

"But he had two years to make things right," she said, revealing the wound that refused to heal. "He didn't even make the attempt."

Max shrugged, his attention turning toward the wolf stalking in their direction with a determined expression.

"You're a big girl, babe, but I think you should give him a break," he murmured.

Before she could retort, Soren came to a halt at her side, baring his teeth at Max.

"Go away, cat," he growled.

"Eat shit, dog," Max countered, flipping him off before he turned to casually stroll away.

"You two are freaks," Cora said as Soren wrapped a possessive arm around her shoulders and turned to urge her away from the rowdy crowd, steadily growing rowdier.

She tensed, already sensing he was subtly trying to herd her toward his cabin. A place she'd deliberately avoided since their breakfast a week ago.

It wasn't that she feared Soren. He would never, ever try to take more than she was willing to give.

No. What she feared was herself.

The burning need for Soren had become a vast, terrifying void. One that threatened to consume her.

She shivered, sucking in a deep breath. Instantly, she was drenched in Soren's rich musk.

Shit. Shit. Shit.

She was obviously going to have to take care of her hunger. It was already making her human half bitchy; soon it would have her cat dangerously aggressive.

So the question was...did she surrender to Soren's exquisite seduction? Or did she find some other male to ease her desire?

Her cat roared in instant denial, her body shuddering with revulsion. Okay. Obviously, finding another male was out of the question.

So that left Soren.

Suddenly, the tightness in her chest seemed to ease, a decadent tingle of anticipation flowing through her.

Perhaps catching the scent of her arousal, Soren allowed his fingers to skim down the curve of her spine, resting on her lower back as he continued to steer them down the path to his cabin.

"Did you like the chocolates?" he asked, his breath a warm caress against her cheek.

"Of course." She glanced up to meet his intense gaze. "You knew I would."

Cognac eyes smoldered with a mesmerizing heat. "I'd hoped."

She nearly stumbled as she felt the damp urgency between her legs. Oh, lord, it'd been so long.

Too long.

"You shouldn't waste your money on me," she

forced herself to mutter.

His fingers moved up her back, threading in her hair that she'd left down this morning.

"I would give my last penny to see you smile," he assured her.

She licked her lips that suddenly felt dry. "Soren."

They reached his front porch, and he halted directly in front of his door, gazing down at her with a tenderness that nearly broke her heart.

"I would give my soul to earn your forgiveness, princess."

She wavered. It would be so easy to submit. To give in to the aching need of her cat. But there was still a part of her that couldn't let go.

Perhaps it was a need to punish Soren. Or to protect her vulnerable heart.

Or perhaps it is simply a very female desire to continue with this delicious game, she wryly conceded. There was, after all, a heady power in having this gorgeous male chase after her.

Whatever the reason, she found herself giving a slow shake of her head.

"I'm not ready."

"I know. I'm sorry." His hand lifted to cup her cheek, his thumb trailing along the line of her jaw. "I can be a pushy bastard. Honestly, I'm happy we can at least be friends."

His light touch sent sparks of pleasure shooting through her body. Swaying forward, she placed her hands on his chest, relishing the feel of his sharp shudder.

"Friends," she said, the word sounding oddly empty.

His thumb found the pulse that was hammering just below the line of her jaw.

"We are friends, aren't we?" he asked.

"I thought..." She deliberately allowed her words to trail away.

"Cora?"

"Maybe we could be friends with benefits," she suggested.

Never stupid, Soren was swift to follow her implication. His muscles tensed, his heart pounding beneath her palm.

"Would those benefits include having you in my arms?" he demanded, his eyes fully wolf as he gazed down at her flushed face.

"If you want-" Her words broke off in a startled shriek as he abruptly grabbed her by the waist and tossed her over his shoulder. "What are you doing?"

Wrapping his arms around her legs, he shoved open the door and headed into his cabin.

"Not giving you the chance to change your mind."

CHAPTER 4

Soren didn't hesitate as he headed to the small room at the very back of the cabin, slamming the door behind him before he dumped a stunned Cora onto his bed.

Friends with benefits?

His wolf growled as he leaned over her.

He'd been oh-so patient. Wooing his wary cat with unexpected surprises and tender touches. Every day he waited for a crack in her defensive walls. Just the slightest hint that he was earning his way back into her life.

And now she'd given him that opening.

To hell with being friends...he intended to claim every silken inch of her. Starting now.

Holding her gaze, he peeled off her clothes with slow enjoyment. Like he was unwrapping an unexpected gift.

As she was a gift.

The female fate had intended to be the other half of his soul.

Planting his hands on the mattress on either side of her head, he leaned down and, without warning, sank his teeth into the tender skin of her shoulder where it met her throat. Not hard enough to taste her blood, but with enough force to warn that he intended to claim his ownership.

"Shit, Soren," she groaned, her claws digging into his shoulders as she writhed beneath him.

Not in fear.

No, this was pure animal excitement.

"Mine," he snarled, his nose pressed just below her ear as if to savor her scent.

She trembled, her cat growling in ready response.

Still, she clearly wasn't about to give in without a fight.

"No," she growled.

He traced his bite mark with lingering kisses before heading down her taut body.

Cora moaned, her fingers shoving into his hair.

"Deny it all you want," he whispered, his teeth teasing the hard tip of her nipple, "but we both know that you belong to me."

She arched her back in silent invitation, even as she denied his claim.

"I told you...I'm not ready."

"Your body recognizes my touch," he pointed out, his lips skimming over the tense muscles of her stomach. "As does your cat."

"Arrogant dog," she muttered.

He chuckled as he shoved himself off the bed, quickly ridding himself of his clothes with minimum fuss. She could call him whatever she wanted, but she couldn't hide her pulsing desire.

The very air was spiced with the scent of her cat's musk.

Rich, evocative, and tempting as hell.

His wolf strained at the leash to pounce on the female who'd haunted his dreams for more nights than he wanted to admit, but Soren took a moment to savor the sight of Cora stretched across the mattress.

His heart twisted. Gods above, she was exquisite.

Her satin curls spilled across the pillows, shimmering with hints of fire in the sunlight. Her features were delicate and her skin a perfect ivory. Her eyes glowed with emerald heat as her cat studied him with a blatant hunger.

Unlike the human part of her that remained wary. His fault, of course.

He'd been young and arrogant and utterly selfish when he'd first met Cora. The last thing he'd expected was to be bewitched by the tiger princess. Which was why he hadn't walked away when he realized that their relationship had gone beyond flirtatious games to something far more dangerous.

Now he knew it was going to take time and patience to earn her trust.

Until then, he fully intended to enjoy what she was willing to offer. Including her delectable body.

Balancing a knee on the edge of the bed, he bent down to kiss a path along the line of her collarbone, pausing to suck at her tender skin. He intended to leave his mark, as well as his scent on this female.

She gave a choked groan as he slowly explored downward over the curve of her breast and the heady perfume of her arousal filled his senses.

Cora reached toward his straining cock, giving a muttered curse when he grasped her wrists and pinned them over her head. There was no way in hell he could endure her touching him. Not when his desire pulsed through him with an edge of violence.

One stroke from her hands and he'd be spilling his seed over her belly.

Sucking the tip of her nipple between his lips, he feasted on her, savoring her tiny moans of pleasure as he used his tongue and teeth to stir her hunger.

"Let me go," she pleaded softly, her body rubbing against him. "I need to touch you."

His lips twitched. She was such a cat.

His wolf, however, was determined to remain in control.

Giving her a punishing nip, he lifted his head to study her with a smoldering gaze.

"Behave yourself, or I'll tie you to the headboard."

She bared her teeth, but when he slowly released his hold on her wrists, her touch was gentle as she reached out to run her fingers over his broad chest.

He allowed himself a second to savor her touch before he returned his attention to the soft satin of her skin, tracing a slow path down her body.

Outside, he could hear the distant sound of his brothers baying at the Pack Games, and the less familiar growl of a tiger passing by the cabin, but Soren's attention was focused on the female beneath him.

The spicy taste of her skin. The rich musk of her scent. The soft purr that rumbled in her throat as he worked his way down the curve of her hip before spreading her legs.

His wolf gave a low snarl of anticipation as he crawled between her thighs, his hands sliding beneath her ass to tilt her to the perfect angle. Only then did he use his tongue to stroke through her moist heat.

"Soren." Her fingers clenched in his hair as he tasted her sweet cream, dipping his tongue into her sweet little tunnel.

He smiled, stroking his way back to the top of her clit. His cat liked having her pussy licked. And he liked licking her.

She tasted like the finest honey.

Pure ambrosia.

Her hips instinctively moved against his mouth, her soft groans filling the air. Her climax was close. He wanted to taste it on his tongue.

Typically, Cora wasn't going to lay back and allow him to be in control. She might be a princess, but she was anything but passive.

"No," she breathed. "I need to feel you inside me."

He turned his head to give her thigh a small nip. "I won't last long," he warned. "I've waited too long to have you."

"I want to see you when I come," she commanded.

"Yes," he breathed.

She was right. There was something intensely intimate in holding a lover's gaze as he thrust deeply inside. With a last, savoring lap of his tongue, Soren flowed upward, branding her mouth in a kiss of pure possession.

He'd waited so long to claim her. Now he would never have enough of her.

Never.

Her arms wrapped around his shoulders, her claws digging into the skin of his back. Soren gave a rough growl. His wolf prowled close to the surface, even as his human body quivered with the need to slam his cock into her. He wanted it rough and raw, claiming her in the most primitive way possible.

Only the fierce reminder that she was a cat, not a wolf, curbed his instinct.

His tiger might occasionally enjoy a hard pounding that led to a swift climax, but she preferred to play.

Locking their gazes, he pressed the head of his cock against her clit, rubbing it through her gathering cream. Her breath caught, her cheeks flushing as she scored her claws down his back.

"Tease," she husked, her eyes shimmering with emerald pleasure.

He leaned down to kiss the tip of her nose. "Christ...I've missed you, Cora."

Her eyes darkened with remembered pain. "Don't."

"Accept us, Cora," he warned. "I have."

"You..."

Her words came to a sharp end as his cock hit her entrance and his tip slid just inside her. The heat of her moist body enfolded his crown.

His breath hissed between his clenched teeth. Shit. He was on the edge of an orgasm, and he hadn't even gotten fully inside of her.

Beneath him, Cora released a shaky breath. "Soren, please."

"This time we take it slow," he murmured. "Next time, my wolf gets to choose his way."

"I never said there would be a next time...oh, hell..."

She arched her back, urging him deeper. Soren pressed forward, giving her another inch.

The air heated, thick with the musk of their mutual arousal.

This morning was about connecting skin to skin, their mutual passions binding them together despite Cora's determination to keep him at a distance.

He tangled his fingers in her glorious hair, lowering his head to kiss her with stark hunger, even as he tilted his hips and surged forward.

Buried deeply inside of her, he held perfectly still, silently absorbing the pleasure that sizzled through him.

"This is what I dreamed of," he buried his face in the silken curls that spread across the blanket, imprinting her scent on the very fiber of his being.

She moaned, her legs wrapping around his waist as he pulled out to the very tip before thrusting deep, over and over. "You. And me. Together."

"Soren," she moaned. "Stop talking."

He chuckled, continuing to plunge into her heat as the pressure of his looming orgasm swelled with alarming speed. Dammit. He'd genuinely intended to make this last the entire night. Or at least a few hours.

But he'd seriously underestimated the force of his need.

Lost in the sensations that were thundering through him, Soren unconsciously sank his teeth into the flesh of her shoulder, holding her in place as her warm pussy clasped his cock, urging him to a savage pace.

She groaned, arching beneath him as her entire body clenched with pleasure. Still, he continued with his ruthless rhythm, waiting until he heard her strangled gasp of completion before he gave in to his own explosive climax.

Groaning, he pumped his seed deep into her womb, slowing his thrusts to a sated pace. Cora ran her hands up and down his back, petting him as his wolf growled in satisfaction.

Yes.

This was what he'd needed.

What he'd longed for since he'd been forced to turn his back on this female.

Raising his head, he studied Cora's flushed features with utter contentment.

CHAPTER 5

Cora snuggled next to Soren, stunned by the shattering pleasure that continued to quake through her.

Good. God.

Sex with Soren had always been fantastic. But this had been...cataclysmic.

They'd never made love with their animals so close to the surface before. It'd intensified each touch, each kiss, until she'd felt as if she were shimmering with an incandescent ecstasy.

Lying on his side, Soren used the tip of his finger to absently trace the tattoo of a pouncing cat on her forearm.

"You're quiet," he murmured.

I'm not the same chatterbox I used to be," she said, not about to admit that she was trying to recover from the spectacular orgasm that had turned her brain to mush.

His ego was quite big enough, thank you very much.

His brows drew together as he gazed down at her. "I hope that's not true."

"Why?"

"I liked your chattering," he said, his fingers lingering on the rough brand that marred her skin beneath the tattoo. A tangible reminder that they lived at the mercy of the humans. "And how you would eat an entire bowl of dough before I could bake a single cookie. And your habit of flitting around the room straightening my messes."

She gave a snort, sternly refusing to admit how fiercely touched she was that he'd remembered so much about their time together.

"Liar. You complained I was OCD."

"Princess, I adored everything about you." Leaning down, he pressed a kiss to the tip of her nose. "Your beauty. Your intelligence. Your frisky love for play." He moved to nibble at the corner of her mouth. "Even your stubborn independence."

"Smooth-talker," she murmured, her hands lifting to stroke over the sculpted planes of his chest. His skin felt like warm satin beneath her palms. Delicious. "You're just trying to get into my pants."

"I've already been in your pants." He swiped his tongue over her lower lip. He had a tendency to show affection by licking her. Sometimes he was such a wolf. "And it was fabulous."

Her lips twitched. Soren was truly irresistible in this teasing mood.

"It was nice," she conceded.

"Nice?" He regarded her with pretend outrage. "My mother's pot roast dinner is nice. Hunting beneath the full moon is nice. The first snowfall is nice." He kissed her, his lips hot and demanding before he pulled back to study her with a piercing intensity. "Fucking you is breathtakingly spectacular."

She released her claws to allow them to press against the skin of his chest.

"Are you fishing for compliments, Soren?"

A low growl rumbled in his throat. "You just can't admit it, can you, princess?"

"Admit what?"

"You belong to me."

She hid a grimace at the stark possession in his voice.

The human part of her might remain stubbornly determined to deny his claim, but her animal was much more basic.

This wolf had captivated her from the second he'd entered her father's home ten years ago. And even when he'd betrayed her, she'd still ached for him with a primitive hunger that refused to leave her in peace.

Today she intended to allow her cat to rule.

"Have I ever told you that you talk too much?" she muttered.

He chuckled, then without warning, he was moving with a fluid speed.

"I'm a wolf of many talents. I can multitask." Cora gasped, finding herself pressed into the mattress with a wickedly amused male perched on top of her. Her eyes widened, excitement exploding through her at the smoldering intensity in his gaze. A hunter who was focused on his prey. No other male had ever made her shiver with such fierce anticipation, his sensuality a physical force that brushed against her. "I can whisper sweet nothings, and at the same time, give you enough pleasure to make you scream out my name."

Her breath was wrenched from her lungs, but she struggled to disguise her violent response.

Soren was arrogant enough without knowing that he was the only lover who could make her heart thunder and her knees weak.

"I'll give you full marks for talking smack," she drawled, her hands grabbing his shoulders to allow her claws to dig into his skin. "But are you more than hot air?"

He leaned down to nip her bottom lip, his hot breath scorching over her cheek.

"Let's find out, shall we?" he husked, his tongue tracing the line of her jaw.

"What...oh."

Cora shuddered as his lips blazed a path down the curve of her shoulder, pausing to nuzzle the bite mark he'd left earlier. His lips traced the sensitive bruise before he was exploring downward.

Pleasure cascaded through her, his lips creating tiny sparks of excitement as he skimmed over the top of her breast, pausing to tease her nipple to a gloriously hard nub that tingled beneath his expertise.

Oh, yes.

Just a few minutes ago she'd been so sated she could barely move, now her body was sizzling back to life with a vengeance.

Perhaps not entirely surprising.

It'd been far too long since she'd had a lover who could excite her to this point of pleasure-pain.

Giving her nipple a last, lingering suck, Soren planted a trail of kisses between her breasts, his dark hair brushing over her skin like a caress. Cora groaned, savoring the rich scent of his musk that filled her senses.

His fingers grasped her hips as he continued to sweep his lips downward, skimming over the clenched muscles of her stomach before he was firmly settling between her legs. Shocks of pleasure raced through her. Lifting herself onto her elbows, she studied the male kneeling between her legs with smug assurance.

She wanted to watch this wolf who'd haunted her dreams for so many years.

As if sensing her need, Soren held her gaze as he lowered his head and slowly licked her gathered cream.

Her heart thundered as she watched his eyes shimmer with a silver fire, his rough tongue teasing over her clit before it was sliding back down to push deep into her body.

She hissed, ecstasy darting through her.

Good lord, he was a talented wolf.

Her hands clenched the sheet beneath her as he continued to arouse her with his tongue, his slow, deliberate strokes designed to take her to the edge without going over.

"Soren," she at last pleaded. "Enough."

To hell with pride. She needed to feel him inside her.

"It will never be enough," he growled, pressing his lips to her inner thigh before retracing a delectable path of kisses back up her body. His wolf glowed in his eyes as he reached for her hand, pressing it against his cock. "I need you."

Not even trying to resist temptation, she wrapped her fingers around his erection. He groaned in approval, tilting his hips to encourage her to pump her hand down to the heavy testicles.

Her lips curved in smug satisfaction.

She liked knowing that she could make this powerful male tremble with need.

Slowly skimming her fingers upward, she circled the broad tip that was already damp with his seed.

"What happened to those sweet words, Mr. Multitasker?" she teased.

He muttered a curse, his claws digging into the mattress as he crouched above her.

"I might have overestimated my ability to concentrate," he muttered. "You...destroy me."

She forced herself not to reveal her intense reaction to his soft words. Not even when something in the center of her chest seemed to melt.

Was it her heart?

No. No. No.

Not again.

Deliberately distracting herself from her dangerous thoughts, she tightened her fingers around his hard arousal, pushing her fist downward with enough force to wrench a groan from his throat.

"Yes," he rasped. "My clever cat."

Continuing to pump up and down, she concentrated on her command over his lean, perfect body. His breath rasped through the air, his back bowing as he neared his climax.

Of course, the pushy wolf couldn't allow her to finish him off in her hand.

Lowering his head, he claimed her lips in a savage kiss before his hands were tightening her on her hips and he was rolling onto his back in one smooth motion.

Caught off guard to discover herself lodged on top of him, she gazed down at his lean, fiercely male face. Planting her hands in the center of his chest, she gave a small wiggle, sighing at the sensation of his large cock pressed against her clit.

Ah, yes.

This was nice. And unexpected.

Soren might be a Beta, but he liked being in control.

Her lips twitched. "You're going to let me be on top?"

His hands moved to cup her breasts, his gaze locked on her flushed face.

"I'm prepared to make you happy, princess," he murmured. "Whatever it takes."

"Soren—"

Her protest was cut short as his fingers strummed over her nipples, sending tiny jolts of ecstasy through her body. She assured herself that she would remind him later that there was nothing between them but sex.

For now, however, all that mattered was the exquisite passion that scorched between them.

Sinking downward, she pressed her nose to the curve of his shoulder, sucking in a deep breath of his musky scent. Then, without warning, she sank her teeth into his flesh.

Soren growled his approval, rubbing his hard erection against her tender nub.

"Is it your turn to be lost for words, princess?" He molded his hands over her hips, sliding the tip of his cock until it rested against the entrance to her body.

In answer, she arched back, allowing her claws to scrape over his chest.

He hissed in pleasure, his head lifting so he could run his lips over the curve of her breast, at last latching onto her aching nipple.

Cora groaned as anticipation exploded through her. She might tell herself this was just sex, but her body knew the difference.

It responded to Soren's touch with a shuddering intensity that wrenched the breath from her lungs.

His mouth moved to torment her other nipple, lapping and pleasuring her with a raw intensity that made her stomach clench.

God almighty. She felt as if she were being burned alive.

As if sensing she was swiftly reaching the point of no return, Soren lowered his head to study her flushed face, his brooding gaze holding more than a little male possession.

Then, reaching up, he grasped her face and pulled her down to cover her lips in a slow, utterly tender kiss. Cora sighed.

During their early flirtations, Soren had enchanted her with his soft, heartrendingly affectionate caresses. They'd been more than just passion. Or lust. They'd been filled with joy, and friendship, and promise.

With a compulsive motion, her hands explored the chiseled planes of his chest. She liked the feel of him. Hard muscles covered by warm, satiny skin.

A true hunter.

Her cat stretched beneath her skin, and with a low purr of pleasure, she dipped her head down to spread kisses along the bottom of his collar.

"I love to hear you purr, princess," he muttered, his hands cupping her ass.

"I bet I can make you purr too, wolf," she whispered, moving ruthlessly lower.

"Shit."

"Do you like?"

"Cora," he rasped as she reached the rigid muscles of his lower stomach. "I'm not sure I can last."

She ignored his warning as she kissed her way to the tip of his massive erection. He'd halted her play earlier before she was done. This time she intended to have some fun.

Holding his gaze, she caught a glimpse of the wolf deep in his cognac eyes as she took the broad head of his cock between her lips.

He cried out in pleasure, his musk spicing the air. She stroked her tongue over the length, pausing to lick the seed at the tip before she sucked him deeper into her mouth.

Soren's hips arched upward, his breath hissing through his clenched teeth as she explored him with her tongue before scraping her teeth down the thick shaft. He released a tortured moan, tugging her by the hair to urge her up his body.

Cora allowed herself to be pulled upward with a pout.

"You are supposed to be making me happy," she murmured. "I wasn't finished."

"I intend to make both of us happy," he rasped, holding on to her hips as he adjusted her over the fierce jut of his cock.

She breathed a harsh sigh; the aching emptiness in her pussy easing as he slowly penetrated her damp channel.

Cora made a sound of fierce approval at the ruthless invasion. She enjoyed playing as much as the next kitty, but there came a time to get down to business.

Widening her knees, she angled herself to sink even deeper onto his cock. Soren hissed, lifting his hips to meet her, his balls pressed against her ass.

They both froze in pleasure, then he tilted back his head, his howl vibrating deep inside of her.

Lifting herself until just the tip of his cock remained at her entrance, she sharply plunged downward. His fingers pressed into her hips, his snarls of pleasure sending goose bumps over her skin.

Refusing to dwell on the sweet intimacy that was weaving a spell of enchantment between them, she concentrated on the sensation of Soren's quickening thrusts; her soft purrs rumbling in the air and her muscles quivering as her orgasm thundered toward a rapturous peak.

Soren muttered something beneath his breath, pumping into her at a furious pace. Squeezing her eyes shut, she sank her claws into his chest, unconsciously marking him as she was thrust into a cataclysmic climax.

Cora trembled in ecstasy, convulsing around him as he gave one more driving plunge of his cock and howled out the pleasure of his own orgasm.

****

The day passed in a sensual haze. Not only were there delicious hours of exploring each other's bodies, re-discovering how to give each other the greatest pleasure, but they'd snuggled on the couch, watching old movies and eating a huge pot of her favorite chili that Soren had insisted on cooking, as well.

It was nearly dusk when they'd tumbled into an exhausted nap, both making up for the past week of sleepless nights.

Cora woke to discover herself tangled in Soren's arms, the shadows in the room warning her that she'd slept longer than she'd intended.

Just for a moment, she allowed herself to savor the feel of the warm male body pressed against her and the scent of musk that clung to her skin.

She'd missed this.

The warmth. The intimacy. The absolute knowledge she wasn't alone.

Torn between the desire to kiss Soren awake and the need to put some distance between them, Cora reluctantly slid out of the bed and pulled on her clothes. After writing a short note, she forced herself to leave the cabin.

Any decisions she made concerning her wolf wouldn't be made when she was still tingling from the pleasure of his touch.

Slipping out the back door, she headed directly through the thick woods that separated the Packs. It was late enough that most shifters would be home with their families, eating an evening meal. However, it was possible there were still a few at the communal area.

Soren's suggestion of casual competitions had been a stroke of genius. It not only allowed the more aggressive Pack members to release their frustrations, it also gave the submissives an opportunity to use their instinctive ability to nurture their people. Soren's efforts along with a few suggestions from her had eased the tensions and promised to build relationships that would hopefully lead to a peaceful future.

But the reduction of potential hostilities meant that shifters felt comfortable mingling in the public areas, and tonight, Cora preferred to avoid being seen. Her thoughts were too muddled to share polite chitchat.

She didn't realize just how muddled they were until she caught the unmistakable scent of humans only a few feet away.

Shit.

She came to a sharp halt, her cat stirring with unease.

It wasn't astonishing that a group of humans had invaded their private compound. The bastards assumed they had the right to make surprise inspections whenever they felt the urge.

But she'd never seen them without an Alpha with them to act as an escort. Or at least that's what the humans had claimed when they'd demanded her father go with them. She privately knew there was a decent chance they would get mauled if they were ever caught alone in the compound.

"Who's there?" she called out, her stomach clenching as she heard the crack of branches and three of the humans circled behind her so she was effectively surrounded. "Show yourself."

A tall male stepped from the shadows dressed in camouflage pants with a matching coat that did nothing to disguise his muscled bulk. His face was broad with heavy jowls, and his hair was buzzed military short.

"Cora Wilder?" he asked.

Her mouth went dry. How the hell did they know her name?

"Who are you?"

He shrugged. "You can call me sir."

Jackass.

"What do you want?"

"You."

She glanced over her shoulder at the men who were blocking the path behind her, acutely aware of how isolated she was in the thick woods.

"Why?"

The man planted his hands on his hips, the gesture emphasizing the gun that was holstered at his waist.

"That will be explained at HQ."

She blinked in shock. HQ. He had to mean the headquarters of SAU.

Every shifter knew that the secretive organization had several nerve-centers spread throughout the world, but only a rare few had ever visited.

Or rather, only a rare few lived to reveal they'd been inside an SAU building, she silently conceded.

Who knew how many had been taken, never to return?

The thought made her break out in a cold sweat. She had to get away, but there was no way she could overpower six men. Even if they were human.

Especially when they were carrying weapons.

She could either attempt to keep them distracted long enough to try and make a break for it, or hope that a shifter might come close enough to sense that she was in trouble.

"I think there must be a mistake." She pasted a stiff smile on her lips. "I have no position in the Pack. If you need to speak with someone, then you should contact my father."

"I'm sure your father will be contacted," the man said, glaring at the soldier behind her that had sniggered at his words. "Once we have what we need."

Cora swallowed the lump in her throat. So, this had something to do with her father. No big surprise. There was no reason for the humans to even know her name if she weren't the daughter of Jonah Wilder.

"What do you need?"

"As I said. You." The male nodded his head toward the nearby fence. "We have your transportation waiting."

Cora took a covert step to the side. There was a large tree just a few feet away. If she could shift fast enough, she could be in the top branches before the guards could catch her.

The trick was going to be turning into her cat before they could shoot.

"If you have questions for me, you can ask them here," she said, taking another step to the side. And then another. "I'm not leaving."

"You're coming with us, cat," the man snapped, pulling his gun from his holster. "We can do this the easy way. Or the hard way."

Dammit. She carefully judged the distance between herself and the tree.

"Fine." She sucked in a deep breath, well aware that it was going to take a miracle to escape. "But first, I need to go by my home and tell my family."

"No."

"They'll worry if I'm not there for dinner," she insisted.

"Trust me, they'll soon know that you've been invited to stay with us."

"Invited?" She gave a humorless laugh. "That implies I can refuse."

"Refuse all you want." The man studied her with all the emotion of a cobra. It truly didn't matter to him if she came quietly or if she struggled and he had to shoot her. For him, she was nothing more than a job that had to be completed. "Take her."

Accepting that it was now or never, Cora shifted in an explosion of fur and fury.

There were several cries from the humans at her abrupt transformation, and hoping to use their shock against them, she headed straight for the nearby tree. Two men bolted in fear at the sight of the two-hundred-pound tiger heading in their direction, but one idiot moved directly in her path, aiming his gun at her head.

With one swipe of her massive paw, she sliced her claws toward his face. He ducked, but not before she managed to draw blood.

The man squealed in pain, dropping to his knees as he clutched his face. Cora didn't hesitate, bounding over him and leaping toward the tree.

She'd managed to dig her claws into the thick trunk when she heard the click of a trigger followed by the sound of the gun firing a shot. She braced herself for the impact of the bullet, but instead, she felt a small prick of pain on her right haunch.

Had the man missed his shot?

She surged up the tree, not realizing that the pain had come from a tranq dart, not the graze of a bullet as she'd originally assumed. It wasn't until her mind began to fuzz and her muscles loosened that she realized the danger.

Cora released a snarl of frustration as she felt her body falling through the air, the darkness closing in.

Oh...hell.

CHAPTER 6

It was the absence of a warm body snuggled next to him that drug Soren out of his nap.

Damn. He hadn't had a decent night's sleep since Cora had arrived at the compound. It'd been the feel of her wrapped in his arms that had, at last, allowed him to relax enough to truly rest.

Now he was more than a little grumpy to wake up alone in his bed.

"Cora?" he called out, his brows drawing together as silence answered him.

Pulling on a pair of gray sweatpants, he headed out of the bedroom, his brows drawing together as he realized that Cora hadn't just snuck out of his bed, but out of his cabin.

He reached the shadowed front room to discovered a short note lying on the battered sofa:

See you around.
Cora

A growl rumbled in his throat as he crushed the paper in his hand and tossed it across the room.

She'd panicked.

Not that she'd admit the truth.

No. Not his Cora. Instead, she would have a thousand excuses for sneaking out like a thief in the night.

She'd say that it was nothing but sex. Or that her father needed her. Or that she had to bake brownies for the picnic they'd planned tomorrow. Or...blah, blah, blah.

But he knew the truth. At some point during the hours of their fierce lovemaking, the barriers that she was so determined to keep between them had shattered.

He'd touched not only her fabulous body, but also the heart that she so jealously guarded.

And now she was on the run, determined to rebuild the walls that kept him out.

"No. Hell, no," he snarled, heading out the front door. "She's not getting rid of me that easily."

Confident that she couldn't have gone far, Soren didn't waste time trying to follow her trail. Instead, he headed down the path that would lead to the communal area. If she wasn't there, then he would go to her father's cabin.

On the edge of the opening in the middle of the compound, Soren slowed his pace as a wolf with light brown hair and blue eyes abruptly moved to block his path.

"Soren."

Soren frowned at his Alpha. "Not now, Holden," he muttered, trying to step around the male.

"This can't wait," Holden warned, planting a hand in the center of Soren's chest.

For a crazed second, Soren considered shoving his friend aside so he could continue his search for Cora. He didn't want to deal with political bullshit. Not tonight.

But something in Holden's tense expression warned him that this was more than just another tedious clash between wolves and cats.

"Trouble?" he demanded.

Holden grimaced, his t-shirt straining across his chest as he planted his fists on his hips.

"I don't know yet."

Soren frowned. "What's going on?"

"Theo was doing a perimeter sweep and caught the scent of six humans who'd come over the fence."

"Over?" Soren frowned in confusion. Although the compound was technically supposed to belong to the shifters, the humans never hesitated to come in and out whenever they wanted. Like the Indian reservations had been years ago. Just a pretense of independence. "Why wouldn't they use the front gate?"

Holden looked grim. "That's the question."

"Are they still here?"

"I've just started my search."

"What about the sentries?"

Holden shook his head. "I prefer to keep this quiet for now, which is why I could use your help."

Soren swallowed a frustrated sigh. He would help his Alpha track the humans, then he was going to find his mate. And once he had her back in his bed where she belonged, he was locking the door and neither of them was leaving until she admitted the truth.

"Let's go," he muttered.

Together, the two males slid through the darkness, moving through the trees with a silence that no human could hope to match.

A thousand scents drifted through the air. The fallen leaves that carpeted the frosty ground. The hint of pine. The smoke from a nearby campfire. And the potent musk of both wolf and feline shifters.

It wasn't until they'd reached the high fence that they ran across the acrid scent of humans.

"This is where the intruders came over the fence," Soren said, bending down to touch the ground where he could see the footprints in the mud.

Even in the darkness he could determine the outline of military boots.

So, these weren't random trespassers who'd entered the compound because of some ridiculous dare or out of mere curiosity.

Holden glanced at the thick trees that grew next to the fence, hiding it from the view of the nearest pathway.

"They obviously didn't want to be seen," the Alpha said.

"But why?" Holden straightened. "It's not like we're in a position to deny them access to the compound, no matter how much we might want to."

Soren's lips twisted with bitter hatred at the thought of the SAU goons who strolled in and out of their private lands as if they were gods.

Jackasses.

"Could they be spying on us?" he asked.

Holden considered for a long moment. Then he gave a sharp shake of his head.

"They're stupider than I suspected if they thought we wouldn't quickly sense their intrusion onto our land," he said. "Besides, if they want to spy, all they have to do is turn their satellites on us."

Soren couldn't argue. They all knew that the government devoted a great deal of money and energy to keeping an electronic watch on them.

"Then they must be searching for something," Soren said.

"Or someone," Holden added.

Soren started to nod his head, only to freeze. Looking for someone...

"Shit."

Fear burned through his blood like acid as he set off at a jog, following the trail of footprints as they led to the center of the thick woods.

Holden was swiftly at his side, darting around the trees with fluid ease.

"Soren, what's wrong?" he demanded.

Soren's concentration remained locked on his surroundings, blocking out the stench of humans to pick up the light threads of a female shifter.

"Cora," he breathed.

"What about her?"

"She would have crossed this area on her way home," he muttered, leaping over a bush that stood in his path.

"So did you finally get her naked?" Holden drawled, abruptly ducking as Soren halted long enough to aim a punch at his face. "Hey," he protested. "You poked your nose into my mating with Arial."

Denied the feeling of his knuckles connecting with his friend's nose, Soren returned his attention to his hunt.

"Because you were clearly out of your mind," he snarled, the hair on the back of his neck standing upright as Cora's scent became more pronounced.

"And you're not?" Holden drawled. "Just because Cora may have passed through this general area doesn't-" His words broke off as Soren abruptly shifted into his wolf form. "Soren?"

Howling in fury, Soren was impervious to the pain of the rapid shift that wrenched his muscles and snapped his bones into place. He was even deaf to Holden's demands for an explanation.

Instead, his mind was filled with a red mist of fury as he caught the unmistakable scent of Cora's blood.

She'd been injured.

And recently.

Bounding over a narrow stream, he skidded to a halt as he came to a small opening.

Here.

Restlessly sniffing the ground, he caught the scent of the humans, as well as his mate. She'd shifted into her cat, he abruptly realized. A fight? He followed her trail to a nearby tree, his hackles rising at the potent scent of her blood along with something else...

Something that made his nose wrinkle in disgust.

His wolf bared its teeth, preparing to go in pursuit of the female who was his heart and soul. But even as he charged forward, he found himself wrapped in a pair of ruthless arms.

Snarling in fury, his animal struggled to break free, even snapping his teeth at the throat of his captor. The male, however, refused to release his steely hold, speaking directly in his ear.

"Soren, come back," the voice commanded.

A shudder raced through his body at the powerful sound of his Alpha. He wanted to ignore the order. His every instinct cried out to rescue his mate from the enemies who'd stolen her away.

But as the voice continued to speak in a voice that refused to be denied, he gave a pained whine. With another blast of agony, he shifted back to his human form.

"I'm sorry, old friend," Holden murmured, laying a hand on Soren's shoulder as he shivered on the cold ground.

"They have her," he rasped, forcing his weak limbs to hold his weight as he lurched to his feet. "She's been drugged."

"Christ," Holden muttered, holding Soren's arm until he managed to regain his balance.

Indifferent to the fact that he was naked in the cold night air, or that his knees felt like jelly, Soren pulled away from his Alpha. Molten anger flooded through him, his fangs still elongated as he hungered for the taste of blood.

"I'll kill them," he rasped, his body vibrating with the force of his fury. "I'll hunt them down and kill each and every one of them."

"We're going to get her back, but the only way to do that is to use our fucking heads," Holden snapped, still in Alpha-mode. "If you give in to anger, you'll put her into even more danger."

The older male was right. Becoming lost in his emotions would only give the humans the upper hand. He had to maintain command of his temper if he were to rescue his female.

"Why would they take her?" he snarled.

Holden gave a lift of his shoulder. "Has she mentioned anything about the SAU?"

Soren struggled to recall if Cora had ever mentioned the agency that made their existence a living hell.

"Nothing more than our mutual hatred of the humans who've imprisoned us," he said at last.

"She doesn't have any inside contacts or intel that might make her a target?" Holden pressed.

Soren gave a sharp shake of his head. His cat was cunning and beautiful and capable, but her talent was creating harmony, not playing spy.

"No."

Holden circled the small opening with a troubled expression, abruptly pausing to lean down and pick up a tiny dart that was trampled in the mud.

"Then she must have been in the wrong place at the right time," he said, holding up the dart. "They were looking for one of our people to take, and she was handy."

Soren battled back another surge of anger. Shit, that had to be how Cora was drugged.

A shudder wracked his body.

*Cool, calm, logic...*he fiercely reminded himself.

"They obviously came prepared," he said between clenched teeth, nodding toward the dart.

Holden gave a slow nod. "True."

"But why kidnap her?" Soren pressed, frustrated by the suspicion that he was missing something obvious. How the hell was he going to help Cora if he couldn't figure out why she was taken? "They could have demanded we send them a shifter if they wanted one." His Alpha growled. By mutual consent, they rarely discussed the shifters who were randomly taken from the compound and never returned. What was the point in agonizing over something that couldn't be changed? At least, not yet. "It wouldn't be the first time."

Holden released a hissing breath, his expression revealing the same irritation that plagued Soren.

"Goddammit." Shoving the dart in the pocket of his jeans, Holden gave a shake of his head. "None of this makes sense."

It didn't. Why would they go to the trouble of sneaking over the fence to kidnap a shifter? And why Cora? She might be precious to him, but there was no reason for the SAU to even be aware of her existence. Not unless it was connected to her role as princess...

Soren made a choked sound as an icy dread clenched his heart.

"Shit," he breathed.

Holden moved to stand directly in front of him. "You've thought of something?"

"Cora may not possess connections to the SAU, but she does have something that no other shifter can claim," he said in thick tones.

"I don't understand."

"Her father's heart."

Holden sucked in a shocked breath; both of them easily able to imagine the catastrophic reaction when the Alpha of the Golden Pack discovered that his only daughter had been taken.

"You're right," Holden muttered, his face pale. "We need to find Jonah."

"You find him," Soren corrected. He'd been rational long enough. His wolf wasn't going to remain leashed. Not when Cora needed him. "I'm going to get my mate."

Holden reached out to grasp his arm. "Soren."

Soren jerked free of his Alpha's grasp. "Don't try to stop me."

Holden grimaced, sensing Soren's feral need to be on the hunt.

"Just don't do anything stupid," he ordered. "I'll work with Jonah to try and get her back without violence."

Soren peeled back his lips to flash his fangs. "Do what you have to do, but I'm not waiting."

Turning on his heel, he ran toward the nearby fence, easily climbing over it and leaping to the other side. Then, halting in the shadows of the trees, he slowly shifted into his wolf.

Agony blasted through him at transforming so soon after his last shift, but he needed his animal's superior senses to track the intruders.

Once he was fully shifted, he gave a pained howl then lowering his head, he went on the hunt.

****

Dr. Frank Talbot paced his office.

What the hell was taking so long?

He'd requested an update from the guards the moment they'd returned to the SAU headquarters. That had been—he cast an impatient glance at the Rolex that was strapped to his wrist—two hours ago.

How long did it take to toss one unconscious female in a cell and lock the door?

Dammit.

He needed to get in and see the shifter before the Director arrived.

Not only would he have a difficult time trying to explain what he was doing there at such a late hour, but there would be no way he could be left alone with the female long enough to take the samples he wanted.

His hands clenched as he turned to pace back across the large office.

He'd assumed that once he became the head of the research department, he'd be given far greater freedom in the laboratory. After all, he was in charge. But instead, he'd found that he was watched closer than ever.

Almost as if Markham suspected that he was hoping to use the blood samples and various specimens to create his very own shifter virus.

Interfering pain in the ass...

Tonight, however, Frank wasn't going to be denied what he needed.

The female wasn't just another shifter. She was the daughter of an Alpha. There was no way he was missing the opportunity to discover if her blood was different.

After all, they didn't know if the Alpha gained the ability to change a human to a shifter after he assumed his role as leader of the Pack. Or if he became leader of his Pack because he could change humans into shifters.

And if his blood were special, wouldn't that mean his daughter would be equally unique? Maybe even capable of producing the same DNA-altering elements in her saliva.

He fully intended to have his answers before they traded her away for her father.

Reaching for the phone to make yet another call to the head of security, he was halted when the door to his office was shoved open and a man dressed in camouflage pants and a tight t-shirt stepped into view.

Speak of the devil.

He glared at the middle-aged man with a broad face and buzzed hair. Richard Grant was a rigid, by-the-book ex-military paratrooper who had the personality of a turnip.

Frank stepped forward, assuming an expression of authority that he'd practiced in the mirror.

"You have her?"

"Yes."

"Any trouble?"

Grant shrugged, folding his arms over his thick chest. "Not after she was tranquilized. Halak got too close before she was under."

Frank arched a brow. "Dead?"

"No, but he's missing an ear," the man said, his voice revealing a lack of concern that was shared by Frank.

The soldiers who did the grunt work for the SAU were nothing more than tools to be used and discarded when they were no longer of value.

As far as Frank was concerned, only the science mattered.

"The female was unhurt?" he asked.

Grant gave another shrug, his resemblance to a turnip more noticeable than usual.

"As far as I can tell," the older man said.

Frank reached for the leather medical bag that he'd strategically placed on his desk.

"Perhaps I should examine her," he said, moving toward the door. "Have her taken to my lab."

"No."

Coming to a halt, Frank turned back toward his companion. "Excuse me?"

The man met Frank's glare with a flat gaze. Did he ever blink?

"My orders were to have her placed in a cell with a guard in front of her door 24/7."

Shit. That's what Frank had feared. And why he was determined to get her into his lab.

"She'll do us no good if she dies before we can get our hands on her father," he snapped.

Grant snorted, his face hard with disdain. "It will take more than a tumble from a tree to kill one of those animals."

"I still need to-"

"If you want the female in your lab, then you need to talk with Director Markham," Grant rudely interrupted, clearly assuming the gun on his hip gave him some sort of power.

Like every other petty bully, Frank told himself.

When he ruled the world, a man would be judged on the size of his brain, not size of his muscles.

"Fine." He forced a stiff smile to his lips, turning back to the door. "I'll do my exam in her cell."

Grant moved until he was deliberately blocking Frank's path, his face impassive, although Frank sensed that the man was taking pleasure in denying him access to the prisoner.

"Not until you clear it with the Director," he informed Frank.

Frank stiffened his spine. How dare this...no-neck idiot treat him as if he were nothing more than just another employee?

"Are you aware that I'm the head of research in this facility?" he bit out.

Grant rolled his eyes. "I'm aware of who signs my paychecks. And it ain't you."

With a mocking nonchalance, Grant swiveled around and strolled out of the office, closing the door behind him with a loud bang.

Frank hissed in fury, his hand slipping into the pocket of his white lab jacket to touch the syringe filled with poison.

Someday.

But not today...unfortunately.

"Neanderthal," he muttered, releasing the syringe as he walked to his desk and took a seat. He took a second to gather his shaken composure before he reached to pick up his cellphone and call the one member of the security division he knew he could trust. "Sinclair, I need you in my office," he commanded as soon as the other man answered.

Tapping an impatient finger on the top of his desk, Frank felt each passing second. How much longer did he have before the Director arrived at headquarters? A quarter of an hour?

Thankfully, Sinclair was in the building, and in less than five minutes, the door was pushed open and the guard stepped into Frank's office.

Unlike Grant, the guard didn't have a military vibe. Instead, he looked like a street thug. He had dark hair hanging to his shoulders and a lean face covered by stubble that needed to be shaved three days before. His body was lean but hard with muscles, covered by a pair of faded jeans and a khaki Henley that stretched across his broad chest.

Strolling forward, Sinclair offered a lazy smile. Frank, however, didn't miss the covert glance around the office to ensure they were alone.

The man wasn't quite as casual as he liked to pretend.

Satisfied there was nothing hiding in the shadows, Sinclair turned his piercing blue gaze in Frank's direction.

"You called?"

"Yes." Frank rose to his feet. "A young shifter was brought in tonight."

The man scowled. "There was a hunt and I wasn't invited?"

Frank held up a hand. He knew that Grant and his men had occasionally taken shifters and put them in the fighting room that was hidden in the lower levels. They seemed to be fascinated by the sight of the various beasts shredding each other to a bloody death.

Or maybe they were just fascinated with the vast sums of money that exchanged hands by betting on the matches.

Either way, it meant nothing to Frank.

So long as he had the opportunity to study the animals, he didn't care what happened when they weren't in his laboratory.

"This particular shifter isn't here for your games," he informed the younger man.

Sinclair's interest was lost as he stifled a bored yawn. "What's so special about this one?"

"She's the daughter of the Alpha of the Golden Pack."

Something flickered in the blue eyes. "A princess?"

Frank blinked. Did the shifters have royalty? He didn't know enough about their politics to be sure.

"I suppose she might be considered a princess," he conceded.

Sinclair shrugged, back to being bored. "What do you need from me?"

Frank hesitated. He paid this man an outrageous sum for his loyalty, but he was careful not to share his secret agenda. He didn't trust anyone.

"The Director isn't here, and Grant is refusing to let me ensure our prisoner is unharmed," he finally said.

Sinclair studied him for a long minute, no doubt sensing there was more than mere concern driving Frank's interest in the female shifter. Then he gave an indifferent shrug.

"Grant's pay-grade is higher than mine."

The mention of the aggravating head of security brought a flush of irritation to Frank's face.

"I'm sure you could make a trade for guard duty," he said.

"I could," he agreed, narrowing his gaze. "What's in it for me?"

Frank hesitated before reaching for the file on his desk.

He'd heard the stories about Sinclair, of course. He knew the man had a twisted obsession with shifter females. And that once he was done with them, they usually ended up buried in the thickly forested park behind the building.

Which was why he'd approached the man in the first place.

A guard without morals would no doubt be willing to do anything. Including deceiving Grant and Director Markham when given the proper...encouragement.

"Her," Frank said, flipping open the file to reveal a picture of Cora Wilder.

Leaning forward Sinclair gave a low whistle. "Nice."

Frank closed the file. "Once she's served her purpose, I'll make sure you have some time alone with her."

A slow, nasty smile curled the man's lips. "Good enough for me." He jerked a thumb toward the door. "Give me five minutes to convince the guard to exchange shifts with me and then come down."

Moving with surprising speed, the guard was jogging out of the office, no doubt anticipating the sick pleasure he intended to take with the female.

Left alone, Frank hid his grimace. His father would tell him that when he was working in the sewers he should expect to come home covered in shit, but there were still times when his conscience pricked.

Sadly, he didn't have a choice. Did he?

He couldn't create a virus without the proper specimens. And with Markham constantly looking over his shoulder, he had to do something.

Right?

Waiting four and a half minutes, Frank left the office and took the emergency stairs down to the hidden basement beneath the parking garage. It was impossible to completely avoid the cameras that constantly monitored the building, but moving with a brisk step, he tried to look as if he were on official business.

He breathed a sigh of relief when he opened the door to the long, subterranean room without being challenged by any of the guards.

With any luck, he would be in and out before anyone paid any attention.

Moving along the cells built against the back wall, he skirted the brightly lit area in the center of the floor and headed toward the far corner where Sinclair was waiting for him.

"She's inside?" he demanded.

"Yep." Standing beside the heavy steel door, Sinclair reached out to place his palm against the electronic reader. Silently, the door slid open. Frank stepped forward, only to come to a sharp halt when the guard grabbed his arm in a painful grip. "Don't forget, doc...once you're done with her, she's mine."

CHAPTER 7

Cora felt like shit.

Her mouth was dry. Her temples pounded.

And her brain felt as if someone had stuffed her head with cotton wool.

And there was a strange pain in her ass.

As if she'd...

Been shot.

With a sharp groan, Cora wrenched her eyes open, not surprised to discover she was lying naked on a cot in a tiny, steel-lined room. She'd known that the gang of wannabe warriors had been sent to kidnap her as soon as the dart had hit her.

Why else use a tranq gun instead of just a traditional bullet to her heart?

What did surprise her was the strange man who was crouched next to the cot, staring at her as if she were a specimen he'd found beneath a microscope.

"Shit," she breathed in horror.

Awkwardly grabbing the blanket that was thrown over her, Cora wrapped it around her naked body and managed to push herself to a seated position. Then, shoving her hair out of her face, she managed to glare at the intruder.

"Easy," the stranger murmured, his thin face deeply tanned and his pale eyes filled with a fanatical glow.

He was staring at her as if he found her a source of endless curiosity.

Creepy...

"Where am I?" she demanded.

He flashed a smile that revealed a perfect row of capped teeth. "Don't worry, you're safe."

She snorted. Was he for real?

"Yeah, I might believe that if I hadn't been shot, kidnapped, and locked in a cell."

"It was an unfortunate necessity," he murmured, trying to sound sincere. "But now that you're here, I can promise that you won't be harmed."

She pressed her back against the steel wall, trying to ease the shivers that raced through her. Until she managed to regain control of her muscles, it would be impossible to shift.

"Who are you?" she asked, her voice raw.

He held out a hand. "Dr. Frank Talbot, Head of Research for the SAU."

She ignored his pretense of civility. They both knew she wasn't a welcomed guest.

"You brought me here to become a specimen for your research," she accused.

He shook his head. "No. Our interest isn't in you as a specimen."

His words were smooth, but she sensed he was lying.

Or at least, not telling her the full truth.

"Then what is your interest?" she demanded.

"Your father."

Cora's fuzzy brain struggled to understand. If they wanted her father, then why didn't they just kidnap him? Why go to the trouble of taking her hostage?

Then, slowly, she managed to shake off the last of the fog that was making it so difficult to think clearly. Obviously, they hoped to control Jonah Wilder by threatening to kill his only daughter.

God almighty.

They had no idea what they were doing.

Her father would be...devastated. But more than that, he would go ballistic.

It terrified her to think what he might do to try and rescue her.

Lost in her dark thoughts, she barely noticed the doctor, who was opening a black bag and rummaging through it. In fact, it wasn't until he reached under the blanket to grab her arm that she abruptly remembered she was in danger.

Stiffening in outrage, she watched as he turned her arm over and brushed his thumb over her skin.

"What are you doing?"

"I want to make sure the drug is fully out of your system."

"I'm fine," she snapped.

He held up a small vial that had a needle on the end. "This won't hurt."

She yanked her hand free. "No."

He pressed his lips together in annoyance. "I just need a small sample."

Holding up her hand, she released her razor-sharp claws. "Blood for blood."

The man was smart enough to jerk back, fear tightening his face. But instead of leaving the cell as she'd hoped, he sent her a warning glance.

"Please don't make me call for the guard," he said. "He enjoys hurting shifters."

Typical. Most of the SAU staff took pleasure in their pain. Why else would they lock them up as if they were worthless monsters?

"Fuck off," she growled.

"Have it your way." Heaving a faint sigh, the man rose to his feet and motioned toward the open door. "Sinclair, will you join us."

Instantly, a large man with long brown hair and a lean face that was scruffy with whiskers stepped into the room.

"Yeah?"

The doctor nodded toward Cora, who remained huddled on the cot, her claw-tipped hand still lifted.

"I need you to convince our guest to cooperate."

"No problem." Walking forward, the guard studied her with a pair of ice blue eyes that sent a chill down her spine. She had no difficulty believing Sinclair enjoyed hurting females. Hell, she wouldn't be surprised if he ate babies for breakfast. As if sensing her thoughts, he pulled his lips back in a humorless smile. "Hey, pussy, pussy."

Even knowing she was too weak to fight, Cora slashed her claws toward the man's face. He laughed, lunging forward so he could wrap his arms around her.

She hissed, but he was far too strong. Stronger than most humans. Obviously, he was one of those vain humans who used steroids. Or maybe the SAU was injecting their soldiers with some new drug.

Maybe they were using shifter power to enhance their employees.

That would explain the doctor, and why he wanted her blood.

Effectively trapped, she was helpless as he turned her back to the waiting doctor. Her nose wrinkled. The man smelled...different.

Not bad. Just different.

If she survived this ordeal, she needed to warn the Alphas that she suspected there was something weird going on with the guards.

"Bastard," she snarled, unable to avoid the doctor as he grabbed her arm to shove the needle into her vein. Swiftly, the vial was filled with her blood. He grabbed another vial, filling it before he removed the needle and tossed it in his bag. Then, pulling out a long swab he pointed it toward her face.

On cue, the steroid-pumped Sinclair grabbed her jaw and painfully forced her mouth open. The doctor reached between her lips with the swab, swishing it against the inside of her cheek before he was hastily pulling back.

Smart man. She couldn't do a complete shift until she'd regained her strength, but she could grow her fangs long enough to bite off his hand.

Talbot reached back into his stupid bag, no doubt searching for something else to poke or prod her with when the man holding her suddenly glanced toward the doorway.

"Someone's coming," he warned.

"Damn." The doctor scowled, snapping shut his bag. "I suppose this will have to do." Scurrying out of the cell like the cockroach he was, he hastily glanced over his shoulder. "Lock the door and don't say a damned word about this."

Hmm...

Cora barely noticed when she was tossed back onto the cot as the guard left the cell and closed the door behind him. She was far more interested in why the doctor wanted to keep his visit a secret. And how she could use the information to her advantage.

Catching a familiar scent, Cora wasn't surprised when the soldier who'd shot her entered the cell. Slimy bastard.

Along with him was a large, gray-haired man who had an air of authority. This was a man who was used to giving orders and having them obeyed.

"So...you're awake," the older man said, tossing her an orange jumpsuit. "Here."

With a grimace, Cora used the blanket as a shield as she pulled on the ugly-ass outfit. Orange really wasn't the new black, she decided as she tossed aside the blanket to look down at the neon-nectarine jumpsuit.

Still, it was better than being naked.

Not that she was about to admit it to her captors. Instead, she sent them a glance of pure disdain.

"Am I supposed to be grateful?"

The man studied her without expression. "Your feelings are immaterial to me."

Cora shivered. The doctor had been creepy, but this man...he was as cold as ice. And she didn't need to be warned that he would kill her as easily as he killed a cockroach.

"Who are you?"

"Director Markham, head of the SAU."

Shit. That would explain his air of authority.

"What do you want?" she asked, her voice not entirely steady.

Reaching into the pocket of his black slacks, he pulled out a small cellphone and tossed it onto the cot next to her.

"I want you to contact your father and tell him to meet me at the Flatirons at midnight," he commanded, referring to the line of rock formations in Green Mountain, southwest of Boulder.

She scowled. "He's not allowed to leave the compound."

"I'll alert the guards that I've given him permission to leave, and text him the exact coordinates once he agrees."

Cora's mouth went dry. The very fact that Markham was suggesting they meet at such an isolated area at midnight meant that this was no government-sanctioned get together. In fact, she would bet her last damned dollar that this was yet another secret SAU mission that was intended to hurt the shifters while giving the humans more power.

"And if I won't?" she challenged.

The older man shrugged. "I'll start sending him your body parts."

The breath was yanked from her lungs at his casual cruelty. What sort of villain could threaten to chop up a person and send her body parts to her father?

It was...evil. Pure evil.

She gave a disbelieving shake of her head. "You hurt me and my father and he'll destroy you," she warned in husky tones.

His nose flared as if he smelled something rotten. "Careful, Ms. Wilder. Shifters who threaten me usually end up dead."

She believed him. She truly, truly did.

She licked her dry lips. "What do you want with my father?"

If possible, the Director's expression became even more arctic.

"Let's just say he's never been eager to assist the SAU," he said, his hatred toward Jonah Wilder a tangible force. "Having you as our guest will hopefully encourage his cooperation." The man's reptilian eyes glittered in the light of the naked light bulb that was hanging from the ceiling. "Make the call."

She tilted her chin despite the fear that thundered through her.

"I'm not going to lead him into a trap," she muttered.

"He won't be hurt," Markham promised. "And neither will you if you do as I ask."

Cora rolled her eyes. Did the humans think she was stupid? "I keep hearing that, but I don't believe you any more than the other man."

The Director stiffened, clearly caught off guard. "Other man?"

Cora licked her lips. Could she play the two men against each other?

At the moment, discord among the humans was her only weapon.

"The doctor who was just in here taking samples," she said.

Markham struggled to conceal his flare of anger. "Doctor?"

"Dr. Frank Talbot."

"He was here?"

"Yes." Cora didn't need her heightened senses to know that the man was furious at the thought of the doctor visiting her without his approval. "Just a few minutes ago."

"What did he want?"

She shrugged. "He took my blood and shoved a cotton swab into my mouth." She deliberately paused, glancing down at her bare toes with a pretense of innocence. "He took off when he heard you coming. I don't know why."

There was a tense silence before Markham leaned forward to snatch the phone off the cot and pressed it into her unwilling hand.

"Make the call, Ms. Wilder."

She glared into his flushed face. "I don't trust you."

"Don't push me," he warned between clenched teeth, his icy composure in danger of shattering. "Either you make the call, or I have Grant start cutting."

Cora hesitated. The last thing she wanted was to put her father in danger. She'd endure any amount of torture if she knew he was safe.

But she wasn't naive.

She knew that Jonah Wilder would go psycho if parts of her started showing up on his doorstep. Hell, he would burn the world to cinders to get her back.

Swallowing a growl, Cora lifted the phone and tapped in her father's number...

****

It'd taken every bit of Soren's skill to track the intruders after they'd climbed into their vehicles. Thankfully, they'd tossed Cora into a Jeep with a loose canvas top that had allowed her scent to escape.

Keeping to the shadows to avoid attracting unwanted attention, he'd followed the trail from the compound to a narrow road that wound along the outskirts of Denver. Somehow, he'd assumed they would be headed to the nearby airbase. Or even the large military hospital. Instead, they continued northward.

At last, the vehicles slowed at the edge of Boulder and turned into a long drive.

Coming to a halt at the heavily secured fence that surrounded a large lot, Soren studied the distant brick building.

The SAU headquarters.

It had to be.

Battling back his urge to storm the front gate, Soren had instead circled to the vast wilderness behind the building. His wolf form was perfect for tracking the intruders, but he couldn't approach the guards as an animal.

He would be shot on sight.

Jogging along a narrow stream, he halted at a human campsite to 'borrow' a pair of jeans and a thick jacket he could use to cover his naked body. He also grabbed a heavy woolen scarf he could wrap around his neck to disguise the collar. Finally, he pulled a stocking hat over his hair and spilled a can of beer over himself.

At a glance, he looked like a drunken idiot who'd become lost in the thick forest.

To emphasize the pretense of helpless stupidity, he swayed and stumbled his way down a narrow path that led directly to the back gate.

He was nearly at the ten-foot fence that surrounded the perimeter when a guard stepped from a small, wooden building and glared at Soren.

Dressed in a heavy camouflage coat and matching pants, the guard towered six-foot-six at least, with the broad muscles of a weight lifter. As if that weren't enough, he held an AK-47 in one hand.

"Stop," he snapped. "This is private property."

Soren stumbled to a halt, smiling with goofy relief. "Oh, thank God," he muttered in slurred tones. "I didn't think I would ever find civilization again."

The man scowled. "Turn around and walk away."

Soren took several swaying steps forward. "Look, dude, I've been lost for hours. My phone is dead and I need to-"

"I said, turn around and walk away," the guard interrupted, lifting his gun in unmistakable warning.

"What the fuck." Soren put his hands in the air even as he continued to stumble forward. "All I need is a phone so I can call for a ride."

"Not here."

"Why not?" Soren tilted back his head, pretending to notice the big-ass fence that blocked his path. "Is this some secret government facility?" Two more steps forward. "Shit. Do you have aliens in there or something?"

"Or something," the man said dryly.

"Cool." Another step. He hid a smile of satisfaction. He was within touching distance. "I wanna see."

Belatedly sensing his danger, the man gave a wave of his gun. "Take one more step and I'll shoot your ass."

"Hey. I pay my taxes." Without warning, Soren lifted his hands to shove them against the man's chest, sending him toppling backward. "I deserve to make a lousy phone call."

Regaining his balance, the man lunged forward, clearly intent on smashing Soren in the face.

"I warned you," the guard snarled, taking a swing.

Soren easily dodged the blow, using the movement to head back toward the nearby trees. As he'd hoped, the infuriated guard followed, taking another swing that missed by a mile.

The guard had obviously never been in actual combat. Otherwise, he would never have allowed his anger to overcome his training.

Two more missed jabs and several feet off the pathway, Soren was finally certain that they were out of camera range.

Waiting for the idiot to throw another punch, Soren grabbed the man's fist, and with one jerk, had him tossed over his shoulder. The man cried out in shock, the gun flying from his hand as he landed on his back with enough force to knock the air from his lungs.

Stepping forward, Soren kicked him in the head, hard enough to knock him unconscious. He preferred to kill his enemies, but if he could get in and rescue Cora without any deaths, it would give the SAU less ammunition to retaliate against the Packs.

With no time to waste, he efficiently traded coats with the guard, along with the uniform hat. Then, he reached into the man's front pocket, a smile touching his lips.

Keys.

Jackpot.

Straightening, he strolled back out of the woods, leaving the gun behind. He could kill quicker and more efficiently with his bare hands. And more importantly, he could do it without making a sound.

Firing off an AK-47 would alert the entire neighborhood that he was breaking in.

With a nonchalant gesture, he lifted a thumb toward the camera on top of the fence, confident whoever was watching the feeds would assume the guard had dealt with the drunk and was returning to his post.

Heading down the pathway, he used the keys to unlock the gate.

Hold on, Cora, he silently pleaded. *I'm coming.*

CHAPTER 8

Soren swallowed a curse as he studied the steel door with the electronic lock that barred him from the lower floors.

He'd managed to use the guard's keys to enter the brick building and search the upper floors. No surprise, there was nothing more exciting than a few offices on the first floor and what looked like a medical lab that took up the entire top floor.

It was obvious they hid their secrets in the basement.

Unfortunately, he didn't have a way to force open the door. Not without a key card to trip the lock.

Shit.

Retracing his steps, he jogged down the hallway, heading toward the back of the building. He'd passed by a security office that was tucked beneath the stairs. There had to be a guard with a key card inside. Or better yet, a way to turn off the entire system.

The last thing he wanted was to get down to the basement and discover he needed yet another key.

Only a few feet from the door, Soren grimaced as he caught the scent of a human male jogging down the stairs. There was nowhere to hide. Not unless he wanted to waste more time by taking the nearby elevator to another floor.

Restraining his burst of impatience, he forced himself to continue forward, ignoring the security door as a uniformed guard arrived at the bottom of the stairs. One problem at a time. Dammit.

He strolled casually past the stairs, only halting when the guard called out.

"Stop."

Turning, he studied the short male with a potbelly and nearly bald head. The man's round face was flushed with a blatant sneer, twisting the flabby features.

"What?"

The male reached to grasp the handle of the gun holstered at his side.

Typical petty bully who'd been given a bit of authority. Always a dangerous thing.

"Where are you going?"

Soren shrugged, moving forward. "Just looking around to get my bearings. I'm new."

The man scowled, but like the previous guard, he didn't seem to notice that Soren was within striking distance.

Obviously, the SAU didn't bother to actually train their staff.

Dumbasses.

"Grant didn't say anything about a new hire," the man said, his hand remaining on the grip of his pistol. "What's your name?"

Soren swiftly searched his mind. He needed to distract the man. He doubted the idiot could pull the gun and shoot him before he could rip out his throat, but he didn't want to risk it. Not with Cora depending on him.

"Chuck. I'm Senator Scott's nephew," he at last said, choosing the name of a politician who was well known for hating shifters. The bastard had made it clear he wasn't going to be satisfied until every shifter had been caged like an animal in a zoo. "He promised me a job here if I wanted it."

"Shit." The man gave a resigned shake of his head. "That's all I need. Some politician sending me his family rejects."

"Hey." Soren leaned forward, raising his voice. "Are you calling me a reject?"

As he'd hoped, the door to the security office was shoved open, and a slender man with short brown hair and a narrow, rat-like face stepped into the hallway.

"What the hell is going on out here?" the man demanded.

Soren shoved his way past the first guard, heading toward the open doorway.

"Whatcha doing in there?" he demanded, covertly making sure that the second man was unarmed. A quick glance revealed that nothing was hidden beneath the black slacks and white cotton shirt. Just the usual IT guy. "You got a TV?"

"They're security monitors, you moron."

"Oh. Let me see," Soren pushed his head through the doorway, making a quick inventory of the long table that was loaded with computers, walkie-talkies, a sophisticated switchboard, and what looked like video recorders. There was also a narrow black box with a line of switches that he bet his left nut was attached to the alarm system.

His attention turned to the monitors that lined one wall, his heart clenching as he caught sight of Cora. Seated on a narrow cot, she was wearing an orange jumpsuit with her hair tangled and her face marred with dirt.

A toxic combination of relief that she was alive and rage at the sight of her locked in a fucking cage sizzled through him. A low growl rumbled in his chest, his fangs elongating as a red mist clouded his mind.

"Get him out of there." He heard the nerd command, feeling his shoulder being roughly grabbed.

"Goddammit. I knew he was going to be a pain in the ass," the first guard grumbled, yanking Soren around to face him. "Look, you entitled piece of shit..." Belatedly catching sight of Soren's eyes that glowed with the power of his wolf and the teeth that were more animal than human, the man took a step back, fumbling for his gun. "Oh, hell."

With a swipe of his hand, Soren knocked the gun from the guard's hand, sending it sliding down the hall to hit the wall with a metallic thud. At the same time, he wrapped his free hand around the man's thick neck and began to squeeze.

The guard made a gurgling sound, desperately reaching up to grab Soren's wrist in a futile attempt to break his ruthless grip.

Soren never wavered, his fingers biting deeply into the spongy flesh. Unfortunately, the bastard took longer than Soren expected to finally pass out. Which meant that the nerd had managed to dart into the security room and slam the door shut.

Shit.

Tossing the unconscious man to the floor, Soren lifted his leg and kicked open the door. It splinted in two beneath the impact. Stepping into the cramped room, he managed to grab the human by the back of his shirt. Giving him a sharp tug, he yanked him away from the wooden desk in the corner.

Just for a second, he thought he'd managed to prevent a disaster. Then, as he lifted the struggling man off the ground, he caught sight of a flashing light over the monitors.

Damn. The nerd must have set off an alarm.

Fear twisted his gut as he slammed the man into the wall, taking satisfaction in hearing his head smack with enough force to knock him out.

Dropping him to the floor, Soren gave him another kick just to make sure he wasn't faking his unconsciousness before stepping over his limp body to grab the black box. With unsteady fingers, he flipped each switch, praying that he wasn't too late.

Then, lifting his arm, he smashed the box against the edge of the table, shattering it into a hundred pieces. Hopefully, that would prevent the doors from being locked down before he could get Cora out.

With a last glance at the monitor that showed Cora now on her feet pacing the cell with obvious unease, he spun on his heel and headed out of the room.

He only had a few minutes to get in and out.

He couldn't waste a single one.

****

Frank had his shifter samples hidden in the small refrigerator that was under the built-in bar, and was hurriedly pulling on his suit jacket when the door to his office was shoved open.

He tensed, knowing who had intruded into his private space even before he slowly turned to watch Markham stroll forward.

"Going somewhere, Talbot?" the older man demanded.

Frank adjusted his cuffs, pretending an indifference he was far from feeling. After all, this was his office. He might not usually work this late, but he could be there if he wanted. Right?

Maybe he could brazen his way out of danger.

"Home," he said, pasting a smile on his lips. "I didn't realize how late it was."

"Yes." The man folded his arms across his chest, his pale gaze studying Frank with an unnerving intensity. "Which makes me wonder why you're here."

Frank waved a hand toward his desk that was stacked with file folders.

"I had some paperwork I needed to complete."

"Paperwork?"

"Yes."

Disbelief was etched on Markham's square face. "And that's the only reason?"

He knew. Frank licked his dry lips. Someone had blabbed the news that he'd been down to the basement.

Now, what?

He cleared his throat, sternly reminding himself that he was Dr. Frank Talbot. He was more intelligent, more ambitious, and more suited for greatness than any other person in this idiotic organization.

Including the barbarian glaring at him as if he'd stolen the Crown Jewels.

"Once I heard that the guards were bringing in Cora Wilder, I decided I should stay," he said in smooth tones.

"An interesting decision." Markham stepped closer, trying to use his size to intimidate him. "Would you like to explain it to me?"

Frank arched a brow, puzzled by the question. "Obviously, I was afraid she might be in need of medical attention."

"Ah." A cold, humorless smile stretched the Director's lips. "And that's why you deliberately went against my orders for no one to enter her cell?"

Frank hid his annoyance. Who'd been snitching on him? Sinclair? The spineless worm who was in charge of the security cameras?

Could it have been the shifter female?

He gave a small shake of his head. It didn't matter. Not now.

With enough cunning, he could salvage his position.

"Grant is no doubt a fine soldier, but he isn't a trained doctor," he attempted to reason with the condescending prick. "The female will be worthless if she dies from internal injuries your men might have unknowingly inflicted when they captured her."

Unimpressed by his logic, the Director took a slow, thorough survey of the office. Almost as if he were searching for something.

"That's why you took blood and swabs?"

Frank resisted the urge to glance toward the refrigerator. There was no way Markham could know where he'd hidden the specimens. Not unless the bastard could read minds.

"They're a part of my exam," he said with a small shrug. "I needed to make sure she wasn't damaged by the drugs that were used to tranq her."

The pale gaze slowly returned to Frank, the heavy features impossible to read.

"No longer."

Frank stilled, sensing that the Director was referring to more than a bit of blood and saliva.

"Excuse me?"

Markham planted his hands on his hips in a familiar gesture that emphasized the bulge of his muscles and the gun at his hip.

"I want you to hand over any specimens you've taken, as well as your keys, and leave the building."

Frank sucked in a shocked breath. "I don't understand."

"Then I'll make it clear." Markham pointed a thick finger in his face. "You're fired."

Was the man demented? He was a brilliant researcher. A genius. In comparison, the rest of the so-called scientists that the SAU hired were talentless hacks.

Only a complete idiot would fire him.

Or a man so insecure in his position of leadership that he couldn't bear to have anyone in his employ that might undermine his authority.

"But-"

Frank bit off his protest as the Director muttered a low curse and reached into his pocket to pull out his cellphone. He pressed it to his ear.

"What?" His blunt features clenched with sudden fury, his pale eyes glittering in the overhead light. "Shit. Put the building on lockdown, I'm on my way." Struggling to regain his stoic composure, the Director shoved the phone back in his pocket and glared at Frank. "You will stay until the lockdown is over, then I want your ass off my property."

Frank felt a genuine stab of fear. Clearly something bad had happened.

Was the shifter out of her cell?

Or worse, had her Pack managed to follow her to the supposedly secret headquarters?

Good lord. Even now, the place could be crawling with the beasts.

"What's going on?" he demanded.

Ignoring Frank's question as was typical, Markham headed across the office.

"Don't leave this office until I return," he warned Frank before he left the room, slamming the door behind him.

"Bastard," Frank breathed, not hesitating to rush to the refrigerator to pull out the various specimens he had hidden in a cooler.

Then, returning to his desk, he unlocked the bottom drawer to pull out the private files that detailed the research he'd done over the past three years. He couldn't take all of them. Not without a damned moving truck. But he could take those that had his most promising results.

Tucking them in his briefcase, he unlocked yet another drawer, pulling out a small pistol. He was a scientist, not a soldier, but he could pull a trigger.

And there was no way he was going to be trapped in this office without knowing what the hell was going on.

Besides, the Director had made it clear it was time for them to cut ties.

It was the perfect opportunity for him to move on to bigger and better things.

As long as he got out of the building alive.

****

Soren inched his way along the ventilation shaft that ran the length of the ceiling.

His first thought had been to charge into the basement and rescue Cora before the guards could stop him. Unfortunately, one glimpse into the long room where Cora was being held revealed a guard standing directly in front of her cell.

He could take the guard, but there was no way to approach without being seen.

And then, he'd caught sight of the silver ductwork that crisscrossed the open beams. It was his only hope of sneaking up on the guard before he could alert others.

Moving with painful slowness to ensure that the thin metal didn't pop or creak beneath his weight, Soren finally reached the end of the room. His jaws hurt from clenching his teeth, and his nose was clogged with dust, but his heart was filled with hope.

Already, he caught the rich scent of Cora.

It helped to ease the animal inside of him that was nearly feral with the need to destroy the enemies who'd stolen his mate.

Coming to a halt, he stretched out on his stomach and peered through the vent. He froze. Shit. The last thing he'd expected was for the guard to glance up.

He hadn't made a sound. Had he?

And no human was sensitive enough to smell his approach.

So what the fuck was the guy looking at?

Releasing his claws, he prepared to slice through the metal and drop down on top of the man. But he was abruptly halted as he caught the scent of another guard rapidly approaching.

Shit.

He would have to wait.

"Sinclair," a male voice snapped.

The guard took a step forward, his face twisted into a scowl.

"What the hell is going on?"

A low growl rumbled in Soren's chest as a man moved to stand directly in front of the guard. He didn't recognize the large, barrel-chested man with the buzzed head, but his scent was familiar.

The bastard had been in the compound where Cora had been taken.

His wolf struggled to break free as Soren fiercely forced himself to cling to sanity. He didn't know how many other guards might be nearby. Getting shot wasn't going to help Cora.

"An intruder has breached our defenses," the older man told the guard.

The guard grimaced, his face twisting with disgust. "Shifter?"

"Who else would break in? The fucking Easter Bunny?"

The guard's hands fisted at the mocking reprimand, but he was obviously too smart to share his annoyance.

"Where is the animal?"

The larger man shook his head, his beefy features hard with anger.

"He managed to destroy the locks before he headed down here."

Well, at least he'd managed to do one thing right.

Soren had known the switches unlocked the doors, but he hadn't been certain that smashing the box would actually keep them disabled.

Which would make it easier to get out. Just as soon as he could get his hands on Cora.

"I haven't seen him," the first guard assured his companion.

"No one has." The leader nodded his head toward the distant door. "I want you to join Clark in searching the building. He may have doubled back in an effort to throw us off his trail."

The guard hesitated as if he were caught off guard by the order.

"What about the cat?" he said. "This might be a diversion to rescue her."

"I'll stand guard."

"But-"

"That wasn't a suggestion," the older man snapped, moving forward until he was nose to nose with the guard. "Go."

Muttering beneath his breath, the guard headed across the long room and out the door. Soren once again prepared to attack, but instead of taking Sinclair's place in front of the cell, the man moved to stand in the center of the room.

Dammit.

There was no way to reach him now. Soren would just have to take the risk.

Using his razor sharp claws, he ripped through the metal duct, making a hole large enough to drop through. Instinctively, he crouched low as his feet hit the hard ground.

That was the only thing that saved him from a nasty injury as two bullets flew over his head.

Rising to his feet, he remained poised to dodge as the man kept the pistol pointed in his direction.

"Stay where you are and put your hands in the air," the man commanded, reaching to grab the walkie-talkie that was clipped to his belt. "Sinclair, I've got him in the basement."

Soren thought he heard Cora call his name, but his concentration was focused on the man who was aiming the pistol at his heart.

"Do you think you can kill me before I rip out your throat?" he asked, taking a small step forward.

He would have only minutes before the other guard returned.

The older man pasted a sneer on his face, although it didn't entirely disguise his fear.

"Don't be an idiot. There's no way you can get out of here alive."

Soren prowled forward. "You always underestimate us. That's what is eventually going to be the downfall of the SAU," he taunted.

The man stumbled back, clearly uncertain whether he could shoot before Soren could tear off his head.

"I have guards surrounding the building..."

His words broke off in a small shriek as Soren abruptly shifted into his wolf and lunged forward.

There was the deafening sound of a gun being fired, followed by sharp pain as a bullet grazed the side of his muzzle and lodged in his shoulder. Soren, however, didn't hesitate. He could already hear the sound of footsteps clomping down the stairs.

It was now or never.

With a last leap, he pounced on the man, his fangs clamping down on his fleshy throat. His prey fell backward, landing flat on the ground with Soren standing on his chest.

Soren growled in satisfaction as he tasted blood on his tongue. At last. But even as he prepared to rip out the bastard's throat, he felt a shockingly painful blow to the back of his head.

With an agonized whimper, he rolled to the side, barely clinging to consciousness as a shadow fell over him.

Sinclair. Looking down at him with an icy gaze.

How the hell had he gotten across the room so fast?

And what had he hit him with?

It felt as if he'd used an iron fist.

"Shit, Sinclair," a new male voice floated through the air. "I had a clean shot."

Soren closed his eyes, pretending to be unconscious as Sinclair turned toward the approaching guard.

"Did you want me to wait and see if you could pull the trigger before the bastard killed our fearless leader, Clark?" Sinclair demanded.

On cue, the older man gave a pained cough. "Shut up, both of you," he snapped. "And help me up."

Soren felt a stab of intense fury.

He'd been shot, the back of his skull split open, and captured before he could save Cora.

The least he could have done was kill one of the bastards.

"Do you want me to put a bullet in his head?" the male that Soren assumed was Clark asked with obvious anticipation.

"Not yet, you idiot," the leader muttered, his voice a rough rasp, as if Soren had done at least some damage. "Markham might be able to use him."

"He's a big boy." Soren felt Sinclair give his haunch a rough nudge with the toe of his boot. "We can always use him in the fights."

Fights? Soren forced himself to remain limp, his eyes closed.

Was that where those missing shifters went? Were the SAU using their authority over his people to use them as some sort of modern-day Gladiators?

"Christ, Sinclair," the older man muttered. "Open the door to the cell."

Soren felt pain jolt through him as the leader grabbed him by one leg and roughly yanked him across the floor. He battled back a growl of agony, not only from the wound on the back of his head, but the bullet that remained lodged in his shoulder.

Until his body managed to work the projectile out of his flesh, he wouldn't be able to heal.

Thankfully, his fur protected his skin as he was dragged over the floor and into the cell. Instantly, he was surrounded by Cora's enticing scent as he sensed her rush forward.

"Stand back, bitch," the guard warned.

"What have you done to him?" Cora demanded.

There was the sound of a low grunt as if Cora had actually run into the man.

"Dammit," the guard snapped. "I told you to get back."

On the verge of opening his eyes and launching himself at the bastard, Soren was halted when Cora abruptly kneeled at his side, her hand stroking over his head in a soothing motion.

"It's okay," she murmured softly.

"Shit." Leaving the cell, the guard slammed the door shut. "Sinclair, keep watch at the top of the stairs," he snapped, his voice harsh as he tried to pretend that he wasn't unnerved by his up-close and personal encounter with a wolf. "We can't be sure he was alone. Clark, stand guard here. Anyone shows up...shoot them."

CHAPTER 9

Cora waited until she heard the two men leave the basement before she leaned down to bury her face in Soren's fur.

"Oh God, Soren," she choked out, shaking with fear.

She'd been terrified when she'd realized that he was in the basement. He had to know that he was risking his life. And then the idiot had charged the guard, getting shot and then hit so hard that she'd been able to hear his skull crack from the impact.

God. She was going to have nightmares for years at the sight of him lying on the floor, so still she thought he was dead.

A deep shiver raced through the wolf before he released a pained groan and shifted back into his human form. With a burst of magic, the fur was replaced by smooth, naked skin and long, muscular limbs that sprawled over the hard floor.

Cora gave a choked cry as she saw the raw wound that continued to seep blood just above his collarbone.

It was even worse than she'd feared.

"Ssh, princess," he murmured, his hand lifting to brush away the tears that ran down her cheeks. "It's okay."

She shook her head. It wasn't okay. Not when he was injured and trapped in this damned cell with her.

"How badly are you hurt?" she asked.

"I'll heal." He grimaced. "Bastards."

Glancing toward the cell door, she could catch sight of the guard who restlessly paced the basement. His human senses weren't acute enough to overhear their conversation, but still, she lowered her voice.

"How did you find me?" she demanded, her fingers running through his tousled hair, careful to avoid the wound on the back of his head.

His lips twitched, his fingers continuing to stroke her cheek.

"There's nowhere in the world I wouldn't be able to track you down, princess," he assured her. "You belong to me."

The tightness that made it nearly impossible to breathe slowly eased as she studied his fiercely beautiful face. He was injured, but he was alive.

Right now, that was enough.

"So arrogant," she teased.

"Determined," he corrected.

She gave a shake of her head, her expression chiding. "And foolish. You could have been killed."

He gave a wry smile, glancing around the cramped cell. "I was trying to impress you with my daring rescue," he told her. "The plan was to rush in, toss you over my shoulder, and take off before the guards realized I was even here. Clearly it didn't work out."

She reached for the blanket that she'd left on the cot, gently folding it over his naked body. As if he needed to impress her.

The mere thought was ridiculous.

"Once we're out of here, I'm going to kick your ass for taking such a risk," she warned.

Cognac eyes darkened as his fingers drifted down to outline her lips.

"Once we're out of here, I'm taking you to my bed. You can do whatever you want to my ass," he promised.

She trembled, easily able to remember holding on to his perfect butt as he surged deep inside of her. Her hand moved to the side of his throat, moving over the collar that she hated before following the line of his shoulder.

"Anything I want?"

"Absolutely." His gaze slid over her face before lowering to the hideous orange jumpsuit. Instantly, his expression hardened. "Did they hurt you?"

"No."

His eyes narrowed as if sensing she wasn't telling him the full truth.

"I could smell your blood where the bastards attacked you."

"They shot me with a dart, and I fell from the tree, but that's it," she said. "I promise."

He held her gaze, searching for the truth before giving a slow nod and allowing his muscles to relax.

"Have they told you why they kidnapped you?"

Her stomach clenched. Just for a few moments, her relief that Soren was alive had driven out her terror for her father. Now it returned with a vengeance.

"They want the Alpha of Golden Pack," she said between clenched teeth.

He nodded, as if he'd already suspected why she'd been taken.

"Why not just grab him?"

She glared toward the door, her cat hissing with fury at the SAU's disgusting lack of morals.

And they called her an animal.

Jerks.

"Because they intend to force him to create shifters. Something he would have refused to do without them threatening to chop me into little pieces."

"Those sons of bitches." He struggled to sit up. "I'm going to kill them."

"Easy." She allowed her fingers to skim down his arm, needing to keep him calm. Until his body managed to rid itself of the bullet, he couldn't fully heal.

The last thing he needed was to become agitated and worsen his injuries.

Perhaps realizing that he wasn't going to be able to do anything until he'd recovered his strength, Soren sank back onto the floor with a grimace.

"Have they contacted your father?"

"Yes. They forced me to call him." She sat back on her heels, futilely trying to disguise her seething frustration. "They're supposed to meet at the Flatirons."

"When?"

"Midnight."

Cognac eyes darkened with a grim determination. "Shit. We have to get out of here."

They did. They had less than an hour to contact her father before he was forced to choose between his daughter and giving into the demands of the SAU.

"We will." Her gaze moved to the bullet wound that continued to seep blood. "As soon as you're healed."

"I'm fine," he muttered, lowering his hand to place it against the cement floor.

"Don't, Soren," she pleaded, already knowing he was going to make another attempt to shove himself upright. "You'll hurt yourself."

"Damn." He squeezed his eyes shut and released a heavy sigh. "This isn't doing much for my image as a super-hero."

She brushed a stray curl from his forehead, at the same time ensuring he wasn't running a fever.

"I don't need a super-hero," she assured him.

"What do you need, princess?"

"You."

"Me?" He opened his eyes, studying her with a raw, aching need that stole her breath. "You're certain?"

"Yes."

"No more walls?"

"No more walls."

"Thank God."

Her fingers lightly traced his brow, her cat purring in satisfaction, even as her heart remained uncertain.

"I just have one question," she said, unable to halt the words despite the knowledge that this was hardly the time or place for this particular discussion.

"What?"

"Why didn't you come to me after..." She floundered beneath his steady cognac gaze. Dammit. Why had she even started this conversation?

"After Leah died?" he finished for her.

She bit her bottom lip, a blush staining her cheeks. "Yes."

He reached to grasp her hand, squeezing her fingers in a grip that helped to ease her regret for mentioning his dead mate.

"I've always told myself that it was guilt that kept me away," he said, his gaze lowering to where their hands were connected.

Cora frowned. "Guilt for what?"

He absently stroked his thumb over her knuckles, his expression unbearably sad.

"For not being able to give Leah my heart because you already possessed it."

Her lips parted on a dismayed sigh.

Crap. She'd been so caught up in her own sense of betrayal, she hadn't really thought about the cost to both Soren and his young mate.

And even if she had, she would never have considered the possibility that Soren would not only continue to love her, but that his feelings for her would have affected his relationship with Leah.

"I'm sorry," she breathed.

His face clenched with soul-deep remorse. "She deserved better."

Leaning forward, she brushed her mouth over his lips in a gentle kiss.

"You did what you thought was best for your Pack," she murmured.

He gave a sharp, humorless laugh. "And hurt everyone in the process."

Cora heaved a sigh. There was nothing she could say to make things better. He was determined to blame himself for a situation none of them could have changed.

Only time would ease his pain.

"You said that guilt was what you told yourself kept us apart," she reminded him, hoping to distract his dark thoughts.

Tightening his grip, he pulled her fingers to his lips. "When I woke up to find you gone from my bed, I felt as if I'd been slugged in the gut."

She wrinkled her nose. "I'm sorry."

He nipped the tips of her fingers. "It made me realize how desperately I didn't want to experience that sense of loss."

"By avoiding me?"

"Yes." He held her gaze. "As long as I kept you as a distant fantasy, then I could cling to the belief that we would eventually be mated. But if I'd come to you and you couldn't forgive me, or worse, if you'd found another male, then I couldn't hold on to my hope." She felt him tremble. "And that would have been unbearable."

****

Soren's wolf pressed against his skin, deeply troubled by Cora's pale face and the weary smudges beneath her eyes.

This was his female.

He wanted to care for her. And that meant getting her out of the man-cage and taking her someplace where she would be warm and comfortable and tucked in his arms.

Unfortunately, that wasn't going to happen until he was strong enough to get off the damned floor. Then, he had to find a way to lure the guard to open the door...

He gave a shake of his head.

First he had to get out the bullet so he could heal.

After that, he could concentrate on getting them out of the cell.

Kneeling at his side, Cora gazed down at him with a troubled expression.

"I wish I hadn't left your bed," she murmured softly.

"Me, too." He deliberately lightened his tone. He hadn't intended to play on her sympathy. Pity from this female was the last thing he wanted. He just needed her to understand why he'd waited so long to come to his senses and claim her as his mate. "We would certainly be having a lot more fun, not to mention a decent bed to sleep in."

Instead of being comforted as he'd hoped, she managed to look even more upset.

"And you wouldn't have a bullet in your shoulder and a cracked skull," she said.

He sucked the tip of her finger between his lips, holding her worried gaze.

"Unless I pissed you off," he teased.

It took a long moment, but as if sensing her distress was agitating his inner animal, she managed to force a smile to her lips.

"I promise that I'll never shoot you," she said. "I might bite or scratch-"

"Mmm," he interrupted with a throaty growl. "You promise?"

"You're impossible." She gave a reluctant laugh, pulling her fingers from his grasp. "I meant that I was sorry I allowed my fear to overcome my desire to stay in your arms."

He studied her pale face. The thought she could ever be afraid of him was...

Horrifying.

He clenched his jaw. "Why would you be frightened?"

"You make me vulnerable," she whispered.

He flinched as if she'd struck him. "You're afraid I'll hurt you again."

His words came out as a statement, not a question.

She shook her head, belatedly realizing that her words had hit him like a blow.

"I think it's more a fear that fate might once again steal you away."

"Nothing is going to separate us, not ever again," he swore, his face abruptly twisting as a searing pain blasted through his shoulder. "Shit."

Instantly, Cora was leaning forward to frame his face with her hands, concern darkening her eyes.

"Soren?"

He tried to speak, but the words were replaced by a hiss of pain as his body went rigid. Christ. It felt as if someone was shoving a hot poker through his wounded flesh.

After what seemed like an eternity, the skin of his shoulder bulged and the bullet was at last pushed from his wounded flesh.

"Damn, I think it hurts worse coming out than it did going in," he muttered.

Taking a minute to catch his breath, Soren savored the sensation of his body beginning to heal. Without the damned bullet, it wouldn't take long for the hole in his shoulder to close and his skull to repair the hairline fracture.

Oh, he was going to have a headache for a while, and he wouldn't be back to full-strength without a few hours of rest and a large meal filled with plenty of protein. But for now, he was as good as he was going to get.

Shoving off the blanket, he planted his hands against the floor and pushed himself to a seated position.

Cora made a small sound of concern, reaching out to try and urge him back to the ground.

"What are you doing?" she protested.

This time, he was strong enough to resist the pressure of her hands. They couldn't remain in this cell.

Not when Jonah would already be traveling to meet the SAU. If the Alpha allowed himself to be taken, the humans could disappear with him before they had any hope of mounting a rescue.

"We can't wait, princess," he reminded her. "We have to get out of here before your father reaches the Flatirons." He glanced across the cell, able to see the shadow of the human who was pacing from one end of the basement to the other. "I need to find a way to force the guard to open the door."

Without warning, she sat back and slipped her hand into the pocket of her jumpsuit.

"I think I can help," she murmured, pulling out her hand to reveal a small metal object.

"A key?" Soren blinked in shock. "How did you get that?"

She smiled, a hint of smug satisfaction glowing in her emerald eyes

"When they dragged you into the cell."

He slowly smiled, pride filling his heart as he recalled the guard's anger when she'd bumped into him. She'd obviously taken advantage of the idiot's distraction when he was hauling Soren into the cell and lifted his key.

"My clever cat," he murmured softly.

Moving with a fluid grace, Cora rose to her feet and moved in silence to peer out the window cut into the door.

"We still need to find a way to distract the guard," she pointed out.

With far less grace, Soren managed to lift himself off the floor, breathing a small breath of relief when his knees didn't buckle.

Shit.

He was still dangerously weak. Something he was determined to hide from his companion. Cora was just stubborn enough to try and protect him. He wasn't going to let her put herself in danger.

"You open the door and I'll snap his neck," he suggested, forcing his feet to carry him across the cell. "That should distract him."

She glanced at him with wry amusement. "I was thinking of something a little more discreet."

"Fine. I'll-" He cut off his words as the second guard abruptly stepped into the basement and gestured for the man to join him at the door.

"Clark."

The guard moved forward. "What now?"

Sinclair lowered his voice, clearly too stupid to realize that a shifter could hear a pin drop a hundred feet away.

"They think we have another intruder," he warned in low tones. "Maybe more than one."

Soren and Cora exchanged a puzzled glance.

More shifters? Could Holden have sent them? It seemed unlikely that he would risk exposing Soren unless he called for backup.

Of course, if he'd found out that Jonah was meeting with the SAU...

Soren grimly leashed his straying thoughts. He couldn't worry about the mysterious shifters. Right now, nothing mattered but getting out of the cell.

"Shit," Clark muttered. "Are they sending more guards down?"

"No." Sinclair studied his companion with a mocking smile. "They want me to go help with the search. You stay here."

"Alone?" There was no mistaking the squeak of fear in the guard's voice.

"You need a babysitter?" Sinclair drawled.

Clark hunched his shoulders. "What if the other shifter tries to rescue the prisoners?"

"You have a damned gun, don't you?" Sinclair demanded. "If something moves, shoot it."

"Smartass," Clark muttered as Sinclair turned to leave the basement.

Sensing the guard was on the edge of panic, Soren leaned against the door, speaking directly through the bars in the window.

"When my friends get here, I'm going to rip out your heart and eat it," he said with a low growl.

"Fuck this," the guard rasped, backing toward the door. "I don't get paid enough."

With a last glare toward the cell, Clark turned on his heel and sprinted out of the basement.

Stepping back, he swiveled around to discover Cora studying him with lifted brows.

"What?"

"Rip out his heart and eat it?" she repeated in dry tones.

Soren shrugged. It might have been a bit...melodramatic.

"It was the first thing I could think of," he said in defensive tones.

She rolled her eyes, moving forward to stick the key into the heavy metal lock.

"You sounded like a cheesy Hannibal Lecter wannabe."

He chuckled. Okay, maybe it'd been more than just a 'bit' melodramatic.

"Hey, it worked, didn't it?"

There was a loud click as she tumbled the lock. Pocketing the key, she sent him a glance as she grabbed the handle.

"Ready?" she asked.

Soren moved forward to frame her face with his hands, lowering his head to claim her lips in a fierce kiss. For a timeless moment, her mouth parted, allowing him to drink deeply of her sweetness.

It wasn't a prelude to sex.

Not that he didn't intend to get her naked and happy at the first opportunity.

But for now, it was simply a physical need to reassure one another that they'd been reunited. And that they could face anything.

Together.

"Let's do this thing," he at last murmured.

CHAPTER 10

Cora pulled open the door, allowing Soren to slip past her as they left the cell and headed out of the basement. It wasn't worth the fight to try and convince him that he was still healing from his wounds and that she should take the lead.

He would be deeply offended if she even suggested he couldn't protect her.

Males...

In silence, they left the basement, Soren indifferent to the fact that he was completely naked. It would make it easier to shift if they were confronted by the enemy.

Cautiously, they began climbing the narrow staircase. Near the top, however, Soren came to an abrupt halt, leaning against the wall as he turned to whisper in her ear.

"There's someone at the door."

She sucked in a deep breath, catching the scent of a human man.

Dammit.

"Is there any other way out of here?" she asked, her voice pitched low enough it wouldn't echo.

Soren glanced up the stairwell, no doubt considering the possibility of climbing to a higher floor before he gave a shake of his head.

"No. The higher we go, the more likely the chances of being trapped," he at last decided. "I'll deal with the guard. You get out of here."

Instinctively, she reached out to grasp his arm. "Soren, you're injured."

"I'm nearly healed," he blatantly lied. As if she couldn't see the blood that still seeped from his wounds. But before she could protest, he held up a slender hand. "I'm fine, I swear I'm not playing the hero."

She narrowed her gaze. "You're not?"

His lips twitched with a rueful smile. "Well, maybe a little," he conceded. "But we both know you have to get out of here and contact your father before he surrenders to our enemies."

"But-"

"Trust me," he murmured, reaching out to brush his fingers over her cheek.

Cora hesitated.

Could she? Could she trust this male who'd once destroyed her heart?

The answer came without hesitation.

Yes.

"Just don't get yourself killed," she muttered.

Relief darkened his cognac eyes. As if he sensed her inner acceptance that they truly were partners.

Mates.

"That's not in the plan," he assured her in husky tones.

Without warning, the door above them was shoved open and Sinclair stepped onto the landing of the stairwell.

"Are the two of you done?" the man demanded, his scruffy face twisted with a sardonic smile. "I mean, it's a touching scene and all, but we don't have all night."

Soren instinctively moved to stand between her and the guard, his claws slicing through his skin as he prepared to attack.

"Run, Cora," he ordered.

The man unexpectedly stepped forward, holding up his hand in a gesture of peace.

"Easy, wolf. I'm trying to help."

Soren growled low in his chest. "Like you helped by hitting me in the fucking head?"

The man shrugged. "Would you rather I'd let my trigger-happy companion shoot your ass?"

Cora pressed against Soren's back. She wasn't prepared to abandon him, but she knew better than to try and step between the two males.

That was a good way to end up dead.

"He held me down in the cell," she told Soren, glaring at the man who sent her a mocking glance. "Don't trust him."

"No problem," Soren assured her, suddenly shifting into his wolf form.

Expecting the guard to react like most humans with a lot of cursing, screaming, and a hasty retreat, Cora felt a stab of fear as Sinclair folded his arms over his chest, studying the large animal about to rip out his throat with remarkable calm.

Then, shockingly, his pale eyes flickered, revealing his inner wolf.

"Now, do you trust me?" he demanded with a growl.

"Soren, wait." Cora leaned down to touch Soren's back, feeling his rigid muscles as he prepared to attack. Once assured the wolf understood that he needed to wait, she straightened to study the male with a flare of curiosity. "You're one of the Unseen?" she demanded.

Nothing else could explain his lack of collar and brand that marked the rest of them as born shifters.

He gave a slow nod. "I am."

She didn't know much about the shifters who'd managed to elude detection by the humans. Which meant she wasn't about to trust him.

Just because he could turn into a wolf didn't mean he was one of the good guys.

"How do you disguise your scent?" she demanded.

"It's a talent many of the Unseen are born with," he smoothly answered.

Hmm. That wasn't particularly reassuring. "You're a shifter and you work for the SAU?"

His features hardened, revealing the deadly predator that lurked just below the surface.

"How better to learn your enemies' secrets than to become one of them?"

Ah. That made sense.

"A spy," she murmured.

"As long as I haven't blown my cover," he muttered, pivoting back toward the heavy steel door to push it open. "Let's move it."

Soren gave a low growl, but Cora reluctantly followed the male out of the stairwell and into the narrow corridor.

What choice did they have?

If Sinclair wanted to hurt them, he could have shot the minute he'd opened the door. There would have been no way they could have avoided being injured, maybe even killed.

And if he was leading them into a trap...well, it couldn't be much worse than being locked in the basement.

That didn't, however, mean she intended to lower her guard.

Keeping a reasonable distance from the stranger, she continued to probe for information.

"I heard the guard say that you made females disappear," she said.

He shrugged, his gaze locked on the doorway at the end of the hall. Was he expecting trouble?

"They assume I enjoy rough sex and that I bury the bodies in the mountains," he explained in off-hand tones. "It's the only way I could smuggle them out of the building."

A portion of her dislike for the man eased. "You rescued them," she breathed.

"Not as many as I would have liked, but I have to be careful not to make my employers suspicious. They're easy to dismiss as stupid humans, but they're cunning and dangerous."

Cora grimaced, recalling how easily they'd managed to kidnap her.

"True."

Sinclair came to a halt in front of a large window.

"I cut the sensors to the alarm, but there are three guards patrolling the grounds." He glanced toward the large wolf, who continued to eye him with homicidal anticipation. "You'll need to keep an eye out for them."

Cora hesitated. She understood that every passing second increased the odds of them getting caught, but she also knew the only way to get away from the SAU was to take off through the nearby parkland. It was too risky to remain in the neighborhood. Who knew which nearby houses might be owned by the secret government agency?

Which meant she would be away from civilization for the next half hour or more.

"I need to contact my father," she said, preparing herself for an argument.

Instead, Sinclair reached into the pocket of his jeans to pull out a small black object. With a lift of his hand, he tossed it in Cora's direction.

"It's a burner phone," he told her.

Snatching it out of mid-air, Cora flipped it open and sent a text to her father in the secret code they'd developed years ago. It was the one certain to make sure that he knew it was her.

Beyond a brief reassurance that she and Soren had managed to escape from the SAU, she sent a short warning that the leader intended to try and force him to use his powers as Alpha to create new shifters.

It took a few minutes, but at last, a short text flashed across the screen that assured her Jonah had received her message and was making plans to deal with their enemies.

Sending up a silent prayer that her father wouldn't do something to get himself killed, Cora shut the phone down and handed it back to Sinclair.

"Here."

"Keep it," he said in tones that indicated he was accustomed to giving orders. "And take this."

She reached to take the folded piece of paper that he'd pulled from his boot. She lifted her brows. He was like a magician producing random items from thin air.

Inanely she wondered how long it took him to get dressed in the morning.

"What is it?" she asked as she smoothed the paper to reveal what looked like a treasure map with a large X marked in the middle.

"A map to an underground bunker that the Unseen use to hide extra food and supplies. You'll find clothing there, as well as weapons, and if you

want, you can take one of the automobiles. We'll have
it picked up later."

"You drew a map?" She glanced up, her lips
twitching with an unexpected flare of amusement.
"You know they have this crazy new invention called
GPS," she said.

He peered down the length of his aquiline nose.
Cora grimaced. Unseen or not, he had to be an Alpha.

"This is disposable," he said, tapping the paper.
"Plus, I can dismiss it as a silly drawing my niece
made for me if it's ever discovered by the SAU."

Knowing she was being subtly chastised, Cora
couldn't resist giving the male a little jab.

"Do we need a secret handshake to enter the
bunker?" she asked in sweet tones. "Or is there a
password."

"No, I'll call and warn the guards that you'll be
dropping by." He deliberately paused. "Hopefully
they won't shoot you."

Okay, she'd deserved that.

The male had risked his trusted position among
the SAU guards—not to mention his own neck—to
help them. It wasn't his fault his natural arrogance
made her want to kick him in the nuts.

Just as she was climbing through the window, she
halted, suddenly remembering his earlier words.

"I assume that your claim about there being more
shifters was just a way to get rid of the other guard?"
she demanded.

"Yep. Until you reach the camp, you're on your
own."

Without waiting for her reply, he headed down
the hallway, opening the distant door and closing it
with a decisive bang.

"I wonder if all the Unseen are so friendly," she
muttered.

At her side, Soren moved to butt her with the top of his head, silently herding her forward.

"Yeah, yeah," she muttered, grabbing the edge of the windowsill again and climbing through.

Dropping to the ground, she heard the scramble of Soren's nails against the tiled floor before he was leaping through the air to land beside her.

She paused long enough to make sure they hadn't been noticed before she was jogging toward the nearby fence.

"Let's go home, big boy," she told her companion.

The sound of Soren's howl echoed through the air.

CHAPTER 11

Holden's argument with Jonah had been short but fierce.

The Alpha of the Golden Pack had been determined to confront the bastards who'd kidnapped his daughter on his own. Holden understood his fear. It was always a danger that the men coming to speak with Jonah would sense Holden and his wolves and punish Cora. The male would do anything to protect his daughter.

Not to mention the fact that they were flagrantly disobeying SAU law by sneaking out of the compound without permission. Which could potentially be a death sentence.

But there was no way in hell that Holden was going to let the Alpha travel to the secluded area alone. The days when shifters could enjoy being enemies were long over. If they were going to survive, it meant facing the humans together.

No matter the risk.

Jonah had grudgingly agreed to his demand that he slip several of his best fighters through a secret tunnel they'd managed to dig beneath the fence, while

Jonah had taken a more visible journey through the front gate.

Now he silently moved among the shifters that he'd spread along the base of the five sharp peaks that ran along the east slope of Green Mountain. Known as the Flatirons by the locals, the area was heavily foliaged and miles from civilization.

Still, he commanded his wolves to patrol the area. Not only to prevent any nasty surprises from sneaking up on them, but to make sure there were no stray campers who might get spooked if anyone decided to start shooting.

He was making his second sweep when Jonah stepped onto a flat rock in the center of a clearing and waved a hand in his direction.

Shifting into his human form, Holden stopped by the Jeep that the cats had driven to the area to pull on a loose pair of sweats. Then, jogging through the pine trees, he joined Jonah, who was in the process of shoving his phone back into the pocket of his slacks.

"What's going on?" he demanded.

The Alpha cat flashed a lethal smile. The kind of smile that indicated he'd just gotten the cream and now intended to slay the mouse.

"I just received a text from Cora."

"Soren found her?"

"Yes."

Relief slashed through Holden. Shit. Until that moment, he hadn't realized just how worried he'd been for his Beta. He'd lost too much.

The thought of Soren being taken from him was...inconceivable.

"Both of them?" he pressed, needing to hear the words.

Jonah nodded, his gaze meeting Holden's with an understanding that only two Alphas could share.

The price of leadership meant that they had to be willing to put those they loved most at risk.

"Both."

"Thank God." Giving himself a second to savor the news, Holden quickly turned his thoughts back to the reason he was standing in the middle of nowhere instead of tucked in his bed with his mate. "Did your daughter say why they were so anxious to get their hands on you?"

Jonah curled back his lips to reveal his elongated fangs. "They think they can force me to create shifters."

"Shit." A combination of guilt and frustrated fury replaced Holden's momentary relief. "I knew that Claire's treachery was going to come back and bite us in the ass," he snarled.

Jonah shrugged. "I suppose it was inevitable that they would learn that particular secret."

Holden didn't know if it was inevitable or not. He only knew that a female he'd trusted had betrayed them all.

"That bitch is going to pay."

"Right now, I'm more concerned with what they intend to do with the shifters they want me to create," Jonah said.

Holden grimaced. His companion was right. Claire's betrayal was over and done with. There wasn't anything they could do to change it.

All they could hope to do was minimize the damage.

"My vote is that we don't ever find out," he said. The mere thought of an Alpha being forced to create a shifter was offensive on a cellular level. And to have the SAU involved...a deep shudder wracked his body. "Let's get the hell out of here."

Jonah held up a hand. "Not yet."

"What are you waiting for?"

"They boldly came into our lands and stole my daughter."

Holden's heart squeezed with dread. Shit. He understood that Jonah was pissed. The mere thought of having the humans enter their territory and take his child would no doubt haunt him for years to come.

But they couldn't afford to create a head-to-head confrontation with the government.

They didn't have the numbers, or the necessary weapons to win that battle.

"And now she's free," he said in soothing tones. "We live to fight another day."

Jonah's eyes flashed with the golden heat of his cat. "We need to teach them that we aren't completely at their mercy."

Holden allowed his gaze to skim the nearby area, making sure none of the wolves or tigers were close enough to overhear their conversation.

The two Alphas had taken special care not to be seen arguing in front of their Packs.

No matter what their disagreement.

"Are you talking war?" he demanded.

"No." Jonah sent him a smile that did nothing to reassure him. "Just a small lesson."

"Damn, you stubborn cat," he muttered in low tones. "You'll get us all killed."

The smile never wavered. "I don't intend to spill blood," he promised Holden. "At least...not tonight."

Holden scowled. Okay. He accepted that Jonah wasn't intending to start slicing and dicing humans, but that didn't mean he wasn't going to cause trouble.

"Then what *do* you plan?"

The male reached beneath the leather jacket he was wearing to pull out a large manila envelope that was embossed with an official-looking emblem on the front. Jonah held it up as if it was the Holy Grail.

"So far, the SAU has managed to convince the public that we're dangerous beasts that have to be locked up for their safety," Jonah said.

Holden snorted. He had little love for the humans who'd so easily turned on them despite the fact that it was shifters who'd saved their damned lives.

"They were eager enough to believe the lies."

Jonah gave a lift of one shoulder. "People always fear what they don't understand. Especially when they've just witnessed a near genocide."

Holden didn't give a shit about what the humans had endured. All he needed to know was whether or not he needed to prepare his people for retaliation.

"Do you have a point?"

"It's time they knew the truth," Jonah said, giving a wave of the envelope.

"What is that?"

Jonah paused, waiting for a patrol of wolves to pass the rock and head for the thick circle of trees before he spoke.

"Files that were smuggled out of the CDC headquarters before it was burned to the ground."

Holden felt a genuine stab of shock. Civilization had crumbled during the worst stages of the virus. There'd been looting, fighting in the streets, and outright anarchy that had included torching of most government buildings.

Which meant that any actual information gathered during the initial outbreak was as rare as gold.

"How did you get your hands on them?" he demanded.

A sly expression settled on the older man's narrow face.

"I have connections with a few humans in leadership roles who aren't completely happy with the SAU and how shifters are being treated," he admitted.

Holden narrowed his gaze. The cunning cat.

"I knew it," he muttered. Silently, he wondered what it would it take to get the names of the government contacts from the tiger.

An Alpha could never have too many friends in high places.

Clearly not ready to share, Jonah glanced at the envelope instead.

"They gave me these when it was obvious that we needed a way to keep the SAU from completely destroying us."

"What's in the files?"

"They trace the original outbreak of the Verona Virus to a human lab outside of Rome," he said, a hint a triumph in his voice. "The defense contractor was attempting to create a weaponized form of the Ebola virus."

"Shit."

It was exactly what he'd always suspected. The virus would never have spread so swiftly, or been so potent, if it hadn't been genetically engineered. Every attempt to halt it had been met with a mutation of the virus that would have wiped out the human race if the shifters hadn't stepped forward and offered their far more potent blood to create a vaccine. The SAU, of course, had steadfastly refused to admit their guilt. Instead, they'd more or less implied that it was the shifters themselves that had been responsible for the outbreak.

To be able to show that the original virus had come from a human clinic...

That was a game-changer.

"You have proof?"

Jonah grimaced. "Nothing that the governments around the world won't try to refute," he admitted. "Nothing less than the actual scientists confessing to the truth will ever force them to reveal what truly happened." He gave a wave the envelope. "But I have enough evidence to create questions among the press."

Holden folded his arms over his chest, his brief flare of hope swiftly fading.

His opinion of the human press wasn't much better than the politicians.

Scuttling bugs that pretended to shine the light of truth, but were, in fact, on the payroll of the highest bidder.

"We've tried to get them to listen to our side of the story before," he growled. "They refused to believe what we had to say."

"It has taken time for the world to recover from the chaos," Jonah said.

"Meaning?"

"Meaning that the humans have started to accept that they aren't in danger of being ravaged by a bunch of bloodthirsty shifters."

Holden wasn't nearly so convinced. Granted, there were no longer protestors who marched outside their gates chanting that 'the man-beasts were going to hell.' Or 'death to the shifters.'

Still, no one was offering to let them move into their neighborhoods.

"If they accepted us, then we wouldn't be living behind fences," he said in dry tones.

"I didn't say they accepted *us*," Jonah corrected. "Only the fact that we haven't become the enemy the SAU tried to create."

Holden shrugged, about to dismiss the male's overly-optimistic opinion of humans, when he was struck by a sudden thought.

"You know, that could be why they're hoping to create their own shifters. They could have them perform any number of heinous acts and blame it on our Packs," he said, easily able to imagine the SAU forcing their homegrown shifters into ruthless, bloody rampages. "It would keep the public terrified of us."

"A possibility," Jonah agreed, his large body stiffening as the sound of vehicles rumbled through the air. "Here they come." He sent Holden a questioning glance. "Are you staying?"

A humorless smile twisted Holden's lips. "Damned straight."

Standing shoulder to shoulder, the two Alphas watched the three large Hummers come to a halt at the edge of the road. Minutes later, a dozen humans were swarming up the hill, their guns out despite the fact that they couldn't see a damned thing in the darkness.

The idiots didn't even know there were both wolves and tigers prowling through the trees just a few feet away.

Idiots.

The head idiot shoved his way past his guards, arrogance chiseled onto his broad features.

"Jonah Wilder?" he demanded, his gaze locked on the tiger Alpha.

Obviously, he'd already seen a picture.

"Yes."

The Director's gaze flicked toward Holden. "I didn't give permission for any other shifters to be out of the compound," he snapped.

Holden shrugged. "Life is filled with all sorts of disappointments."

The man glared at him before returning his attention to Jonah. Almost as if he hoped by that ignoring him, he could pretend Holden didn't exist.

"I'm Director Markham of the SAU," he said, planting his fists on his hips. "Do you intend to come with us peacefully?"

"As a matter of fact...I don't."

A flush of anger stained Markham's face as a tangible shock raced through the chilled air. Laying his hand on the holster strapped to his side, he puffed out his chest and took a step forward.

"Then we do this the hard way," he blustered.

Jonah shrugged. "Your men try to take me, and they'll become dog food."

The guards stiffened, belatedly glancing toward the trees where large predators were circling them with hungry eyes.

The Director licked his lips, glaring at Jonah. "That's a very foolish threat. Your daughter-"

"Is safely on her way home," Jonah interrupted with obvious relish.

Markham made a choked sound. It seemed his boys hadn't kept him updated.

"Lies," he rasped.

Jonah shrugged. "Check for yourself."

Turning, Markham pointed toward the nearest guard. "Call HQ," he snapped.

The man scrambled to pull out his phone, his gaze darting toward a nearby tiger who crouched near the clearing as he pressed a speed dial number. Within seconds, he was connected to the mother ship and being given the news that the prisoners were missing.

The Director clenched his teeth as he slowly turned back to meet Jonah's mocking glance.

"I didn't travel all this way to leave empty-handed," he snapped. "The SAU has need of an

Alpha. It's in my right to demand that you accompany me to headquarters."

Jonah shook his head. "No."

"You're refusing a direct order?"

"Yes."

The guards shuffled their feet, clearly wishing they were anywhere but the isolated park surrounded by lethal killers.

"I have the authority to take you—and every shifter here—into custody," Markham continued to bluff.

Jonah prowled forward, ignoring the guns that were suddenly pointed in his direction as he shoved the envelope into Markham's hand.

"You bother me or my family again, and the press will receive these documents first thing in the morning."

With a scowl, the Director pulled out the stack of documents, tilting them to the side as one of the guards rushed forward to shine a flashlight on them.

Seconds ticked past, the man's face growing pale as he shuffled from one page to another.

He was seemingly smart enough to realize that they could pose a danger to the authority of the SAU.

"You expect the public to believe such blatant lies? The papers are clearly forgeries," he at last muttered, lifting his head to glare at the two Alphas.

"It only takes one reporter to start asking questions," Jonah drawled, leaning forward in a gesture of unspoken intimidation. "Are you willing to risk what they might find?"

Markham instinctively stumbled backward, only to halt when he realized what he was doing. Then, clearly embarrassed by his revealing retreat, he grabbed the papers and ripped them in two.

"You can shove your threats up your ass," he snapped, tossing the paper to the ground.

"Those are copies," Jonah warned, his smile revealing his elongated fangs. "I have a hundred more all printed and ready to go by courier post at daybreak."

The Director deliberately glanced toward the collar that encircled Jonah's neck. A reminder that the government considered shifters second-class citizens.

"You don't frighten me."

"I should. You crossed a line." Jonah pointed a finger in the man's face. "You and the SAU will pay for that."

"No. You're the one who'll pay." The two men glared at one another, but in the end, it was the human who was forced to back down. Trying to pretend he hadn't been neatly outwitted, the Director spun around and stomped back down the hill. "Come on," he commanded his guards.

Watching the humans scramble back into their Hummers and speed away, Holden glanced at his companion.

"You think this is over?"

Jonah grimaced, rubbing a weary hand over the back of his neck.

"Nope. But I think they realize that we're not going to be spineless victims forever," he muttered.

Reaching out, Holden laid his hand on Jonah's shoulder. "Let's get the hell out of here."

****

A week later, Soren snuggled on the bed with his beautiful mate.

The trip back to the compound from the SAU headquarters had been a gut-wrenching effort. Even after they'd managed to slip out the back gate and disappear into the woods, he'd been terrified they were going to be tracked down before he could get Cora to safety. And if he'd hoped for more than the basic necessities from the Unseen bunker, he was destined to be disappointed.

Following the map, they'd come to a small cabin where they'd found a couple of pairs of sweats, some water, and the keys to a pickup that was older than Soren. He assumed that at least one or two of the elusive shifters were nearby, but they'd refused to show themselves.

With no choice, Soren had urged Cora into the truck, and they'd chugged their way through the thick forest, wincing as the stupid engine backfired loud enough to alert any human within a ten-mile radius.

Thankfully, no one had stopped them, and they'd eventually made their way back to the compound.

Over the past few days, they'd worked to put the past behind them, determinedly concentrating on building their future together. And the evening before, they'd formally celebrated their mating with a communal dinner followed by the mating marks.

Holden had insisted on personally doing Soren's tattoo, adding an exquisite cat to the Pack symbol and blending it seamlessly with the mark he had done when he'd mated Leah. It'd been Cora who'd urged him not cover up his previous tattoo. She understood that the young female wolf had claimed a part of his past, and instead of trying to banish Leah from his memory, insisted that they celebrate her too-short life.

Jonah had done Cora's tattooing, pretending to be horrified, even as he'd created a large wolf that stood guard next to a smaller tiger.

Soren knew exactly what her father was demanding of him.

Mate. Protector. And most importantly...partner.

Leaning his cheek against the top of Cora's head, he watched as she lightly traced her new tattoo. The morning sunlight slanted through the window, warning that the day had already started, but he was in no hurry to move.

Not when Cora's naked body was pressed tightly against him.

As far as he was concerned, this was where he intended to spend the next few hours.

"Well?" he murmured as she continued to stroke her fingers over the mating mark.

"It's beautiful," she murmured.

He buried his nose in her reddish-gold curls, breathing deeply of her scent.

"Now the world knows that you belong to me," he said, smug satisfaction laced through his tone.

She reached to touch his tattoo, her own smile filled with satisfaction.

"And you belong to me," she said.

"Forever."

"Forever," she echoed.

A peaceful silence settled in the cozy room. A peace that Soren was reluctant to break. There was, after all, a hope that they could enjoy another bout of hot, sweaty sex within the next half hour.

But, dammit, after a week of waiting for Cora to take the initiative, he was tired of waiting. She was his mate, and it was time for her to take the final step.

Clearing his throat, he lifted his head so he could watch her reaction to his words.

"Now that we are officially mated, I think it's time you move in with me."

Her lips twitched. Was she laughing at his gruff tone, or the idea of living with him? Neither did anything for his male pride.

"Yes," she at last murmured.

His wolf stirred with a restless annoyance. "You could be a little more enthusiastic," he muttered.

Tilting back her head, she met his searching gaze. "We're going to have to discuss some guidelines."

Her teasing tone eased his wolf and allowed him to shake off his brief flare of nerves.

"Guidelines, hmm?" He leaned down to kiss the top of her nose. "Why do I think I'm about to be nagged by my wife?"

A flush touched her cheeks. She was still enchantingly vulnerable at the newness of their mating.

"Because you're a slob," she muttered, waving a hand toward the clothes he'd tossed on a nearby rug. "You can't just drop your clothes on the floor."

He arched a brow, wise enough not to remind her that she'd helped him strip off a few of those clothes in their eagerness to get naked last night.

"Why not?"

"It's disgusting."

He chuckled. "Ah, my finicky cat."

"Not finicky," she protested. "Just opposed to growing mold in my bedroom."

"I see." He allowed his fingers to thread through her glorious hair, his thoughts becoming distracted by the sight of the sunlight warming her ivory skin. He was fairly certain that he'd tasted every inch of her, but it wouldn't hurt to make sure. "Anything else?" he asked in distracted tones.

She made a choked sound as his hand moved over the hateful collar to find the sensitive skin at the base of her throat.

"You can't hog all the covers," she managed to say.

His lips brushed her forehead, his fingers continuing to explore her satiny skin.

"And?"

She shivered as he followed the tempting curve of her upper breast.

"And you have to promise to make me pancakes with warm maple syrup every Sunday."

"I think that can be arranged," he murmured, his lips moving to trace the curve of her cheek. At this moment, he'd promise this female anything she wanted. "Now can we discuss my rules?"

She lifted her arms to circle them around his neck, studying him with emerald eyes that were darkening with a ready hunger.

"What are your rules?"

His hand boldly cupped her breast, his lips skimming to whisper directly in her ear.

"Hold me and never let go."

Her fingers threaded in his hair, her slender body arching beneath him in a silent invitation.

"You're easy," she teased.

"Hey." He gave a faux frown as if he'd been insulted. Then, he flashed a wicked smile. "Okay, I'm easy." He rubbed his foot up and down her leg. "Have your way with me."

Her hands moved down his back, sending tiny jolts of electric pleasure through his bare skin. His wolf gave a low growl, enjoying the sensation of being petted.

"I just had my way with you."

"Only once," he protested, refusing to count the half-dozen times he'd turned to her during the night.

"Soren," she breathed as his fingers circled the hardened tip of her nipple. Then, without warning, she was pushing away his hand. "Did you hear that?"

"What?"

"I think someone is at the door."

Lifting his head, Soren sniffed the air. Wolf.

"Ignore it," he growled, kissing a path over her cheek before finding her lips.

Her hands pressed against his chest. "I can't," she protested.

At the same time, there was the sound of a fist slamming against the front door.

"Soren, open up," Holden shouted.

With a furious growl, Soren forced himself to climb out of the bed and pull on a pair of sweats.

"I'm going to kill him," he muttered, watching as Cora hurriedly slipped on a robe to join him as he left the bedroom and crossed the narrow living room.

He was beginning to understand why humans chose to hop on a plane or a cruise ship after their wedding. Clearly the only way to have time alone with his new mate was to go far, far away.

"You can't kill him," Cora took away his only comfort. "He's your Alpha."

"Watch me," he said. Reaching the door, he grabbed the knob and yanked it open, glaring at the large male who was pacing the porch with a tangible impatience. "What the hell?"

Whirling on his heel, Holden stomped his way back to the door, his expression clenched so tightly he looked like he had a lemon shoved up his ass.

"We have troubles," the older male snapped.

Soren slammed his fists on his hips, glaring at his Alpha. "I'm on my honeymoon."

"I truly am sorry, Soren," Holden said, his expression softening with genuine regret. "But this is important."

Cora moved forward, standing at Soren's side. "What's going on?"

Holden grimaced. "You know we've been waiting for the other shoe to drop after our little powwow with Markham from the SAU?"

Soren's muscles clenched. Holden had shared the details of his and Jonah's meeting with the Director of the SAU, including Jonah's bluff with the files he'd received from the CDC.

They'd all been waiting for the bastards to retaliate.

Now, Soren could only hope that it wouldn't come to bloodshed.

"Are they here?" he demanded, instinctively moving to shield Cora from the narrow pathway that ran in front of their cabin.

"No. But they sent their retribution," Holden warned, moving to jog down the steps of the porch. "Come with me."

Spinning toward his mate, Soren reached up to place his hands on her shoulders.

"Cora-"

"Don't even think about it," she interrupted, her voice filled with a warning not even a male lost in his fierce need to protect his mate could miss. "You start treating me like a helpless little woman and I'll slice off your nuts."

"Give it up, Soren," Holden called over his shoulder.

Soren heaved a sigh, reaching out to enfold her fingers in his hand. They were both right.

As much as he wanted to keep his female safe, he couldn't exclude her from the troubles that they would be facing in the coming days.

She was a vital part of their Packs.

He couldn't diminish her worth.

Threading her fingers with his, Cora pressed herself close to his side as they followed Holden through the nearby trees toward the communal area of the compound.

They'd reached the fringes of the opening when a large male brushed past them, his expression grim.

Soren frowned. "Who the hell..." His words trailed away as he caught the unexpected scent. "Was that a bear?"

Holden gave a short, humorless laugh. "They shut down the Ursine Compound."

A very bad feeling inched down Soren's spine. "What do you mean they shut it down?"

Holden waved a hand toward the communal area that was suddenly seething with unhappy bears.

"Meet our new neighbors."

Soren gave a slow shake of his head, already sensing the shit-storm that was about to hit with all three predators forced to share the cramped space.

"God. Damn."

Look for more of the Branded Packs series with ABANDONED AND UNSEEN coming soon.

A Note from Alexandra and Carrie Ann

We hoped you enjoyed reading **STOLEN AND FORGVEN**. This is just the start of our dark and gritty Branded Packs series. With more to come, we can't wait to hear what you think. If you enjoyed it and have time, we'd so appreciate a review on Goodreads and where your digital retailer. Every review, no matter how long, helps authors and readers. You won't have to wait long for more in this series! Happy Reading!

The Branded Pack Series:
Book 1: Stolen and Forgiven
Book 2: Abandoned and Unseen (Coming Sept 2015)

Abandoned and Unseen

Next in the Branded Packs series:
Abandoned and Unseen – Coming Sept 15th – 2015

Abandoned

When bear shifter, Anya Tucker fell in love with the wrong man, the only thing she left with was a broken heart—and her two bear cubs. Now she's mended her wounds and learned that in order to raise her babies she can only trust herself. When her sons meet the lazy cat next door and fall heads over tails for him, she'll do whatever she takes to protect them—even from a past she'd thought she'd left behind.

Cole McDermott is a jaguar on a mission. Long naps, a willing woman, and a full stomach is usually all he needs when it comes to relaxing after a long day of protecting his Pack. Then he meets Anya and the burn of temptation is silky and tantalizing indeed. When a horror from Anya's past threatens everything she loves, Cole will put everything aside and fight for her family—as well as his own.

Unseen

Nicole Bradley had no reason to live after the humans murdered her son. Not until she learns to hunt down those responsible for his death. Shifting into her wolf form at night, she slips out of the compound, determined to do as much damage as possible. The last thing she expected was to discover secrets that could destroy the SAU.

Polar shifter, Tucker Stone, lives off the grid. It's the only way the Unseen can avoid being rounded up by the humans and tossed into a compound. Besides, he's a loner by nature. But he can't walk away when he sees the pretty female wolf in danger. Risking exposure, he takes her to his hidden den and tries to heal her wounds.

Can a reclusive polar bear and a wolf with a death wish find happiness together?

About Carrie Ann and her Books

New York Times and USA Today Bestselling Author Carrie Ann Ryan never thought she'd be a writer. Not really. No, she loved math and science and even went on to graduate school in chemistry. Yes, she read as a kid and devoured teen fiction and Harry Potter, but it wasn't until someone handed her a romance book in her late teens that she realized that there was something out there just for her. When another author suggested she use the voices in her head for good and not evil, The Redwood Pack and all her other stories were born.

Carrie Ann is a bestselling author of over twenty novels and novellas and has so much more on her mind (and on her spreadsheets *grins*) that she isn't planning on giving up her dream anytime soon.

www.CarrieAnnRyan.com

Redwood Pack Series:
Book 1: An Alpha's Path
Book 2: A Taste for a Mate
Book 3: Trinity Bound
Book 3.5: A Night Away
Book 4: Enforcer's Redemption
Book 4.5: Blurred Expectations
Book 4.7: Forgiveness
Book 5: Shattered Emotions
Book 6: Hidden Destiny
Book 6.5: A Beta's Haven
Book 7: Fighting Fate
Book 7.5 Loving the Omega

Book 7.7: The Hunted Heart
Book 8: Wicked Wolf

The Talon Pack (Following the Redwood Pack Series):
Book 1: Tattered Loyalties
Book 2: An Alpha's Choice (Coming Aug 2015)
Book 3: Mated in Mist (Coming Soon)

The Redwood Pack Volumes:
Redwood Pack Vol 1
Redwood Pack Vol 2
Redwood Pack Vol 3
Redwood Pack Vol 4
Redwood Pack Vol 5
Redwood Pack Vol 6

Dante's Circle Series:
Book 1: Dust of My Wings
Book 2: Her Warriors' Three Wishes
Book 3: An Unlucky Moon
The Dante's Circle Box Set (Contains Books 1-3)
Book 3.5: His Choice
Book 4: Tangled Innocence
Book 5: Fierce Enchantment
Book 6: An Immortal's Song (Coming Soon)

Montgomery Ink:
Book 0.5: Ink Inspired
Book 0.6: Ink Reunited
Book 1: Delicate Ink
Book 1.5 Forever Ink
Book 2: Tempting Boundaries
Book 3: Harder than Words
Book 4: Written in Ink (Coming Soon)

The Branded Pack Series:
(Written with Alexandra Ivy)
Book 1: Stolen and Forgiven
Book 2: Abandoned and Unseen (Coming Sept 2015)

Holiday, Montana Series:
Book 1: Charmed Spirits
Book 2: Santa's Executive
Book 3: Finding Abigail
The Holiday Montana Box Set (Contains Books 1-3)
Book 4: Her Lucky Love
Book 5: Dreams of Ivory

About Alexandra and her Books

Alexandra Ivy is a *New York Times* and *USA Today* bestselling author of the Guardians of Eternity, as well as the Sentinels, Dragons of Eternity and ARES series. After majoring in theatre she decided she prefers to bring her characters to life on paper rather than stage. She lives in Missouri with her family. Visit her website at alexandraivy.com.

Guardians Of Eternity
When Darkness Ends
Embrace the Darkness
Darkness Everlasting
Darkness Revealed
Darkness Unleashed
Beyond the Darkness
Devoured by Darkness
Yours for Eternity
Darkness Eternal
Supernatural
Bound by Darkness
The Real Housewives of Vampire County
Fear the Darkness
Levet
Darkness Avenged
Hunt the Darkness

A Very Levet Christmas
When Darkness Ends

Masters Of Seduction
Masters Of Seduction Volume One
Masters Of Seduction Two:
Ruthless: House of Zanthe
Reckless: House Of Furia

Ares Series
Kill Without Mercy

Bayou Heat Series
Bayou Heat Collection One
Bayou Heat Collection Two
Raphael/Parish
Bayon/Jean Baptiste
Talon/Xavior
Bayou Noel
Sebastian/Aristide
Lian/Roch
Hakan/Severin
Angel/Hiss
Michel/Striker

Branded Packs
Stolen And Forgiven
Abandoned And Unessn

Dragons Of Eternity
Burned By Darkness

Sentinels:
Out of Control
Born in Blood
Blood Assassin

18132505R00175

Printed in Poland
by Amazon Fulfillment
Poland Sp. z o.o., Wrocław